THE SUBSTITUTE BRIDE

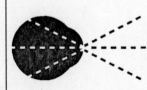

THE SUBSTITUTE BRIDE

JANET DEAN

THORNDIKE PRESS
A part of Gale, Cengage Learning

GALE
CENGAGE Learning

Detroit • New York • San Francisco • New Haven, Conn • Waterville, Maine • London

GALE
CENGAGE Learning™

LIBRARY OF CONGRESS CATALOGING-IN-PUBLICATION DATA

Dean, Janet.
    The substitute bride / by Janet Dean.
        p. cm. — (Thorndike Press large print christian historical fiction)
    ISBN-13: 978-1-4104-3558-3 (hardcover)
    ISBN-10: 1-4104-3558-X (hardcover)
    1. Debutantes—Fiction. 2. Mail order brides—Fiction. 3. Farm life—Iowa—Fiction. 4. Marriage—Fiction. 5. Large type books.
    I. Title.
    PS3604.E1516S83 2011
    813'.6—dc22   2010052333

Published in 2011 by arrangement with Harlequin Books S.A.

Printed in Mexico
2 3 4 5 6 7 15 14 13 12 11

And we know that all things work together for good to them that love God, to them who are the called according to his purpose.

— *Romans* 8:28

To my wonderful Steeple Hill
editors Melissa Endlich,
Emily Rodmell and Tina James.
Thank you for your
encouragement and wisdom.
To my beloved grandchildren
Tyler, Drew, Lauren and Carter.
God bless you for giving me
fresh eyes, endless joy and
hope for the future.
To the Daves, our sons
by marriage, and my husband,
Dale — your steadfast faith is a
role model for our family.

CHAPTER ONE

Chicago, spring of 1899

Elizabeth Manning had examined every option open to her. But in the end she had only one. Her heart lurched.

She had to run.

If she stayed in Chicago, tomorrow morning she'd be walking down the aisle of the church on Papa's arm. Then, walking back up it attached to Reginald Parks for the remainder of his life, which could be awfully long, considering Reginald's father was eighty-two and still going strong.

Papa said she had no choice, now that their circumstances had gone south like robins in winter. He'd reminded her that as Reginald's wife, she'd be kept in fine style. Probably what the keepers said about the tigers at the zoo.

She scooped her brush and toiletries into a satchel, then dropped it beside a valise crammed with clothes. No, she couldn't rely on mortality to get her out of the marriage.

And as for God . . .

Martha had promised God would help her. Well, Elizabeth had prayed long and hard and nothing had changed.

Her breath caught. Perhaps God had washed His hands of her. If so, she could hardly blame Him.

The time had come to take matters into her own hands. Once she got a job and made some money, she'd return — for the most important person of all.

She dashed to her four-poster bed, threw back the coverlet and yanked off the linens, then knotted the sheet around the post, jerked it tight and doubled it again for good measure. That ought to hold her weight.

A light tap. She whirled to the sound.

"Lizzie?"

Elizabeth flung open the door. Skinny arms and legs burrowed into her skirts. "I don't want you to go," her brother said, his voice muffled by tears.

"I don't want to, either. But I've explained why I must."

Robby's arms encircled her waist, hanging on tight. Her breath caught. Could she do this? Could she leave her brother behind? "I'll be back, as soon as I find a job. I *promise*."

With few skills, what job could she do? Could she find a way to support them? All those uncertainties sank like a stone to her stomach. Refusing to give in to her fear, she took a deep breath and straightened her shoulders. She would not fail her brother.

"What if you can't?" Robby's big blue eyes swam with tears. "What if —" he twisted a corner of her skirt into his fist "— you don't come back?"

Looking into her brother's wide eyes filled with alarm and hurt, Elizabeth's throat tightened. Was he afraid she'd die like Mama had?

"I'll be back." She knelt in front of him and brushed an unruly lock of blond hair out of his eyes. "We're a matched set, remember?"

Robby swiped at his runny nose, then nodded.

"We go together like salt and pepper. Like toast and jam. Like —"

"Mashed potatoes and gravy," Robby said, voice quavering.

"Exactly." The smile on Elizabeth's face trembled but held. "In the meantime Martha and Papa will take good care of you."

"But — but when we move, how will you find us?"

One month until the bank tossed them

out on the street. One month to forge a new life. One month to save her family. Her stomach dropped the way it had at nine when she'd slipped on the stairs and scrambled to keep her footing. She hadn't fallen then and she wouldn't fail now. "I'll be back before the move."

Tears spilled down his cheeks. "I want to come with you."

If only he could. But she had no idea where she'd go. What conditions she'd face. "Eight-year-old boys belong in school." Elizabeth forced the words past the lump in her throat.

Tugging him to her, she inhaled the scent of soap, thanks to Martha's unshakable supervision. A sense of calm filled her. She could count on Martha, who'd raised her brother since Mama died, doting on him as if he belonged to her.

Robby's eyes brightened. "Can you get a job on a farm, Lizzie? So I can have a dog?"

His request pressed against her lungs. What kind of a father gave his son a fluffy black-and-white puppy for Christmas, then turned around and sold it in January? Reversals at the track, he'd said. As always with Papa, luck rising then falling, taking their family and their hearts with it.

A chill snaked down her spine. What if

Robby caught Papa's fever for gambling? If she didn't get him away from here, her brother might spend his life like Papa, chasing fantasies.

"I can feed the pigs and chickens," Robby pleaded, his expression earnest.

"I don't have the skills to work on a farm, sweet boy, but once we're settled, you'll have the biggest dog I can find." She kissed his forehead. "I promise."

Yet another promise Elizabeth didn't know how she'd keep.

A smile as wide as the Chicago River stretched across Robby's face. "You mean it?"

"Have I ever failed to keep a promise?" She ruffled Robby's hair. "Now promise me you'll be brave while I'm gone."

His head bobbed three times. "I will."

She wrapped her brother in one last lingering hug. "I love you." She blinked back tears. "Now, tiptoe to your room and crawl under the covers." She tapped his nose with her fingertip. "Sweet dreams."

His lips turned up in a smile. "I'm gonna dream about a black-and-white fluffy dog."

She forced up the corners of her mouth as Robby took one last look back at her then slipped out the door.

No longer able to hold back her tears,

Elizabeth leaned against the wall, fingering the cameo hanging from the delicate chain around her neck, the last tie to her mother. She would miss her room, her home, the place she'd lived all her life. Her watery gaze traveled the tiered moldings, crystal chandelier and wood-planked floor. Once this bedroom had held a mahogany writing desk, hand-carved armoire and handsome Oriental rug.

Here one day, gone another.

Like her life.

"Elizabeth, we miss your company."

Papa's booming voice was followed by the muffled mumblings of her want-to-be groom.

She swiped the tears from her cheeks, then hustled to the half-open door and caught snatches of Reginald's conversation. "Tomorrow . . . at my side . . . ceremony."

"I assure you, Reginald, she'll be there," Papa said, his voice carrying up the stairs, putting more knots in her stomach than she'd tied in her linens.

He'd promised her to Reginald Parks much as he had the armoire he'd sold to Mrs. Grant last week and the cherry breakfront he'd shipped to the auctioneer the week before. He expected her to bail him out as Mama's fortune had, until he'd squandered every dime and worried poor Mama into an early grave.

How could Papa believe Reginald was the answer? She couldn't abide the man. He had no patience with Robby, even hinted at sending her brother to boarding school, as if losing his mother hadn't been enough upheaval in his young life.

Surely God had another answer.

She sighed. If only she and Robby could have a real home where a family shared their meals and the day's events at a dining table that stayed put, where a man considered his family first, where love didn't destroy.

"Elizabeth Ann!" Papa called. "Reginald is waiting."

She heard the familiar creak of the first step — Papa was on his way up. With her heart thudding in her chest, she eased the door shut and turned the key until the lock clicked. Then she jammed her hands into her kid gloves, grabbed her handbag and the small satchel stuffed with necessities and tore to the open window.

She looked down. *Way* down to the lawn and shrubbery along the back of the house. She gulped at the prospect of following her possessions out that window. Now was not the time to lose her nerve. She dropped the satchel. It bounced but stayed shut. When the valise hit, the latch sprung, scattering clothing across the lawn. Praying she'd hold up better when she alighted, Elizabeth flung the rope of sheets over the sill.

A rap on the door. "Be a good girl and come downstairs."

She grabbed the footstool and set it below the window.

"Reginald promised you a lovely matched team and gilt carriage as a wedding present," Papa said, his tone cajoling.

Elizabeth hiked her skirts and took a step up.

He pounded on the door. "Elizabeth Ann Manning, I'm doing this for your own good!"

Papa might believe that, but in reality, her father had one goal — prosperity. Through the door, she heard him sigh. "Sweetheart, please. Don't embarrass me this way. I love you."

Her fingers fluttered to her mouth as tears filled her eyes. "I love you, Papa," she whispered.

How could she abandon him? She stiffened her spine. *He'd* made the choice to gamble away their money, not her. Years of watching him take them on this downward spiral had closed off her heart. In her mind, he had only himself to blame.

Well, she and Robby wouldn't go down with him. Together they'd start a new life. She'd find a job somewhere, then return for her brother. After they got settled, she'd find a way to help Papa. She'd find a way to save them all, a way that didn't involve marriage to Reginald Parks. *To anyone.*

Papa slammed his body into the door. Elizabeth gasped. The hinges quivered but held, thanks to Mama's well-built family home, a home far enough west to have survived the great fire. A home they'd soon lose.

With one leg in and one leg out the window, she clung to the sheet and somehow managed to get a knee up on the ledge. Soon both legs dangled from the second-story window. Gathering her courage, she lay on her belly, ignoring the metal stays of her corset pinching her ribs.

The pounding stopped. She heard a creak on the stairs. Papa must've gone in search of Martha and her ring of keys. He'd soon be back.

Holding her breath, Elizabeth relaxed her fingers, and down she went, faster than a sleigh with waxed runners — until her palms met a knot and broke her grip. She landed on the boxwood with a thud, and then tumbled backward onto the lawn.

For a moment, she lay sprawled there, dazed, then gathered her wits and scrambled to her feet. No time to gather her clothing. She snatched up her satchel and purse and darted for the cover of the carriage house. Slipping inside, she tore through it and out the back, easy to do since Papa had been forced to sell their carriage.

Out of sight of the house, she sprinted down the alley past the neighbors', no small feat in silk slippers. By the time she reached Clinton Street, her breath came in hitches.

Once Papa found a key and got her door open, he and Reginald would be out searching for her. Two doors down, a hack rounded the corner and dropped off a passenger. She slid two fingers into her mouth and let out one of the peace-shattering whistles that had sent Mama to her bed with a cold compress draped across her brow.

The hack pulled up beside her. "Where to?"

Robby's words marched through her mind. *Can you get a job on a farm? So I can have a dog?*

Her brother yearned to live in the country, a good place for a boy. Not that she knew the first thing about the life, but a farm would be far from Reginald.

Perhaps a farmer's wife would want help

18

with . . . whatever a farmer's wife did. Elizabeth was strong. And she could learn.

She gave the driver her destination. Then she settled into the corner of the coach and wiggled her hand into the slit she'd made in the lining of her purse. And came up empty.

A moan pushed past her lips. Papa had taken the small stash of money she'd hidden for just such an emergency. How low would her father stoop to feed his compulsion? She dug to the bottom of her bag and found enough coins to pay the driver. She wilted against the cushions.

How would she buy a ticket out of town?

Well, she'd face that later. Knowing she had no money, Papa wouldn't look for her at the depot, at least at first.

She wasn't going to walk down an aisle tomorrow morning, so how bad could her situation be?

Right before dawn, Elizabeth woke. She'd tossed and turned most of the night, as much as the bench would allow, listening in the dark to every sound. But Papa and Reginald hadn't come. In fact, no one had paid the least bit of attention to her.

She twisted her back to get out the kinks, sending three sections of the *Chicago Tribune* sliding to the floor. Thankfully the news that she'd bedded down at the depot wouldn't make the Society Page. Not that anything she did these days merited a mention.

Carrying her possessions, she tossed the newspapers into the trash and strolled to the lavatory. Through the window, the rising sun lit the sky with the promise of a new day. What would this day bring?

In front of the mirror in the large, tiled room, she pulled a brush through her hair, twisted it into a chignon, and then pinned her hat in place.

The distant shriek of a whistle shot a shiver along Elizabeth's spine. She grabbed her belongings and hustled to the platform. Porters hauled trunks and hatboxes to baggage carts while soon-to-depart travelers chatted or stood apart, sleepy-eyed. Her heart thumped wildly in her chest. A ticket. She needed a ticket. But tickets cost money. What could she do?

Smokestack belching and wheels squealing, the incoming train overshot the platform. Amid clangs and squeaks, the locomotive backed into position. Soon passengers flowed from the doors to retrieve luggage and hail hacks.

Elizabeth had to find a way to board that train. Her stomach piped up. Oh, and a spot of breakfast.

Near one of the station's exits a robust, plainly dressed young woman huddled in the corner weeping. Passersby gave her a brief glance then moved on. The stranger met Elizabeth's gaze. Her flawless skin glowed with health, but from the stricken look in her eyes, she was surely sick at heart.

Some inner nudge pushed Elizabeth toward her. "Can I help?"

"I . . . I can't go through with it. I can't marry him."

Another woman running from matrimony. "Who?"

"The man who sent me this." Out from the woman's hand stuck a ticket, a train ticket. "Eligible bachelors are few and far between, but . . ." Tears slid down her ruddy cheeks. "I'm homesick for my family already and I've only come as far as Chicago."

Pangs of longing for Martha and Robby, even Papa, tore through Elizabeth. She'd left a note, but that wouldn't stop them from worrying. Worse, Papa and Reginald might appear at any moment.

"That's my train." The stranger pointed to the rail cars across the way. "I feel terrible for spending his money on a trunk full of clothes, then leaving him in the lurch. He's a fine Christian man and doesn't

21

deserve such treatment."

Elizabeth's stomach tangled. A twinge of conscience, no doubt for neglecting church since Mama died. For not heeding the Scriptures that Martha read each morning while Papa hid behind the headlines and she and Robby shoveled down eggs. No doubt the reason God hadn't heard her prayers.

Her gaze latched onto her means of escape. "I need to leave town. What are you going to do with your ticket?"

Brushing at her tears, the young woman's sorrowful eyes brightened then turned thoughtful. "The ticket is yours — if you want it."

"You're *giving* your ticket to me with no strings?"

"Well, not exactly no strings." The woman gave a wan smile. "More like a tied knot."

"What do you mean?"

"My groom's expecting Sally Rutgers . . . me. If you're up to starting a new life, take my place."

Elizabeth took a step back. "I couldn't."

"If you don't like his looks, use this round-trip ticket to take the next train. That was my plan."

As Elizabeth scanned the throng milling on the platform, her mind scampered like hungry pigeons after a crust of bread. *Marry a stranger?* There had to be another way to take care of Robby without marrying *anyone.*

Her heart skipped a beat. Not fifty yards away, Papa, looking handsome, vital and by all outward appearance, prosperous, stood talking with Reginald. From under Reginald's bowler, white tufts of hair fluttered in the breeze.

Twisting around, Elizabeth grabbed Sally's arm. "Tell me about this man."

"He lives on a farm." Sally sighed. "Oh, I doubt that appeals to a fine lady like you."

A farm. Robby's dream. Was this God's solution? "How will I know him?"

Sally removed a stem of lily of the valley from the collar of her traveling suit and pinned it to the bodice of Elizabeth's dress. "Wear this, and he'll find you." She checked the nearby clock. "Better hurry. Your train leaves in ten minutes."

Elizabeth glanced over her shoulder. Papa and Reginald had stopped a porter, probably giving her description. She had nowhere to go except back to Reginald. She'd rather ride a barrel over Niagara Falls.

That left her one alternative. Wear the lily of the valley and take a gander at the groom.

"Where to?" she asked.

23

"New Harmony, Iowa."

Where was that in Iowa? Did it matter? In Iowa was a farm, the answer she sought.

Clutching the ticket in her hand, Elizabeth thanked Sally, then dashed for the train. She boarded and found her seat, careful to avert her face. Within minutes, the engine worked up steam and lumbered out of the station. Once she'd presented her ticket to the conductor, she lost the hitch in her breathing.

The seat proved far more comfortable than the depot bench and she nodded off. Her last thought centered on the man who had sent for a bride.

What would she find in New Harmony, Iowa?

New Harmony, Iowa

Pickings were slim in New Harmony.

One last time, Ted Logan started down the list of the single women in town. There was the schoolmarm who'd bossed him like one of her errant pupils before they even made it out the door. He wouldn't let himself be pulled around by the ear. Or subject his children to a mother who wore a perpetual frown.

And then there was Ellen, Elder Jim's daughter, a sweet, docile creature who

24

quoted the Good Book at every turn. With the church and all its activities at the center of her life, he doubted she possessed the gumption to live on a farm.

Strong as an ox, the blacksmith's daughter could work alongside any man. But Ted couldn't imagine looking at that face for the rest of his life. Well, he might've gotten used to her face, if she'd shown the least bit of interest in his children. From what he'd seen, she preferred the company of horses.

Then there was Agnes, the owner of the café, who came after him with the zeal of a pig after slop and appealed to him even less. Something about Agnes set his teeth on edge. Maybe because she forever told him he was right and perfect. Was it wrong to hope for a woman with a bit of vinegar? One who wasn't afraid to set him straight when he went off on some tangent? And how would she handle his home, family *and* the café?

All godly women, but most weren't suitable mothers for Anna and Henry. And nothing about any of them drew him.

That left his bride-by-post.

God's solution. A woman of faith who loved children and life on the farm.

Ted tugged the brim of his hat lower on his forehead and scanned the passengers

25

leaving the train. A young woman stepped to the platform, wearing the sprig of lily of the valley pinned to her clothing. His pulse kicked up a notch. Sally, his bride.

Gussied up in a fancy purple dress, not the garb of a farmer's wife. Even gripping a satchel, she carried herself like a princess, all long neck and straight spine and, when she moved, as she did now, her full skirts swayed gracefully. He could hear the petticoats rustle from here.

She turned her head to sniff the flower, putting her face in profile. The plumed hat she wore tilted forward at a jaunty angle, revealing a heavy chignon at her nape.

He swallowed hard. Sally was a beautiful woman. He hadn't expected that. She didn't have a recent likeness. And he couldn't have sent the only picture in his possession — of him and Rose on their wedding day. In the three letters he and Sally had exchanged, he had described himself as best he could, even tried to be objective, though he hadn't told her everything.

It appeared she'd taken liberties with her description, too. Light brown hair, she'd said. Well, he'd call it more blond than brown, almost as blond as his.

Blue eyes, she'd written, though from this distance, he couldn't confirm it.

Tall and robust, she'd promised. Tall, all right, but slender, even fragile.

He noticed a nice curve to her lips.

And a jaw that said she liked having her way.

Sally didn't look strong enough to handle even part of the chores of a farmer's wife. Well, he'd prayed without ceasing for a suitable wife and God had given him this one. He couldn't send her back like he'd ordered the wrong size stovepipe from the Sears, Roebuck Catalog.

His stomach knotted. When a man prayed for wisdom, he shouldn't question the Lord's answer. Still, the prospect of marrying what amounted to a stranger was unsettling.

But Anna and Henry needed a mother to look after them. This morning, and countless others like it, left no doubt in his mind. He didn't have what it took to manage the farm, the livestock and his children. Never mind the house and cooking.

Even if Sally couldn't handle heavier chores, she'd said she could cook, clean and tend a garden, as well as Anna and Henry. That'd do. With all his qualms forming a lump in his throat, he moved out of the shadows. Might as well get on with it. The preacher was waiting.

He strode across the platform, nodding at people he knew. New Harmony was a nice town, though folks tended toward nosy. The news Ted Logan was seen greeting a woman down at the depot would spread faster than giggles in a schoolhouse.

When he reached his bride, he stuck out a hand. "I'm Ted."

Not a spark of recognition lit her eyes. Had he scared her? He was a large man. Still, he hadn't expected the blank stare.

"The flower . . . in the letters, we agreed —" He clamped his jaw to stop the prattle pouring out of his mouth. "You're Sally, aren't you?"

Her eyes lit. He gulped. They were blue, all right. Like forget-me-nots in full bloom.

"Oh, of course." She offered her hand. "Hello."

He swallowed it up with a firm shake. She winced. He quickly released his hold then held up callused palms. "Sorry, chopping wood, milking cows and strangling chickens have strengthened my grip."

Her rosy skin turned ashen, as if she might be sick. How would he manage if he married another woman in failing health?

CHAPTER TWO

Elizabeth swallowed hard. She'd never considered how fried chicken or cold milk arrived at the Manning table. Drat, she'd have to scrub her glove. Not that Sally's intended looked as if he didn't wash. He smelled clean, like soap, leather and sunshine.

Mercy, the man was brawny, wide at the shoulders with a massive neck, chest and powerful forearms. Not someone she'd care to cross. White creases edged his eyes in his tanned face, evidence of long periods spent in the sun. Those intense blue-gray eyes of his appeared to see right through her.

She hoped she was wrong about that.

But all the rest . . . well, she couldn't find anything to complain about. She'd expected another Reginald Parks and another reason to run. But something about Ted Logan kept her rooted to the spot, unable to look away.

Decency demanded she tell him she wasn't his bride. But if she did, would he insist she take the next train back? She needed time to think. To take a look at the town and see if she could find employment here.

She couldn't forget the importance of that farm, the fulfillment of her brother's dream. If only that didn't mean she had to marry the man, and all that entailed. She shivered. Well, she wasn't foolish enough to give her heart to this man.

Through narrowed eyes, he looked her over. "I expected you to have brown hair."

She gulped. "You don't like my hair?"

"The color of your hair doesn't matter a whit."

"Glad to hear it." She leaned toward him. "And so you know, I happen to like the color of yours. It's lighter than I expected, but it's tolerable."

His lips twisted up at one corner, as if they tried to smile without his approval. "I can't decide if I like a woman talking to me like that. Especially one I'm about to marry."

Elizabeth's stomach flipped at the mention of matrimony, a subject she intended to avoid. Her gaze traveled to a field of cows grazing not far from the tracks. "It's better than talking to the cows, isn't it?"

With a large hand, he gently tilted her face to his. "Yep. And a far sight better view."

A woozy feeling slid over her. Without thinking, she grabbed hold of his arm for support. And found rock-hard muscle. Beneath her feet, the ground shifted. She hadn't eaten in what seemed like forever. That had to be the reason for her vertigo.

He gave her a smirk and pulled away. "I'll get the rest of your things."

"Things? Oh, my luggage." Once he discovered she had no trunk, he'd send her back. Without money for food or housing, how would she take care of Robby? Moisture beaded her upper lip. "I, ah, left the trunk unattended in Chicago, only for a minute." With guilt at her lie niggling at her, she added, "When I returned, it was gone."

"Everything you bought with the money I sent — is gone?"

She nodded. Twice. "I'm sorry."

"Didn't you think to check it?"

"Didn't you ever make a mistake?" she fired back.

"Sure have," he said, arms folded across his chest, "but I've never lost all my clothes."

She grabbed a fistful of skirt. "Well, neither have I."

He sighed. "We'll have to stop at the mercantile."

If only she'd had time to gather her clothes scattered across the lawn. "I'll make do."

Waving a hand at her dress, he arched a brow. "With only that frippery to wear day and night?"

"That frippery is silk shantung, I'll have you know." She poked the rumpled lapel of his suit. "Do you think you're qualified to judge *my* fashion sense?"

He grinned, a most appealing smile. Or would be if he wasn't the most exasperating man she'd ever met.

"It's not your *fashion* sense I'm questioning."

Determined to stare him down, she held his gaze. Neither of them gave ground as travelers swept past them, tossing an occasional curious glance their way. "I'm smarter than you think."

"Smart enough to sew a new dress?"

"I can sew." She ducked her head. *Did embroidering pillow slips count?*

"We'll purchase fabric, whatever you need later."

Perhaps the store could use a clerk. The possibility eased the tension in her limbs. Instead of arguing with him, she'd better keep her head if she hoped to escape this mess. But without food she could barely keep on her feet.

Ted plopped his straw hat in place then took the satchel from her. "Better get moving. The preacher's waiting."

His words cut off her air supply as effectively as if he'd wrapped those large hands of his around her windpipe and squeezed. "So soon?"

"Did you expect to be courted first?"

She'd expected to remain single but wouldn't say that. "Well . . . no."

Behind them, the locomotive emitted a whistle, the call of "All aboard!" Wheels turned, picking up speed as the train chugged out of the station, taking with it her means of escape.

Elizabeth's eyes roamed what appeared to be the town's main street. Maybe she could find work here, though not a solitary establishment looked prosperous. She gnawed her lip and faced the truth. Unless a shop needed a clerk who could recite the multiplication tables while pouring tea, she had slim chance of finding employment.

Hysteria bubbled up inside her. She clamped her mouth shut, fighting the compulsion to laugh. Breathe in. Breathe out. Breathe in. Thankfully, the giddy sensation passed, replaced with the heavy weight of responsibility. Robby was depending on her, not a laughing matter.

Ted took hold of her elbow and ushered her along the platform. "We both know this marriage is one of convenience, a business arrangement."

Exactly what she wanted to hear, wasn't it? Then why did his words sting like a slap? Well, business arrangement or not, how could she wed a stranger? Elizabeth dug in her heels and yanked out of his grasp. "I . . . I can't. I can't marry you."

Ted turned to her, searching her face. His expression softened. He took her hand in his and ran his thumb along the top. Her stomach dipped. His gentle touch gave her a measure of comfort . . . and far too much awareness of the man.

"This isn't easy for either of us," he said, his eyes filling with tenderness. "But I want you to know, I'll be kind to you. Work hard to provide for you. I don't have much, but all I have is yours."

Elizabeth didn't want to marry, but what choice did she have? She didn't know a soul in this town. Didn't have a penny to her name. Didn't have a single idea what to do. That made her — a desperate woman.

A desperate woman with a proposal on the table.

A proposal that would solve all her problems.

Except this proposal was permanent — *and* offered to another woman. What would Ted say once he knew her true identity?

"My farm isn't much," he continued, his voice steady, calm. "But with God providing the sunshine and rain, the earth gives back what I put into it."

Such a simple yet profound statement. This man gave instead of took. He relied on hard labor, not luck. Ted Logan had planted his feet, appeared as solid as the earth he worked, the exact opposite of her father.

"I have cows, pigs, chickens, horses." He paused, then chuckled. "A dog."

Elizabeth's heart skittered. "What does your dog look like?" She held her breath, every muscle tense as she waited for his answer.

"Black and white. Shaggy." Ted shrugged. "Lovable."

Goose bumps rose on her arms. The exact description of the puppy Papa had given Robby, then taken away.

Martha always said there was no such thing as coincidence, not for a praying believer. Could Ted Logan be God's answer for Robby? Without a doubt her brother would adore this hulk of a man. Yes, Rob-

35

by's dream stood before her with the promise of a wedding band.

Ted held out an arm. "Are you ready?"

A business arrangement he'd said. Maybe
if she dealt with the marriage that way, she
could go through with the wedding.

For Robby's sake she would.

She slipped her hand into the crook of his
waiting arm. They strolled along the street.
The occasional passerby gave them a speculative look, but by now most people had left
the station.

Ted stopped at a weathered wagon with
nary a speck of gild, nor springs or leather
on the wooden seat to soften bumps in the
road. Two enormous dark brown horses
wearing blinders swung their heads to get a
better look at her, their harnesses jingling a
greeting. Her carriage waited. The matched
pair were built for hard work not preten-
sion, like Ted.

"That's King and his missus, Queen.
They're Percherons," Ted said, a hint of
pride in his voice.

Elizabeth didn't know much about breeds
to work the farm, but Ted obviously cared
for his animals, another point in his favor.
She ran her hand along a velvety nose.
"They're beautiful."

"And mighty curious about you."

36

Clearly she'd traded a fancy carriage for a rickety wagon, but a far more suitable groom. Her fingers toyed with the lily of the valley pinned to her dress. Could she go through with it? Could she marry a stranger?

Before she knew what happened, Ted handed her up onto the seat with ease, as if she weighed no more than dandelion fluff, then swung up beside her. Elizabeth shifted her skirts to give him room, while the memory of those large hands, warm and solid through the fabric of her dress, spun through her, landing in her stomach with a disturbing flutter.

She glanced at Ted's square profile, at this strong, no-nonsense man. The eyes he turned on her spoke of kindness. Even excluding Reginald Parks, she could do far worse. No doubt Ted Logan was a good man. He'd be kind to Robby. To her. That is if he didn't retract his offer of marriage once she revealed her true identity.

He clicked to the horses. "I left my children at the neighbor's. I'll pick them up tomorrow after breakfast."

Elizabeth swayed on the seat. "Children?"

"Don't tell me you've forgotten Anna and Henry?"

Sally hadn't mentioned children. "I'm just . . . tired."

How old were they? Since Mama died, Robby's care had been left to Martha. Sure, Elizabeth had read to her brother, taught him to tie his laces, but she had no experience caring for children.

What did she know about husbands for that matter?

And the tomorrow-morning part — did he intend a wedding night?

Well, if he had that expectation, she'd call on her touchy stomach. No bridegroom would want a nauseous bride.

Though if she didn't get something to eat — and soon — there wouldn't be a wedding. For surely the bride would be fainting on the groom.

CHAPTER THREE

On the drive through town, Ted's bride glanced from side to side, worrying her lower lip with her teeth. From the dismay plain on her face, the town disappointed her. Ordinarily he wasn't the edgy type, but this woman had him feeling tighter than a rain-soaked peg.

Not that Ted thought the town paradise on earth, but he hoped she didn't look down her aristocratic nose on the good people of New Harmony.

Silence fell between them while she plucked at her skirts. "I'm . . . I'm sorry about my clothes."

"No use crying over spilt milk."

Though money was always a problem. Because of her carelessness he'd have to spend more. Would he rue the day he'd advertised for a wife?

No, if Sally was kind to Anna and Henry, he could forgive her most anything. From what she'd said in her letters, she liked children and would be good to his.

If not, he'd send her packing.

His stomach knotted. He hoped it didn't come to that. Since Rose's death, his well-planned life had spun out of control. Every day he got further behind with the work. Every day his children got less of his attention. Every day he tried to do it all and failed.

To add to his turmoil, he'd felt the call to another life.

A life he didn't seek. Yet, the unnerving summons to preach was as real, as vivid, as if God Himself had tapped him on the shoulder.

Him.

He couldn't think of a man less qualified. Yet the command seared his mind with the clarity of God speaking to Moses through the burning bush.

As if that wasn't enough to leave a man quaking in his boots, his bride, the answer to his prayers, now harbored second thoughts.

Lord, if this is Your plan for our lives, show us the way.

Up ahead, Lucille Sorenson swept the entrance of the Sorenson Mercantile. The broom in her hand stilled as she craned her

40

neck to get a look at the woman sitting at his side. He tipped his hat as they rolled past, biting back a grin at the bewildered expression on her face.

They passed the saloon. Mostly deserted at this hour.

"Does that tavern foster gambling?"

Ted's breath caught. "Reckon so. Never been in the place."

"I'm glad." Sally smiled. "I'm sure I'll like . . . the town."

"I've lived a few places and the people here are good."

"Good in what way?"

"Folks pitched in after Rose died. Insisted on caring for the children and doing my chores. They've kept us supplied with enough food to feed an army of thrashers. I owe them plenty."

"People like that really exist?"

He raised a brow. "Aren't farm folk the same in Illinois?"

A flash of confusion crossed her face, but she merely shrugged. A prickle of suspicion stabbed at Ted. Something about Sally didn't ring true. Before he could sort it out, they reached the parsonage.

Ted pulled on the reins, harder than he'd intended. No reason to take his disquiet out on his team. "Here we are."

"Already?"

"Doesn't take long to get anywhere in New Harmony."

He set the brake, climbed down and walked to her side, reaching up a hand to help her from the seat. She took it and stood, wobbly on her feet. Was she sick? He looked for signs she'd be depositing her lunch in his hat brim. But all he saw was clear skin, apple cheeks and dazzling blue eyes.

He'd never seen bluer eyes, bluer than the sky on a cloudless day. His attention went back to her skin — smooth, fair with a soft glow about it. He'd have no trouble looking across the table at that face.

Or across the pillow.

Why had he thought she wouldn't suit?

He wrapped his hands around her waist, so tiny the tips of his fingers all but touched, and lowered her with ease. With her feet mere inches from the ground, their eyes met and held. Ted's heart stuttered in his chest. His gaze lowered to her mouth, lips slightly parted . . .

"Are you going to put me down?" she said, color flooding her cheeks.

"Sorry." He quickly set her on her feet.

She sneezed. Twice. Three times. Then

42

motioned to the road. "This dust is terrible."

Ted looked around him, took in the thick coat of dust on the shrubs around the parsonage, further evidence of the drought that held the town in its grip. Unusual for New Harmony.

"Is it always dusty like this?"

" 'Cept when it rains, then the streets turn to mud."

She wrinkled her nose. "Can't something be done?"

"Like what?"

She waved a hand at the road. "Like paving it with bricks."

"No brickyards in these parts."

"Hmm. If the dust turns to mud, why can't that mud be made into brick?"

An interesting point, one he hadn't considered.

"Well, I shall have to think about the problem," she said, tapping her lips with her index finger.

Thunderation. She sounded like the governor. Did she mean to send him out with a pickax and set to work making a road before sundown? "What are you, a reformer?"

She raised a delicate brow. "Would that bother you?"

"Hardly think you'll have time to reform

much more than my kitchen." His gaze swept Main Street, mostly deserted at this time of day. Folks were working either at home, in the fields or the town's businesses. All except for Oscar and Cecil Moore lazing on a bench in front of Pete's Barbershop, whittling. "Even if you did, you'll find nothing much gets done in New Harmony."

"Why? Are people here lazy?"

"For a farmer's daughter, you don't know much about farming. Farmers don't have time to fret about roads and such. We work and sleep. That's about it."

"What do you do for fun?"

"Fun?" He opened the gate of the picket fence and offered his arm. They strolled along the path to the parsonage door.

"Don't you have socials? Parties?"

"Some, but this isn't the city. We're a little . . . dry here."

The breeze kicked up another cloud of dust and she sneezed again. "*That* I believe."

He chuckled and rapped on the wooden door, which was all but begging for another coat of paint. Jacob kept his nose tucked in the Bible or one of the vast number of books he owned. And let chores slide. Maybe Ted could find time to handle the job on his next trip to town.

Lydia Sumner opened the door, neat as a

pin and just as plain, wearing a simple brown dress with a lace-trimmed collar, nut-brown hair pulled into a sensible bun. She had a heart of gold and, like now, a ready smile that she turned on Sally.

"Lydia, this is Sally Rutgers. My mail — Ah, fiancée."

"Hello, Miss Rutgers. Please come in." She stepped back to let them enter the small vestibule, then motioned to the closed door of Jacob's study. "My husband's working on Sunday's sermon. He'll only be a moment."

Ted doffed his hat and they followed Lydia into the parlor, where dollies and doodads covered every tabletop. "Glad we didn't hold him up."

"Can I offer you a spot of tea?"

Ted shook his head. "No thank —"

"Oh, I'd love a cup," Sally chimed in. "Do you have some cookies, perhaps? I'm famished."

"Why, Ted Logan, you didn't think to feed her?"

At half-past three? "Uh . . ."

Lydia patted Sally's arm. "The ladies at church vie over appeasing my husband's sweet tooth. I'll just be a minute."

Bald head shining like a beacon in the wilderness, Jacob passed his wife leaving the room. Tall, long limbed with the begin-

45

ning of a paunch, most likely the result of that sweet tooth, his pastor beamed. "Sorry to keep you folks waiting."

Once again Ted made introductions and he and Sally took seats on the sofa, leaving a chasm between them wide enough for a riverboat to navigate.

Jacob clapped Ted on the shoulder. "Shall we get started?"

"Yes," Ted said.

"No," Sally said.

Ted's jaw dropped to his collar. "No?"

She gave a sweet smile. "I hoped to have that tea first."

Used to cramming every waking moment with activity, Ted reined in his desire to hurry her along. Unsure this feisty woman would comply if he did.

Once Sally devoured two cups of tea and three cookies, she dabbed her lips with the snowy napkin. "Thank you, Mrs. Sumner."

Ted lowered his half-filled cup to the saucer. "Now are you ready to get married?"

She shot him a saucy smile. "I thought you'd never ask."

A chuckle rumbled in his chest.

Jacob slipped his glasses out of his coat pocket. "Do you have the license, Ted?"

"It's ready to go, filled out with the information Sally sent me in her last letter."

46

He withdrew the neatly folded paper from the inside pocket of his suit and handed it over.

Jacob scanned the document. "Everything appears in order."

Sally lifted a hand, then let it flutter to her lap. "Pastor Sumner, you . . . ah, might want to change one teeny thing."

He readied his pen. "Be glad to. What would that be?"

"The name."

All eyes swiveled to Sally. Ted frowned. What in tarnation?

The ticking of the mantel clock echoed in the sudden silence, hammering at Ted's already shaky composure.

"I'm, ah, not Sally Rutgers. My name is Elizabeth Ann Manning."

Had Ted heard correctly? The woman at his side wasn't Sally? He frowned. That would explain her odd behavior on the way over. Clearly his children had come as a surprise to her. No wonder she hadn't remembered anything from those letters he'd exchanged with Sally.

He'd been duped.

Pulse hammering in his temples, Ted rose to his feet, towering over her. "Why did you lie about your name all this time?"

"I haven't lied *all* this time." She lifted her

chin. "I've lied for less than an hour."

Jacob stared at the bride as if she'd grown two heads, one for each name. Lydia wilted into a chair, her smile drooping.

"What are you talking about?" Ted shoved out through his clenched jaw, his tone gravelly.

"Have you ever been down on your luck, Ted Logan?"

The question caught him like a sharp blow to the stomach. He shifted on his feet. "Well, yes, of course."

She ran a hand over her fancy dress. "Despite what you see, I'm destitute. So when the real Sally changed her —"

"What?" he bellowed.

"You're making me nervous, glowering at me like that. It's not my fault Sally got cold feet."

His pastor laid a hand on Ted's shoulder. "Let's stay calm. We'll get to the bottom of this."

Ted staggered back. "Who are you?"

"I told you. Elizabeth Ann Manning, your bride. That is —" she hesitated then forged ahead "— *if* you can ignore a small thing like an identity switch."

"A small thing?" He pointed toward the door. "Use the other half of that ticket. Go back to where you came from."

Wherever that might be.

Tears glistening in her eyes, she slumped against the sofa, her face pale and drawn. "I can't."

Lydia hurried to the impostor's side and patted her hand. She shot Ted a look that said she blamed him for this mess.

Him!

"I should've told the truth right off, but I was afraid you'd send me back," she said, her voice cracking, tearing at his conscience. "I'll get a job and repay you for the ticket."

Unable to resist a woman's tears, Ted bit back his anger. Something terrible must've happened to compel this lovely, well-bred woman to marry a stranger. Still, she'd deceived him.

Not that he hadn't made plenty of mistakes of his own. God probably didn't approve of his judging someone, especially someone with no place to live, no money and, in this town, whether she knew it or not, little prospects of either.

Still, something about her claim didn't ring true. If she was destitute, then it must've been a recent development.

"Our marriage is one of convenience," she whispered. "Weren't those your words?"

"Well, yes," he ground out.

She gave a weak smile. "Sally's not here. I

am. How much more convenient can I be?"

Lydia released a nervous giggle. Looking perplexed, Jacob's brow furrowed. Obviously nothing in those books of his had prepared him for this situation.

Scrambling for rational footing, something Ted took great pains to do, he struggled to examine his options. He'd spent most of his cash bringing his mail-order bride to Iowa. He couldn't afford the time or money to begin another search.

Still, could she be hiding something else? "Are you running from the law?"

She lurched to her feet and planted fisted hands on her hips. "Most certainly not," she said, her tone offended.

Unless she was a mighty good actress, he had nothing to fear there. Trying to gather his thoughts, he ran a hand across the back of his neck. "Will you be good to my children?"

"Yes."

"Do you believe in God?"

She hesitated. Her hands fell to her sides. A wounded expression stole across her face. "Yes, but God's forgotten me."

God forgot no one. Elizabeth's forlorn face told him she didn't know that yet.

Had God ordained this exchange of brides? Ted had prayed without ceasing for

God to bring the wife and mother He wanted for him and his children. Had this woman been God's answer all along?

Lord, is this Your will?

A potent sense of peace settled over him, odd considering the circumstances. "Well then, let's get on with it."

His pastor turned to Elizabeth. "You do realize the vows you are about to exchange are your promise before Almighty God."

Elizabeth paled but whispered, "Yes."

Though Jacob didn't look entirely convinced, he changed the bride's name on the document.

Lydia unpinned the flower on Elizabeth's dress and handed it to his bride, her bridal bouquet, then reeled to the organ in the back corner of the room. Her voice rose above the strains of "Love's Old Sweet Song" while Jacob motioned them to a makeshift altar. The song ended and Lydia slipped in beside Elizabeth.

"Dearly beloved, we're gathered here today to . . ."

Ted considered bolting out the door. But he couldn't plant the crops with Anna trailing after him and Henry riding on his back like a papoose. He had priorities that demanded a wife, even if he hadn't picked this one. He trusted with every particle of his being that God had.

"Ted, did you hear me?"

"I'm sorry, what?"

"Join hands with your bride," Jacob said in a gentle tone.

Ted took Elizabeth's ungloved hand, soft, small boned, cold, like his. Under that forceful exterior lived a woman as uncertain and unsettled as him.

"Elizabeth Ann Manning, do you take Theodore Francis Logan to be your wedded husband, to live together in holy marriage?"

She swallowed. Hard. "I do."

Ted gave her credit for not getting weepy on him. He couldn't handle a woman's tears.

"Do you promise to love him, honor and obey him for better or worse, for richer or poorer, in sickness and health, and forsaking all others, be faithful only to him so long as you both shall live?"

Elizabeth glanced at Ted, at the preacher, then back to him. "I'm . . . I'm not sure I can do the . . . obey part."

A strangled sound came from Lydia. Jacob frowned into the book he held, as if searching for a clue on how to respond. Ted opened his mouth but nothing came out.

"But I promise to try," Elizabeth added

with a feeble smile.

Jacob yanked out a handkerchief and mopped his brow, then the top of his head. "Is that acceptable to you, Ted?"

He nodded, slowly. This woman had nerve, he'd give her that. She wasn't one bit like Rose. Good thing they weren't standing up in front of the congregation. If they were, after this, every man he passed would be guffawing.

Looking eager to get the knot tied, Jacob righted his glasses. "All right, Miss Manning, do you agree, then, to what I just said, except for adding the word *try* to the obey part?"

Elizabeth beamed. "I do." Then she repeated the vows after the preacher, cementing her to him.

"Will you repeat after me, Ted?"

This marriage would be legal, binding like a business arrangement, but far more than that. As his pastor said, Ted would make his promises to this woman before Holy God, the foundation of his faith and his home.

Ted gave his "I do" promise, then Pastor Sumner recited the words, words Ted echoed in a voice hoarse with strain.

"I, Theodore Francis Logan, take thee, Elizabeth Ann Manning, to be my wife." *What was he letting himself in for?* "To have and to hold —" *Would she allow that?* "—in sickness and in health, for richer and for poorer —" *She could count on the poorer part.* "— and promise my love to you until death do us part." *He'd try to love her about as much as she tried to obey him.*

He turned his gaze from the preacher to his bride. She licked her lips, no doubt a nervous response, sending his stomach into a crazy dive.

Next thing he knew, Jacob had Ted digging in his pocket for the ring, a slender gold band he'd ordered from the catalog. It had cost him over a dollar, but he'd ordered fourteen-karat so the metal wouldn't discolor her skin.

"Slip it on her finger. And repeat after me."

Ted did as he was told, repeating the words, "With this ring, I thee wed."

He released her hand. Elizabeth looked at the ring as if a ball and chain hung from her finger.

"Inasmuch as you have pledged to the other your lifetime commitment, by the power vested in me by the State of Iowa, I now pronounce you man and wife in the name of the Father, the Son and the Holy Ghost." Looking around as though he addressed a church full of witnesses, he

54

warned, "Those whom God has joined together, let no man put asunder." Smiling, Jacob rocked back on his heels. "You may kiss the bride."

Ted had forgotten that part. He lowered his head as she turned her face. Their noses collided.

"No need . . ." she said softly.

Well, he had no intention of letting her believe he couldn't manage a simple kiss. He cupped her jaw, tilted up her face. Her eyelids fluttered closed, revealing long, dark lashes. He leaned forward and brushed her lips with his. She tasted of tea and sugar, all sweetness with a bit of bite.

Her eyes opened. Startled, bright blue, a man could get lost in those eyes. He had an impulse to pull her to him and kiss her more thoroughly. But kissing her like that would most likely stand Lydia's hair on end. And scare his bride. After all, she hadn't married for love. And neither had he.

Like a racehorse crossing the finish line, Jacob blew out a gust of air. "I've got to admit, this has been the most unusual wedding I've ever performed."

"And for the handsomest couple," Lydia said, beaming. "We hope you'll be very happy."

The wary look in Elizabeth's gaze no

doubt mirrored his, but they murmured their thanks.

Jacob ushered them to a desk, dipped the pen into the inkwell and handed it to Ted. "Now all you have to do to make this legal is sign the license," Jacob said, examining their faces as if expecting one of them to refuse.

Ted signed and passed the pen to Elizabeth.

She wrote her name with a wobbly hand, then glanced at Lydia. "Could I bother you for a couple more cookies?"

"Why, of course." Lydia giggled. "You have quite the appetite."

A few minutes later, Ted ushered his new wife, clutching a fistful of cookies, into the sunshine. A cardinal chirped a greeting from the top branch of the ancient maple sheltering the lawn. His horses twitched their tails, chasing away flies. The sun still hung in the heavens.

Around him, nothing had changed. Yet in less than an hour, everything had.

A troubling truth struck Ted. He knew more about his livestock than about the woman he'd just married. But then she must feel the same disquiet about him.

One thing was obvious. Unlike Sally Rutgers, Elizabeth Manning had courage. Courage based on desperation, not on the desire for a family. What had driven his wife to switch places with his mail-order bride?

What was she hiding?

What other lies had she told?

CHAPTER FOUR

Outside the parsonage, her new husband turned to Elizabeth, the chill in his steely gray-blue eyes raising goose bumps on her arms. "I've got to ask. Where are the clothes I bought?"

Elizabeth looked away. "With Sally."

His mouth thinned. "When you said someone stole your trunk, you lied."

She swallowed. "I didn't know how to tell you the truth."

Suspicion clouded his eyes. "If you're lying about anything else, I want to know it. Now."

Elizabeth dropped her gaze. She did have one more lie, a three-and-a-half-foot, blue-eyed whopper.

But if she told Ted about Robby, about the real reason she'd run from Chicago and into this marriage of convenience, he'd march her into the preacher's and demand an annulment. What would become of her brother then?

"I'm sorry I lied. But Sally's clothes wouldn't fit me."

His gaze traveled over her, bringing a flush to her cheeks, and a rosy hue beneath his tan. "Reckon not."

He helped her onto the wagon seat, then scrambled up beside her, released the brake and pulled back on the reins. "We'll stop at the mercantile to pick up what you need."

As they rode down the street, Elizabeth's focus settled on the rumps of the horses. How long before she could bring Robby here?

How long before Ted lost patience with her inability to handle a household? Or care for his children? Her stomach lurched. What would happen then?

Well, she wouldn't fail. Couldn't fail. Too much depended on it.

She scrambled for a change of subject, a way to smooth the rough waters between them. "Pastor Sumner performed a lovely service."

Ted gave a curt nod.

Wonderful. A husband of no words. Well, she knew how to fill the gap. "He didn't seem like one of those hellfire-and-brimstone preachers."

"Jacob can rise to the occasion if it's warranted."

Elizabeth cringed. Would she be the topic of his next sermon on deceit? She tamped down the thought. Perhaps she had a way to get him to open up. "Were you born here?"

"No."

Talking to Ted was like pulling teeth with a fraying thread. "Then where?"

"St. Louis."

"What made you leave?"

"No reason. Just looking for something, I guess."

Elizabeth couldn't imagine what he'd been looking for that had stopped him here.

One street comprised New Harmony's downtown. A blacksmith stood at a forge in front of his shop, hammering a red-hot horseshoe while a young woman prepared the steed's hoof. A few doors down, a man wearing bib overalls entered the bank. Two women stood talking outside Sorenson Mercantile, the younger bouncing a baby on her hip. Signs tacked to the fading exterior advertised a post office and seed store in the back. Make *one* stop and you'd be done for the day.

The door to a café stood open to catch the afternoon breeze. A barber's red-and-white-striped pole caught her eye among the other nondescript buildings. Not much of a town compared to Chicago, compared to most anywhere.

Still, New Harmony provided more chance to socialize than being tethered to a farm. That might be Robby's dream and she'd done all this to give it to him, but she dreaded life in the country. How would she survive for the next ten, twenty, goodness, forty years? Still, her situation could be worse. She could be wearing Reginald Parks's ring.

Once she handled Ted's household reasonably well, she'd have the courage to tell him about Robby. At the prospect of reuniting with her brother, her mood lifted, putting a smile on her face. Robby was the warmest, sweetest little boy. He never judged. Never manipulated. Never let her down.

In the meantime, maybe a neighbor would befriend her. Or were these people as shallow and unfeeling as her so-called friends in Chicago, once word got out about the Manning reversals?

Ted said he'd be kind to her, take care of her and give her all he possessed. But if she didn't fulfill her end of the bargain to his satisfaction, would he forget all his fine words? Were Ted's promises as meaningless as Papa's?

She fingered the gold band encircling her finger. Like most young girls, she'd dreamed of her wedding day, marrying a man she adored, a man who cherished her in return. But her parents' marriage had taught her that real life didn't measure up to fantasy.

The wheels caught in a rut in the street, jostling the wagon. Clinging to the seat, Elizabeth glanced at her husband, the flesh-and-blood man sitting next to her. Firm jaw, solid neck, wide shoulders. Ted had called their union a business arrangement, a binding contract. No matter what she told herself, Ted Logan didn't look like a line on anyone's ledger.

At Sorenson's Mercantile, he pulled back on the reins, set the brake, then jumped down and tied up at the hitching post. His long strides brought him to her side. He lifted her to the street, his hands strong yet gentle. If only she could trust Robby's future to this man.

Up ahead a plumpish woman made a beeline toward them, the ribbons on her bonnet flapping in the breeze. "Hello, Ted. Who's this?"

"Afternoon, Mrs. Van Wyld. This is Elizabeth, my wife."

Her blue eyes twinkled. "Well, imagine that? I hadn't heard about your marriage."

She turned to Elizabeth. "Call me Johanna."

Obviously this woman kept up with the news. Still, her warm greeting brought a smile to Elizabeth's face. "We just came from the ceremony."

"You did? Well, congratulations!" She beamed. "Why, I must be one of the first to know." She said goodbye then rushed off, calling to a woman down the way.

Ted harrumphed. "No need to put an announcement in the paper now that Johanna knows."

Elizabeth's optimism tumbled at the expression on his face. They'd have no friends. No family. No party to celebrate. "Were you hoping to keep our marriage a secret?" *In case it didn't work out.* But she didn't finish the thought.

"No." He opened the mercantile door. "It would've been nice to get used to it ourselves before the whole county knows."

Inside, Elizabeth gaped at the wide array of goods filling every table and ledge. The scent of kerosene, vinegar and coffee greeted her. Behind the long counter, shelves stocked with kerosene lamps, china teapots, enameled coffeepots, dishes and crocks rose from floor to ceiling.

Barrels of every size and shape lined the front of the counter, leaving enough space

63

for two customers at the brass cash register. Overhead, lanterns, pots and skillets hung from the ceiling. Picture frames, mirrors and tools of every size and description lined the walls.

Ted pointed to a table in the center of the room piled with bolts of fabric. "Get yourself some dresses."

"I . . . don't see any dresses."

He gave her a curious look. "Uh . . . that's because they aren't made yet."

"Oh. Right." She marched toward the bolts. "I'll take the fabric to the dressmaker's —"

He laid a hand on her arm and then jerked it back, as if afraid to touch her. "Dressmaker's?"

"Well, yes, won't she —" The look on his face cut off Elizabeth's protest. "Oh." Her fingers found her mouth. "I'm the dressmaker?"

"You said you could sew."

She avoided his eyes. "I may have . . . exaggerated." She'd figure out how when the time came.

He chuffed but let it go. "Don't take too long making your selection. It's getting late."

Elizabeth glanced at the afternoon sun streaming in through the front windowpanes. "Late?"

64

"I'd like to get us home before dark."

A jolt of awareness traveled through her, squeezing against her lungs. She gulped for air then forced her attention to the material, trying to ignore the implications.

Lovely bolts of restful blue gingham, cheerful yellow dimity, sweet sprigs in pink twill. She ran a hand over a length of lavender checked cotton, cool to the touch. Not exactly the silks and velvets of her gowns back home, but nice.

"The blue would look pretty with your eyes," he said, his gaze warm and intense.

His inspection set her hands trembling, a silly reaction. Clearly she needed a meal, far more than a few cookies. "Then I'll take this one," she said, indicating the blue.

"Get enough for two, one to wear and one to wash."

Laundry, another to add to the long list of chores she'd never done.

Thinking of the closet full of dresses in Chicago, she bit back a sigh. Then she remembered Ted's concern about money. Offering two was generous. She motioned to her dress. "I can wear this."

"To church maybe, but you'd make a pretty scarecrow wearing that in the garden." He hesitated. "Get enough to make three."

Had he just called her pretty? And offered three dresses?

Yes, and called her a scarecrow, too. Her new husband could use lessons in chivalry.

Heavenly days, she didn't know how to make *one* dress. Still, she couldn't refuse his gift. Under his rough exterior, Ted Logan possessed a soft heart.

A woman wearing her salt-and-pepper hair in a tight bun and a crisp white apron over a simple blouse and skirt lumbered over, her smile as wide as her hips. "Why, Ted Logan, who do we have here?"

Ted made introductions. The shop owner jiggled all over at the news.

"Well, I'll be! *Huuubert!*" she cried, the way Martha had when, as a child, Elizabeth had ignored her calls to come inside. "Come here and meet Ted's new wife!"

"I ain't deef, missus." A ruddy-faced splinter of a man, his suspenders crossing his humped shoulders, moseyed in from the back, carrying a bag of seed. He laid it on the counter then ambled to where they stood. Smiling at Elizabeth, he shook Ted's hand. "Well, Ted, you married yourself a looker."

"Oh, she certainly is," Mrs. Sorenson said. "Resembles one of those ladies in the Godey's book, all fancied up and pretty."

Heat climbed Elizabeth's neck. "Thank you."

"How long have you two been married?"

Ted shifted on his feet. "We just came from the preacher."

"Why, I saw you ride past. You must've been on your way to the parsonage then." Mrs. Sorenson elbowed her husband in the ribs. "Tell them congratulations, Hubert."

"I'm about to. Much happiness." He turned to Ted and clapped him on the shoulder. "You're a lucky man. Can't say I recall seeing your missus before. If I had, I'd have remembered." He smiled at Elizabeth. "Are you from around these parts, Mrs. Logan?"

Elizabeth's new name socked her in the belly. She was a missus now. Her belly flipped faster than Martha's Saturday pancakes. "No, I —"

"We're here to buy a few things," Ted interrupted.

He must not want people to know she was a mail-order bride, and not the original bride at that. Did he believe they'd think she popped up under a rosebush?

Mr. Sorenson waved a hand. "What can I get you folks?"

Ted motioned to the stack of bolts Elizabeth had selected. "She needs enough fabric to make a dress from each of these."

Mrs. Sorenson stepped forward, her gaze running up and down Elizabeth's frame, muttering gibberish about yardage and seam allowances. She grabbed up the three bolts Elizabeth indicated and lugged them to the long counter.

Elizabeth and Ted followed, watching as Mrs. Sorenson unrolled the blue gingham, sending the bolt thumping across the counter. Soon she'd cut and stacked all the fabrics in a neat pile. "Will you need thread, needles?"

Elizabeth glanced at Ted.

"Plenty of thread at home, needles, too." He glanced away. "But Elizabeth does need . . . a . . . few other things."

Mrs. Sorenson nodded. "Like what?"

Ted tugged at his collar, squirming like a liar on a witness stand. He may have been married, but as a gentleman, he couldn't speak of a woman's unmentionables. "Get her two of whatever she requires."

"Of course." Mrs. Sorenson grinned. "Right this way, Mrs. Logan."

As Elizabeth followed the older woman to a table at the back of the store, she wondered if she'd ever get used to hearing herself referred to as Mrs. Logan.

Ted stayed behind, talking grain with Mr.

Sorenson. Grateful not to have to select undergarments with her new husband looking on, Elizabeth unfolded a pretty white nightgown, a sheer, lacy thing.

"Oh, your husband will love that," Mrs. Sorenson whispered, her voice warm with approval.

Glancing back at Ted, she found him watching her. She dropped the gown like a hot biscuit and grabbed a long-sleeved, plain, high-necked nightgown. Not exactly body armor, but close.

"It's hot around here in the summer," Mrs. Sorenson put in.

Heeding the hint, Elizabeth selected a sleeveless square-necked gown with no trim. Ugly and plain. *Perfect.*

"That's serviceable, but this is beautiful." Mrs. Sorenson pointed to the sheer, lacy gown.

"It's too . . . too . . ." Elizabeth grabbed up the tag. "Pricey. You know new husbands."

"Yes, I do," the older woman said with a wink, "which is why I suggested this one."

Elizabeth quickly gathered up two pairs of drawers, an underskirt and two chemise tops in cotton, all simple and unadorned, whether Mrs. Sorenson approved or not.

At the counter, the shop owner totaled

the purchases. When Elizabeth heard the number, she gasped. A sudden image of her father harassed by creditors popped into her mind. Had she and Mama spent too much money on clothes? Jewelry? Had mounting bills forced Papa to gamble? If so, why hadn't he gotten a job like most men?

"Add that to my account," Ted said, his voice thick and gruff as if saying the words hurt.

Was she to witness yet another man's financial ruin? She vowed to watch her pennies. Well, when she had pennies to watch.

Mr. Sorenson opened a book, the pages smudged and crammed with names and numbers; cross outs and additions. Elizabeth couldn't imagine how he kept track of who owed him what in such a messy ledger.

Mrs. Sorenson wrapped the purchases, then handed two bundles to Elizabeth. "I look forward to seeing you again, Mrs. Logan."

Elizabeth blinked.

Mrs. Sorenson chuckled. "Why, Hubert, she forgot her name."

"Oh. Yes." She gave a weak laugh. "Thanks for your help, Mrs. Sorenson."

"Anytime! Enjoy the sewing."

Ted took her elbow. If she could find an

excuse to linger, Elizabeth could ask Mrs. Sorenson's advice about dressmaking.

The store's proprietor turned to Ted. "Are the children at the Harpers'?"

Ted grabbed up the seed. "Yes, Anna loves their new baby."

"Hubert, get that precious child some candy."

"I am, missus, if you'd stop issuing orders long enough to notice."

Elizabeth bit back a groan. Another model of wedded bliss. Why had she taken such a drastic step?

Mr. Sorenson removed the lid from a large jar of peppermints on the counter, dipped out a brass scoopful and dumped them into a small sack, then handed it to Elizabeth. "These are for Anna."

Ted raised a palm as if to refuse, then nodded. "That's thoughtful. Thank you."

"Give a kiss to Henry," Mrs. Sorenson added.

These shopkeepers were warm and generous, different from those Elizabeth had known in Chicago.

"We'd better be on our way," Ted said. "I promised dinner at the café."

"Could I speak to you, Ted?" Mr. Sorenson asked.

"Sure." He turned to Elizabeth. "Will you

be all right for a minute?"

"Of course," Mrs. Sorenson said for her. "That'll give us a chance to talk. Maybe your wife will share a favorite recipe."

Elizabeth gulped. Unless calling the maid for tea constituted a favorite recipe in these parts, she was in deep trouble. Surely only the beginning of her woes.

CHAPTER FIVE

Ted stowed the seed in the wagon, then took the packages from Elizabeth and wedged them in tight. For a man in a hurry, he had a patient way about him. She'd never been patient about anything in her life. A trait like Ted's could either drive her to distraction or make life easier.

Right now, he dallied when her stomach demanded speed. "I'm starved."

"Getting married must give you an appetite," he said, giving her a smile.

Mercy, the man set her off-kilter with that lopsided grin of his.

They walked up the street to Agnes's café. Inside the spotless, simple dining room, he led the way to a table in the corner. He murmured greetings to the diners they passed, but didn't stop to introduce her. The way people put their heads together, the room suddenly abuzz, Ted must have lost his wish for privacy.

He sat across from her, studying his menu while she studied him.

Ted looked up. Met her gaze. A baffled expression crossed his face. "What?"

Her face heated and she grabbed the menu. "I'm thinking about my order."

"Good evening, Ted." Carrying glasses of water, a round-faced, dark-eyed woman with black curly bangs smiled at Ted. When she looked at Elizabeth her warm smile faltered. "This must be your wife," she said, stumbling over the word *wife.*

"News travels fast. Elizabeth, this is Agnes Baker, proprietor of this establishment and the best cook in town."

Agnes and Elizabeth nodded a greeting while Ted scanned the single sheet as though he'd never laid eyes on a menu before. "What's the special today?"

"Your favorite. Chicken and dumplings."

"I'll take a plate of that." He turned to Elizabeth. "Know what you want?"

Elizabeth's stomach rumbled. The cookies and tea had kept her on her feet, but her stomach had met her backbone a long time ago. "I'll have the same." She smiled at Agnes. "I'm glad to meet one of Ted's friends."

A sheen of sudden tears appeared in Agnes's eyes. "It'll only be a minute," she

74

said, then sped toward the kitchen.

Elizabeth glanced at Ted, who fidgeted with his silverware. Did he realize this woman adored him?

If so, why had he sought a bride by mail?

The gazes of their fellow diners burned into Elizabeth's back. Apparently everyone knew everybody else in a town this size. Well, she'd rather be here, the topic of speculation, than on the way to the farm with Ted. And the night ahead.

Her heart lost its rhythm.

A tall man loped over to their table. "Reckon this is your missus, Ted. Johanna came in earlier, making her rounds." He cackled. "Thought I'd say howdy to your bride, seeing I'm the mayor of sorts." He looked at Elizabeth. "Not that I'm elected, but mayor's what folks call me." He stuck out a hand. "Name's Cecil Moore."

"Nice to meet you, Mr. Moore."

Agnes arrived, two steaming plates in her hands.

"I'll let you lovebirds eat in peace," Cecil said, moseying on to the next table where the occupants looked their way, smiling.

Agnes set Ted's plate in front of him. "Hot and piled high, the way you like it."

"Thanks, Agnes." Ted blushed, actually

blushed, no doubt aware of Agnes's devotion.

Then the proprietor plopped Elizabeth's dish down on the table without a glance and returned to the kitchen.

Elizabeth's gaze dropped to her food. Her portion didn't measure up to Ted's but, far too hungry to fuss about it, she attacked her food. Mmm, delicious.

She glanced at Ted's untouched plate and lowered her fork.

"I'll say grace," he said, then bowed his head.

Cheeks aflame, Elizabeth bowed hers.

"Lord, thank You for this food. Walk with Elizabeth and me in our new life as man and wife. Amen."

Elizabeth's gaze collided with Ted's. She quickly looked away. Not that Elizabeth had neglected praying about her problems, but God had withheld His answer.

Well, she'd found her own. And he sat across from her now.

Ted picked up his fork. "How long since you've eaten?"

His words reminded her to take dainty bites, not pig-at-the-trough gulps. "I had tea and cookies at the parsonage."

His brow furrowed. "You didn't eat on the train, did you?" he asked softly.

She stared at her plate. "No."

"Look at me, Elizabeth."

She raised her chin and looked into his eyes, which were now clouded. Was it with dismay?

"I may not have much in the way of money, but my cellar's stocked. You won't go hungry. At least if you're a good cook," he added with a chuckle.

She fiddled with her napkin. "I'm sure I can."

"You've never tried?" he said, his tone laden with amazement.

Elizabeth took a swig of water. "I grew up in a home with maids, a cook, laundress, tutor, butler, even a nanny."

Ted frowned. "You said you were destitute."

"I am. Of late."

"What happened?"

"What happened isn't a topic for good digestion."

She wanted to ask how long it had been since Rose had died, but it didn't seem like the right time, either. Instead she returned to her food.

Ted took a bite, obviously enjoyed the tasty dish and ate every morsel, and didn't end the meal with a belch.

Uninvited, a memory invaded her mind.

Of the three red-faced, ho-humming, toe-tapping times she'd sat in the parlor with Reginald after dinner, swishing her fan until her arm ached, trying to dissipate the silent belches rocking his spindly body and the unpleasant odors chasing after them. She'd tried to be kind, to turn the other nostril, ah, cheek, but he'd been . . . distasteful.

Papa had said Reginald Parks was short on manners but long on cash so he had to be forgiven. Instead of forgiving Reginald, she'd defied her father. A heavy weight squeezed against her lungs. Would Papa find it in his heart to forgive her?

Would Ted forgive her once he knew about Robby?

She looked up to find Ted studying her in that quiet way of his. He wiped his lips on the napkin. Nice lips. Full. At the memory of Ted's kiss at the end of the ceremony, Elizabeth's pulse leaped. His lips had been soft. Gentle. Enticing.

The one time Reginald had lowered his whiskered face to hers, he'd triggered spasms in her throat that threatened to make her retch.

Another point in Ted's favor.

Though, at the moment, her stomach tumbled. Too many uncertainties churned inside her.

The door burst open and in marched Mrs. Van Wyld, followed by a knot of ladies, beaming like sunshine. Johanna led the procession to their table.

"The folks of New Harmony, leastwise those I could round up, are here to give you newlyweds a party." She gestured to Cecil Moore. "If I know the mayor, he's got his harmonica. His brother will be along with his fiddle."

Grinning, Cecil flipped the instrument out of his pocket and played a few merry notes. Ted looked as if he wished the floor would open up and swallow him, but Elizabeth's toe tapped under her skirts.

People came over, shook Ted and Elizabeth's hands, offering their congratulations.

"Would you like a piece of Agnes's pie?" Johanna said, once the crowd cleared.

Ted took a step toward the door. "We really need to be going."

"My treat," Johanna persisted. "Sorry it's not cake, but it's mighty good."

In case she needed to escape tonight, Elizabeth couldn't risk putting the sheets to the test. She turned to Ted. "Is your house one story or two?"

"One."

"Oh, I'll have a slice of pie, then. A big one." She smiled at Ted, resting her chin on her palm. "Pie is my weakness."

Johanna waved to Agnes. "They'll have pie. I'm paying."

Agnes appeared at their elbows. "I've got sugar cream and cherry today."

"The sugar cream, please," Elizabeth said.

Ted frowned as if he didn't approve of the turn of events. "None for me."

"Don't be silly," Johanna said. "This is your wedding day. Your bride shouldn't eat pie alone."

Ted sighed. "All right —"

"Cherry and coffee black," Agnes said, obviously familiar with Ted's tastes.

With Johanna issuing orders, diners moved the tables, opening space in the middle of the room. The mayor let loose on his harmonica. A heavyset, squat fellow strode in carrying the fiddle and joined in. Cecil's brother Oscar, Johanna informed Elizabeth.

Four couples formed a square, moving up and back, square dancing or so Johanna explained.

Agnes arrived with coffee and pie. Flaky golden crusts piled high with luscious filling. Elizabeth thanked her, and then dug in. Mmm, cinnamon. Sugar. Cream. She licked her lips, capturing a speck from the corner of her mouth. "This is delicious." She glanced at her husband.

Ted sat motionless, his fork hovering over his plate. Did the man pray before each course? No, he was staring at her lips. Had she missed a crumb? She dabbed at her mouth with the napkin.

His face turned a deep shade of red. Blue eyes collided, hastily looked away and then back again. He dropped his gaze to his plate, slicing his fork into his pie and then lifting a forkful of cherries and crust to his mouth. Her stomach dipped. When had pie ever looked better going into someone else's mouth besides her own?

In all of Elizabeth's years she had never been unable to finish a piece of pie. But tonight, her wedding night, she pushed the plate away. "I'm stuffed."

Ted smiled. "Glad I finally got you filled up." He glanced out the window. "Time to head for home."

"We can't leave." She waved a hand. "Your friends have done all this for us. To celebrate our marriage."

"Johanna's turned our wedding dinner into a spectacle."

"My dreams for my wedding day hardly match our ceremony."

Ted had the decency to look contrite. He rose and offered his hand. "May I have this dance, Mrs. Logan?"

"If you'll teach me the steps, Mr. Logan."

"It'll be my pleasure."

Her pulse raced at the warm, steady pressure of his hand on her back. At the warmth radiating from his very masculine body. At the breadth of those powerful shoulders.

No doubt Ted could protect her from any danger. Yet she'd never felt more threatened. More out of control.

Surprisingly light on his feet for a hulk of a man, Ted led her through the dance. But even with the unnerving awareness that others watched every move they made, smiling and nodding approval at her attempt to join in, she wanted to stay. Leaving would mean being alone with her husband.

Right now, if she could, she'd stamp Cancel on their mail-order nuptials. But that meant she couldn't give Robby a home.

So like a self-assured bride, she smiled up at her groom, but under her skirts, her knees were knocking.

What had she gotten herself in for?

Neither Elizabeth nor Ted said much on the trip to the farm. As dusk crept in and a full moon rose overhead, lights appeared in the houses they passed. Elizabeth kept her gaze off the man beside her, who took up more

82

space than a mere man should, and focused on the fields. The turned-over earth exposed parched soil as cracked as old china. An owl hooted overhead, an eerie, lonely sound that crawled along her skin, raising the hair on her nape.

"You mentioned a weakness for pie. Any other flaws I should know about?" Ted said at last, his voice laden with humor.

No doubt an attempt to ease the tension crackling between them. Well, she'd do her part. "I'm emotional. A talker."

He turned toward her, his pupils reflecting the moonlight. "What do you mean, emotional?"

She squirmed under his stare.

"Are you a weeper?"

"Just the opposite. I have a temper." She pinched her fingers together then opened them a tad. "A teeny temper."

"Ah, I see." He chuckled. "Thanks for the warning."

"Do you?" Elizabeth asked.

"Do I what?"

"Have a temper?"

"Nothing makes me mad, except deceit. How can you trust a man if he can't be taken at his word?"

Fortunately for her, he didn't say *woman.*

Elizabeth fidgeted with her ring. "Couldn't

there be a good reason a person would lie?"

"The truth sets people free."

She'd be set free, all right. If Ted learned about Robby, he'd rip this simple gold band off her finger and get an annulment faster than Johanna Van Wyld could spread the news.

Ted shifted on the seat. "Seems odd to be married and know so little about you."

"I feel the same."

"It'll take some getting used to, especially for my children."

Elizabeth gulped. She'd forgotten about Ted's children. From what she could remember about Robby, babies cried a lot and forever needed a change of clothes. "How old are they?"

"Anna's seven and scared, I think. She understands a lot."

Robby had been six when Mama died. Even though Martha had taken care of her brother when Mama took sick, Robby had cried for his mother. Rose's death had to be even more traumatic for Ted's daughter.

"Henry's fourteen months. All he cares about are his meals and a soft lap." He lifted a brow. "That is, if you're one to cuddle a baby."

She'd cuddled Robby. No problem there. Besides, a lap meant sitting and from all

Ted's talk about work, sitting sounded good. "I'll have a lap anytime he needs one — at least when you're not available."

"As long as you're gentle with my children, you have no need to worry about overstepping. I'll expect you to mother them whether I'm in the fields or in the house."

Elizabeth suspected little ones cared not a whit about who you were, how much you owned or where you came from. Long as they had that lap and a ready meal.

But cooking, well, she hoped Ted and his children had low expectations, bottom-of-a-burned-pan low.

Approaching a house near the road, a dog barked a greeting, leaping along the bank as they passed. Inside, people gathered around the table. Good people who lived by the toil of their hands. Not trying to make money without working for it like Papa had, and losing most every time.

Still, as furious as Papa's gambling made her, she still loved him. He was an affectionate, jovial, handsome man who had a gift with words. In that careless manner of his, he loved her, too, and was probably worried about her now.

Tears pricked at her eyes. She'd propped a note on her dresser, assuring him of her love. But love might not heal the breach she'd crossed when she'd defied him.

Her attention drifted to Ted, which didn't do much for her peace of mind. She shifted, trying to ease the tightness between her shoulder blades. How could she relax, knowing once they reached the farm, she and her new husband would be totally alone?

Ted had made no move to touch her, other than to help her from the wagon and a polite offer of his arm. Still, they'd signed a marriage license. And surely he'd noticed that baffling attraction between them at the café.

She wrung her hands in her lap while the pie and noodles waged war in her stomach. He'd better keep his distance. They'd only scarcely met.

Desperate to end the silence between them, she said, "I don't mean to criticize, but Mr. Sorenson's ledger could use some organizing."

"Sorenson has a heart of gold, not a head for bookkeeping. He asks me for advice, but can't seem to implement it. Sometimes I think the store is too much for him."

Elizabeth's heart skipped a beat. Could this be the solution for earning the money to bring Robby to New Harmony?

"We're not far from my place." In the

gloom, Ted's deep voice made her jump. "Sorry, did I scare you?"

"I don't frighten that easily."

"Me, either," he promised.

She stiffened. "You should be scared, at least of me."

"Oh, I thought you only had a teeny temper. I'm not afraid of that." He chuckled. "Appears my wife's the timid one."

"Me?"

"Yes, you." He tipped a finger under her chin for a brief, heart-stopping moment and then went back to the reins. "I don't see any other wives around, do you?"

"Well, maybe I am, a little."

He laughed. "Thank goodness, because I'm terrified of you."

Laughter burst out of her into the clear night air. For the first time in ages she felt more in control of her situation.

She cocked her head at her new husband. "You're a handsome man, Ted Logan. And from what I've seen of New Harmony, probably the most eligible male in town."

Eligible for Chicago, too. Anywhere. But she wouldn't tell him that.

He looked mildly uncomfortable with her appraisal. "I'm a married man, remember?"

As if she could forget.

"Why would you advertise for a wife when

I suspect you could've had Agnes, probably a number of other women, too, by simply saying the word?"

He cleared his throat. "I thought it better to marry for convenience rather than marry someone who'd expect love."

Obviously Ted held no illusions that this marriage would lead to love. Good. Love wasn't her goal, either. She only wanted a happy home for Robby.

"Would you be marrying anyone if you didn't have two children to care for?"

The reins hung limp in his hands. "No."

"That makes you as desperate as I am."

He flashed some teeth, pearly white in his tan face. "Reckon so. So why did you decide to take Sally's place?"

That quickly Ted gained the upper hand. Unaccustomed to feeling out of control with beaux, too young, too old or too self-absorbed to be taken seriously, Elizabeth's brow puckered.

"I came to Iowa to . . ." She took in a deep breath. "To get away from a marriage my father arranged . . . to a much older man, a man I couldn't stomach marrying."

"Why would your father insist you marry someone like that?"

"Money. The man's rich." She sighed. "So I ran."

"Into marriage with me. Guess I should be flattered you consider me the lesser of two evils."

"To be honest, I'd planned to find a job here, not a husband. But one look at the town destroyed that strategy."

He chuckled. "No danger of getting a swelled head with you around. Not sure I've ever met a female like you."

Ted's tone held a hint of awe. Did he understand the tedium of propriety, the yearning for something she couldn't name? "I'll take that as a compliment."

He reached across the space between them and brushed a tendril of hair off her neck. "You know, Mrs. Logan, this marriage might just be fun."

His wife scooted about as far from Ted as she could get without tumbling from the wagon. Not a typical bride. But then not a typical wedding, either.

He stood over six foot tall. Hard work had broadened his shoulders and strengthened the muscles in his arms, an ox of a man, some people said. Was she afraid of him?

Well, if so, she needn't worry. He was far more afraid of this slip of a woman from Chicago. If she smelled any sweeter, he'd need to sleep in the barn instead of the children's room, his plan for tonight.

The decision made, he felt an odd sense of relief. Elizabeth might be his wife, but she was a stranger. A charming stranger at that. She made him laugh, something he hadn't done in far too long. And as now, he could barely tear his gaze away from the curve of her neck, her tiny waist —

"What happened to your wife?"

Her question doused his interest like a glass of cold water in his face. "Rose died of nephritis." He tightened his hold on the reins. "Her kidneys began shutting down after Henry's birth."

"I'm sorry."

Nodding an acknowledgment, he turned the horses into the lane leading up to the house, relieved to reach his farm. And avoid the topic of his deceased wife.

As they bounced over the ruts, he remembered his citified wife's complaints about the condition of New Harmony's streets. He made a mental note to haul rocks from the creek to level the surface after he'd finished planting.

The road curved around to the back of his house. They passed the garden plot. In the barnyard, he stopped the horses and set the brake. Tippy bounced into view, barking. Ted climbed down and gave the dog a pat.

Night was falling, putting the farm in shadow, but Ted knew every building, fence and pasture. He'd earned all this off others' pain. A straight flush had paid for the house, a full house repaired his barn and a four of a kind had bought his livestock.

Yep, the best poker player on the Mississippi, that had been him. Not that he'd planned on being "Hold 'Em" Logan when he'd joined the crew of that riverboat.

He'd seen men die over a game of cards, women toss their hearts after gamblers who loved their whiskey and the hand they held more than any female. He'd watched men and women lose everything they owned. Not a decent life. A life he now detested.

He'd started over here. Put his mark on this land. Everywhere he looked he saw evidence of his hard work, his daily penance for his past.

Shaking off his dreary thoughts, Ted walked to Elizabeth's side. Even in the dim light she looked tired, worn to a frazzle, as his mother would've said. He encircled her waist with his hands and she laid a gentle hand on his shoulder for balance. Light in his arms, she surely needed fattening up if she hoped to handle the chores. Her hand

91

fell away and he quickly released her. A strange sense of emptiness left him unsteady on his feet. Must be the strain of this eventful day.

Elizabeth bent and ran a hand along his dog's shaggy back. His white-tipped tail wagged a greeting.

"Tippy is gentle as a lamb," Ted said, "and the best sheepdog in these parts."

While Elizabeth got acquainted with Tippy, Ted retrieved their purchases from the back of the wagon. When he returned to her side, she gave the dog one final pat, like she'd met a good friend and didn't want to say goodbye.

"Go on in. The door's unlocked." Ted handed her the packages. "I'll be along as soon as I bed down the horses and feed the stock."

She turned to face him, hugging the bundles close. "I've got to ask . . ."

He waited for her to say whatever she had on her mind.

"Where will you be sleeping?"

Ted gave her credit for asking him straight out. "In the children's room. If that's agreeable with you."

"That's fine. Perfect." She released a great gust of air, her relief palpable in the soft night air. "You're a good man, Ted Logan."

Would she still say that if she knew about his past?

CHAPTER SIX

With the sleeping arrangements settled, Elizabeth walked toward the house with a light step, suddenly curious about her groom's home. At the back door, a whiff of lilac greeted her, transporting her to the ancient, mammoth bush behind the Manning carriage house. To the gigantic vases Mama filled to overflowing, giving off the heady fragrance of spring. *Home.*

Tears stung her eyes but she blinked them away. Refusing to dwell on what she could not change, she whistled Tippy inside. She'd found a friend and had no intention of leaving him behind.

The door led into the kitchen, a huge room that ran the entire depth of the house, from back to front, cozy, if not for the chill in the air. A stack of newspapers all but covered the faded blue cushion of a brown wicker rocker.

In front of the chair, Elizabeth spied dried

mud in the shape of a man's boots. Didn't Ted shed the footgear he wore in the barn before entering his house? Well, if he expected her to clean, that would have to change.

A large table, legs sturdy enough to support an elephant, dominated one end of the kitchen. Its porcelain castors sat in a sea of crumbs. "Come here, Tippy." The dog made quick work of the tidbits. Elizabeth patted her personal broom.

A high chair was set off to one side of the table. A spoon was glued to the wooden tray with oatmeal and, from the smell of it, soured milk. On the back of a chair, a garment hung haphazardly.

"Oh, how cute." Elizabeth picked up a tiny blue shirt that stuck to her fingers. "Uh, maybe not."

She put the oatmeal-painted apparel back where she found it. Tippy sat on his haunches watching her every move, as if he wanted to oblige her by licking her hands clean.

At this preview of marriage to Ted, her knees wobbled and she slumped into a chair.

She should leave. Maybe Reginald Parks wasn't so bad after all. Well, no, *he* smelled like sour milk. Far worse.

She surveyed the smudgy oilcloth covering the table. Over the center Ted had tossed a blue-checked square, covering whatever lay underneath. Hide it and run — a cleaning plan she could relate to. She lifted the corner of the lumpy cloth, exposing a sugar bowl, a footed glass filled with spoons and one nearly empty jar of jam.

In the sink, a pile of oatmeal and egg-encrusted dishes filled a dry dishpan. As if waiting for her. *Welcome home, little wife.*

Obviously Ted needed help. Well, she might not know the first thing about housekeeping, but she could handle this clutter better than Ted. Couldn't she?

A mirror hung over to one side of the sink. An odd place for it. She unpinned her hat and then couldn't find an uncluttered spot to lay it.

Carrying her hat, she climbed the two steps leading to the living room. Nothing fancy here — two rockers around a potbelly stove, a kerosene lamp in the center of a round table stacked with *Prairie Farmer* magazines. On either side of the table a navy sofa, chair and ottoman looked comfy. A sloped-top desk stood under the window with a ladder-back chair tucked beneath. Not so much as a lace curtain to soften the glass.

Nothing like their parlor at home with its

lavish velvet curtains, brocade sofa, wing chairs and prism-studded chandelier. Well, that room had been stuffy and suffocating.

Now it stood empty.

Shaking off the maudlin thought, she walked to the four-paned side door that opened onto a covered porch. The shadow of some kind of a vine blocked her view of the lawn and sheltered a wooden swing at the far end. A pleasant place to read. Though farmer's magazines hardly interested her.

Well, she'd see about changing that on her next trip into town. Surely New Harmony had a library.

She crossed the room and opened a door. A small rumpled bed clung to one wall. A crib hugged another. Anna and Henry's room — the place where Ted would sleep tonight. He'd surely be uncomfortable curling his massive frame onto that small space.

A bureau filled the niche between the beds. Tiny clothing dangled from three open drawers. Elizabeth stuffed the garments inside. As she pushed the drawers closed, her gaze rested on a framed photograph on top of the dresser.

She recognized Ted immediately. Wearing a suit, face sober, he looked vaguely uncomfortable, as though his collar pinched. In front of him sat his bride, her dark hair covered by a gauzy veil, gloved hands clasped in her lap. Rose. Elizabeth studied the mother of Ted's children. She read nothing in her expression but quiet acceptance.

Along the opposite wall a rocker was positioned next to a washstand. A cloth floated in a bowl of scummy water and a still-damp towel hung from the rails of the spindled crib. Her new husband couldn't be accused of fastidiousness.

When her father no longer had the money to pay servants, Martha had gladly taken over all the duties in their house. She'd be in her glory here. Elizabeth cringed. Now *she'd* have to play Martha. Well, she'd spiff this place up in a matter of hours. Show Ted she could handle the job of wife.

Back in the kitchen, she shivered. How long did it take to bed down a pair of horses? She should start a fire. She bent toward the black behemoth. *Home Sunshine* in raised letters on the oven door hardly fit her mood. She took hold of a handle and opened a door. Ah, ashes. Must be where the fuel should go.

She grabbed a couple of small logs from a large, rough-hewn box, then squealed when a bug crawled out of one of them. She tossed the infested firewood into the stove.

98

Where were the matches? Her gaze settled on a metal holder hanging high above little hands. A flick of the match against the side and it flared to life. She tossed it on the wood and stepped back in case of sparks.

The match went black. She needed something smaller than that log, something more flammable. She crumbled a big wad of newsprint, lit another match and tossed the whole thing into the stove. The paper lit and blazed. Soon the log would ignite.

She glanced at the dog. "See, nothing to it."

Tippy whined.

Elizabeth shut the stove's door. "You're a worrywart."

Once the fire took off, she'd heat water and wash these dishes. That would show Ted his new wife could carry her weight, *and* his, by the looks of this place.

The acrid odor of smoke reached her nostrils. Tippy barked. Elizabeth dashed to the stove and flung open the door. Black smoke poured out of the gaping hole, enveloping her in a dark, dirty, stinky cloud. She coughed and choked, waving at the smoke hanging stubbornly around her, stinging her eyes.

The screen door banged open. Ted raced to the stove, tossing his suit coat on the rocker as he passed. He turned a knob in the pipe and slammed the door shut. "Didn't you know to open the damper before you lit the stove? You could've burned the house down!"

She sniffed and swiped at her burning eyes. "Are you going to yell at me on our wedding day?"

The sour expression he wore turned troubled. "No, I don't suppose I should." He met her gaze. "I'm sorry."

He yanked up the windows over the sink and opened both doors, then cleared the smoke with a towel. She watched the muscles dance across his broad back. When he turned around, he caught her staring.

"Ah, thanks for taking care of the smoke," she said weakly.

With a nod, he inspected the kitchen, as if trying to get his bearings. "As soon as the fire gets going, we can have a cup of coffee. Or tea, if you'd prefer."

"Tea would be lovely."

He swiped his hands across his pants, and then filled a shiny teakettle with water. "Sorry about this mess. I wanted the place to look nice."

"It's, ah . . . homey."

"I meant to get the dishes done before we left, but things kept happening." Ted set the teakettle on the stove. "Henry spilled his milk. Anna tried to wipe it up but slipped and bumped her head on the high chair. They both needed holding before it was over. Everything takes more time than I expect."

Elizabeth smiled at the look of dismay on Ted's face. This father cared about his children, loved them. Like Papa loved Robby and her. A nagging unease settled over her. Could Papa love her when he'd tried to use her to discharge his debts?

But of course he did. Hadn't he always told her so?

"What's the dog doing in here?"

Tippy hung his head, appeared to shrink into himself. "Doesn't he live here?"

"Not inside, he doesn't." He opened the back door. The dog gave one last pleading glance at Elizabeth. "Out you go, boy. You know better than to come inside."

"I don't see why he can't stay."

"He's a working dog, not a house pet. And the way he sheds and attracts mud, you'll be glad of it, too."

"Then that must be his mud in front of the rocker?"

He harrumphed.

She smothered a smile.

The teakettle whistled. Ted gathered two

cups and a blue willow pot, then rummaged through a cabinet, mumbling. His broad shoulders filled every inch of space between the wall and table. Elizabeth squeezed past him as if she thought he would bite, then pulled a container marked *Tea* from behind a bag of cornmeal.

Her gaze lifted to his. She swallowed hard. "Here it is."

He reached for the tin, his fingertips brushing hers. "I . . . ah." He blinked. "Thanks. I spend half my time searching for things."

She smiled, remembering Papa's inability to find something right in front of his nose while she could spot a sale on gloves from three stores away. She picked up the kettle and filled the teapot with water, dividing the rest between the two round pans, then added dippers of cold. She chuffed. And Martha said she didn't have a domestic bone in her body.

Ted waved a hand at the mess. "They'll wait till morning."

"No time like the present." She sounded smug even to her own ears. But keeping busy meant avoiding her new husband.

The sink hung in a wooden counter supported with two legs at one end and a cabinet at the other, the space under the sink skirted. What an odd arrangement.

"What's the mirror for?" she asked.

"I shave there sometimes. And it helps me keep track of Henry." He smiled. "Like having eyes in the back of my head."

In no time, Elizabeth worked up some suds by swishing a bar of soap in the pan, then dipped a plate through the bubbles, but dried yellow food still clung to the plate. She scrubbed with the dishrag. Still there. Running her thumb over the hardened mess, she crinkled her nose as the nasty stuff filled the space beneath her nail. Well, she wouldn't let dried-on egg yolks defeat her. She rubbed harder. Her thumbnail gave way and tore. She dropped the plate into the pan. It hit bottom with an ominous clunk.

Ted stepped up behind her. "What was that?"

Elizabeth brought up the plate. It looked fine. Fishing beneath the water, she found a cup, a handle-less cup. "Oh, my."

Ted didn't say a word, merely turned away, but from the tight expression around his mouth, she imagined he blamed her for squandering his possessions.

"The cup isn't the only thing that's broken. My nail is practically down to the quick."

"Around here nails take a beating."

Obviously she'd get no sympathy from Ted. Well, she'd finish washing these dishes if it cost the nails on both hands.

Careful not to let them slip between her fingers, she attacked bowls of dried oatmeal. The fork and spoons ranked the nastiest. Finally she'd laid the last utensil to dry and dumped the water down the drain, smiling at her achievement.

Then she shrieked. Water gushed over her shoes — her only shoes, and formed a puddle of water and debris on the planks.

Pulling himself away from staring out the back door while she killed herself in his kitchen, Ted grabbed two towels off the hook alongside the sink and mopped up the mess.

"The drain leads to a bucket under the sink. Reckon it needed emptying."

"What kind of a drain does that?" she wailed, looking at her shoes.

His brow creased into a frown. "*My* drain," he said in a want-to-make-something-of-it tone.

He gathered the drenched towels and draped them over the lilac bush out back. She stepped aside so he could return to the kitchen where he heaved the large bucket out from beneath the skirted sink.

"The other bucket under here is a slop jar for the pigs. They eat most anything so you can dump table scraps and peelings into that one. Don't mix them up. Pigs aren't partial to soap."

He grabbed the full-to-the-brim drain bucket by the bail and carried it to the door. Beneath the weight, his biceps bulged. Her stomach did a strange little flop. As the door slapped shut after him, Elizabeth slumped into the wicker chair.

She removed her beautiful silk slippers, now water stained. Irritating tears stung her eyes. What had she gotten herself into? She buried her head in her hands. "I can't do this."

"Yes, you can," Ted said softly. Ted wadded up a few newspapers, stuffing them into the toes. "That'll help keep their shape. You can wear my mom's boots until I can get a pair of shoes made."

"You make shoes?" She hiccuped.

"They won't be Sunday-go-to-meeting shoes but you can work in them. And save these."

She sniffed back her tears. Ted Logan might not spoil her like Mama had, nor bribe or cajole her like Papa, but the man could be kind. She'd give him that.

He took her hand, his grip sending unwelcome heat through her veins. "Let's have that tea."

At the table, Elizabeth tucked her stocking toes over the rungs of the chair and added a teaspoon of sugar to her cup. Ted drank his plain, the way he drank his coffee. While she stirred her tea, she thought about Ted making those serviceable shoes.

What did he expect her to do besides work in the kitchen? "A farmer's wife must be busy cooking, doing dishes and . . ." She let the words trail off, hoping he'd supply her with a list. A short list.

"Besides caring for the children, Rose baked bread for the week, cleaned, mended, washed and ironed and weeded the garden. Oh, and collected the eggs. In the fall, she canned."

"With all that to do, how will I find time to sew dresses?"

"Oh, you'll find the time." He gestured at her frock. "That won't last long hoeing and gathering eggs."

Hoeing? Whatever that was, it sounded hard. The prospect of doing all those chores weighed her down. "What do you do all day?" she snapped.

"Milk the cow, feed and care for the livestock, work the land from planting through harvest." He ticked off each chore on his fingers. "Plow the garden so you can plant. I've got machinery to mend, the barn to muck, tack to clean and repair and firewood to chop. Now a pair of shoes to make." He'd used his last finger so he stopped. "Always plenty to do."

"Can't you get in some help?"

His expression turned troubled. "I know I don't have much to offer you, a woman who's accustomed to a staff waiting on her."

"Those days are gone."

"What happened?"

"Bad investments." She threw a hand over her mouth to stifle a sudden yawn and further questions.

"You'd best get to bed," Ted said. "The day starts early."

How early? she wanted to ask but didn't dare, certain she wouldn't like the answer. She gathered her purchases. "I'll say goodnight, then."

He flicked out a section of the paper. "Good night." He gave her the briefest glance then returned to the farm news.

In the bedroom, she turned the lock, satisfied by the firm click that followed. Not that Ted had given her reason to fear him. But something about the man made her insides tremble.

She lit a kerosene lamp on the nightstand.

An open Bible filled most of the space. Sally had called Ted a godly man and so he appeared. Compared to his untidy kitchen, Ted's bedroom was immaculate. A chamber pot, dry sink with white pitcher and bowl, even a fresh towel. Under the window sat a black contraption with a spool of white thread on top. A sewing machine — another reminder of all she had to do with no inkling of how to do it.

The bedroom had a chill in the air. Shivering, she didn't waste time getting into her nightgown, new and soft as down. Inside the chifferobe, she found Ted's clothes and a few items of women's clothing, obviously Rose's. Did Ted still love his wife so much he couldn't get rid of her things?

She pulled a robe from the hook and tried it on. Though it barely covered her shins, the robe would cover her nightgown in the morning. She didn't relish donning her soiled dress, especially if she got an opportunity for a bath. But with no bathroom in the house, where would she find privacy?

She sighed and slipped between the sheets. They smelled clean, sweet and fresh. Obviously Ted had managed to change the linens. She stretched out her body, thankful to sleep in a bed.

Long before this, Robby would be tucked

in for the night, an extra pillow clutched in his spindly arms, while Martha heard his prayers. She hoped he wasn't missing her or, worse, crying. Her heart squeezed. To give her brother his dream, she must first find a way to manage Ted's home and children. Tonight proved she could handle the cleaning. Learning to cook should soften Ted up enough to tell him about Robby.

She had less than a month to become a passable farmer's helpmate, less than a month to earn the money for two return train tickets. If Mr. Sorenson needed help, she might be able to handle his books.

But how would she get to town?

Who'd take care of Ted's children so she could get away?

She had plenty of questions, but no answers. She sighed. Take it one step at a time. Tomorrow she'd learn to cook. Martha had tried to interest Elizabeth in the culinary arts, or so the nanny called meal preparation. Up till now, Elizabeth had only one interest in food. Eating it. She suspected that was about to change.

CHAPTER SEVEN

The clatter of pans brought Elizabeth straight up in bed. For a second she didn't know where she was. Then memory hit with the force of a gale wind, tossing her back against the pillows.

She'd awakened in Ted Logan's house. Married to the man. No doubt that was Ted, her dear, considerate husband, up and raising a ruckus in the kitchen.

Through the curtain, she could see the slightest glow from the rising sun. A rooster crowed, heralding the day. Gracious, why was everyone in such a hurry?

Yawning, she tossed back the covers, slid out of bed, shivering when her bare feet hit the floor. It might be spring but during the night the temperature had dropped. She slipped on the robe, cinched the belt tight and padded to the kitchen. Today she'd prove herself by handling the cooking.

Ted sat at the table, bent over at the waist,

pulling on his boots. His thick blond hair showed the tracks of a comb. A sudden urge to run her fingers through the silkiness brought a hitch to her breathing.

Raising his head, Ted took in her attire with a silver-blue disapproving gaze. He opened his mouth as if to say something and then clamped it shut.

Elizabeth looked down at the robe. "I hope you don't mind if I wear this." A war of emotions waged on his face, telling her plenty. She turned to go. "I'll take it off."

"No, you need a robe and that's a perfectly good one."

"You're sure?"

"Yes, seeing you . . . just surprised me is all." He jammed his stocking foot into the second boot. "I'm heading out to the barn. Can you manage breakfast?"

"Of course." She'd handled the dishes, hadn't she?

"I started the stove and made coffee." He rose, towering over her, then grabbed a jacket from a hook near the back door and shrugged it on. "I should finish the morning chores in about an hour."

"Wonderful." She put on her best smile but the robe fit her far better. "Uh, what do you usually eat?"

"Fried eggs, bacon, biscuits. Nothing

fancy." He tossed the words over his shoulder as he strode out the door.

She sank onto a chair. Eggs, bacon, biscuits? Couldn't he ask for something that matched her experience? Like cold cereal and milk. Well, she'd drink a cup of coffee to get her brain working, maybe two. Then find a cookbook. And start on the road that led to Robby's dream.

Martha was a nanny, not a cook, but she'd whipped up plenty of meals. How hard could cooking be?

Butterflies fluttered in her stomach. *Hard* was the arrival of Ted's children later today. If only she knew a recipe for motherhood.

Two cups of coffee and a roar from Elizabeth's stomach motivated her to unearth *The Farmer's Guide Cook Book.* Rose had apparently put the volume to good use, judging by the stains on the cover and looseness of the spine.

Under Breads — Quick, she read, "The ability to make good biscuits has saved the day for many a housewife."

Well, it better. On page eleven the list of ingredients for baking powder biscuits read like Greek. Flour, baking powder, salt, lard and . . . sweet milk. What on earth was sweet milk?

Inside the cabinet near the pantry door,

112

she found the baking powder and lard. The flour had to be here somewhere. Pulling back a sliding panel, she discovered a metal contraption with a spout at the bottom and a wire sticking out from the side. She gave the wire a couple flips and a volcano of white poured onto the work surface, soaring into the air and onto the front of Rose's robe.

Elizabeth sneezed then sighed. She'd get to the mess later. Maybe when Ted came in the back, a big gust of wind would blow through and send the flour out the front door.

Yeah, that was about as likely as Papa giving up gambling.

Rummaging through the doors and drawers, she dug out a large brown crockery bowl, measuring cups and spoons, then washed her hands.

The ever-helpful cookbook read, "Sift together 2 cupfuls flour and 4 teaspoons baking powder with half teaspoonful salt." Sift? Did that mean mix? She shrugged and scooped flour off the work surface into the cup then dumped it into the bowl. Twice.

"Add 2 tablespoonfuls lard and work well with tips of fingers."

Ew. Whose fingertips?

She sighed. No one here but her.

The clock ticked away at an alarming speed. Best get it over with. With one hand, she attacked the lard, squeezing it through her fingers. It stuck, seeped under her nails until her hand looked like a dough ball. She tried to scrape it off with her other hand, but the mixture stuck to that hand, too. Her stomach somersaulted. Cooking was nasty.

The clock struck behind her. A half hour until Ted returned. She'd better get the rest in. Add seven-eighth's cup sweet milk. Well, cow's milk with lots of sugar would have to do. She grabbed the pitcher from the icebox, guessed how much less than a cup she needed then added sugar. She tried to stir it into the flour mixture with a spoon but resorted again to her fingers. The dough had become a gummy, thick mess.

She read, "Roll lightly to half inch in thickness and cut any size desired. Bake 15 minutes." Thankfully, they wouldn't take long to bake.

She grabbed up the blob and plopped it on the floury work surface, sending more flour into her face. Her nose itched. She ran the back of her hand across it.

The door opened. "I forgot to mention that you'll need to feed the fire so —" His eyes widened. "What happened to you?"

She followed Ted's gaze first to her robe,

dusted with white, then to the planks in front of the cabinet where she could plainly see her tracks in the flour. She swiped her hands over her middle, then rubbed a hand over her cheek. "The flour bin exploded."

A grin curved across his face. His light blue eyes sparkled with humor. He let out a chuckle that became a howl. "Looks like you've been in a pillow fight and you lost," he said, once he got himself under control.

"You should've seen my opponent," she said with a toss of her head.

He chuckled again. "You missed some. Here." He stepped closer and brushed the tip of a finger along her jaw, sending tingles down her neck, dispelling every trace of mirth between them. "And here." He moved to a spot on her cheek.

Their gazes locked. Something significant passed between them, drawing her to Ted like filings to a magnet. Her spine turned to jelly while Ted lurched toward the wood box, grabbed a log, fed the fire and, without a backward glance, headed to the barn.

Disoriented, as if cobwebs filled her brain, she struggled for her composure. What had just happened? Whatever it was, she wouldn't let it occur again. If she hoped to bring Robby here and find a modicum of peace, she'd need to keep her wits. And hang on to her heart.

Returning to the task, she laid her hands in the flour then rolled the dough around until it took the form of a loaf of bread. Using a large knife with a razor-thin blade, Elizabeth whacked off slices, making some thick for Ted, others thin for Anna and Henry.

What to bake them on? She opened and closed cabinets until she found a metal pan. With her finger she drew a daisy on a few. Once she got the hang of it, cooking was kind of fun.

She washed the mess off her hands, not an easy task, then picked up the pan of biscuits, a feast for the eyes. She grabbed the knob on the oven door, almost dropping the pan. First rule to remember — stove handles are hot.

Once she'd safely tucked the biscuits inside, she wrapped her hand in a wet dishrag and tied a knot in it with her teeth. She rummaged in the icebox, emerging with a crock of eggs and a slab of bacon.

By the time Ted hit the back door the second time, she had the bacon and eggs draining on a platter and the bottom-burned biscuits pried from the pan and piled on an oval glass plate that read "Bread is the staff of life."

Well, this batch had nearly killed her.

Ted washed up at the sink then wiped his hands, smiling at her. "Smells good in here." His expression turned wistful. "I'm starved."

Something suggested he meant more than his stomach. Elizabeth hurried to the table, putting as much distance between them as she could, and wilted into her chair. To sit at the table with Ted, just the two of them alone in the house, had her feeling tauter than an overwound clock.

She'd been up a little over an hour but felt she'd worked half the day. She took in the floury mess and smears of dough on the handles of the cabinets. Tippy wouldn't relish lapping up this.

Ted bowed his head and gave thanks for the food and this time Elizabeth remembered to wait for prayer before diving in.

He picked up the platter and scooped two eggs and four slabs of bacon onto his plate. After pulling off the undersides of two biscuits, he buttered the salvageable parts.

"Remember to put the bottoms in the slop jar. The pigs will be glad to get them."

Maybe Ted hadn't meant anything by it, but more than likely she should feel insulted. She would if she had the energy.

He raised a bite of egg to his lips and chewed, then caught her watching. Nodding, he turned up the corners of his mouth, lifting a weight from her shoulders.

With enthusiasm, she took a bite, only to find the egg much too salty. When she cut into the side meat, one end shattered into a hundred pieces while the other wiggled beneath her fork. Even minus the burned bottoms, the biscuits tasted terrible, bitter in spots and hard as stones.

Her shoulders sagged. Nothing resembled their cook's food in Chicago. Or Martha's, once she took over the household.

Ted took another bite, grimaced and swallowed. "Not bad," he said gallantly, and then cleaned his plate.

The man had a strong stomach. She'd give him that.

"Why not be honest?" Elizabeth said. "The breakfast is terrible."

Ted took her hand and gave it a gentle squeeze. "I won't criticize the answer to my prayers."

"How do you know I'm the answer to your prayers when I'm not the woman you planned to marry?"

He released her hand and studied her, probably wondering how to quickly retract his statement as he had his hand. "I'll admit the switch threw me at first. But God's

given me a sense of peace about our marriage."

"What do you mean by a sense of peace?"

"God laid a gentle hand on my spinning
thoughts, calming them like He did the Sea
of Galilee. Like Peter, I felt called to take a
step out of my boat and onto the water with
Him."

Whatever was Ted talking about?

"I'll get the Bible and read that passage."

No doubt he'd seen on her face the confusion she felt.

He disappeared, returning with the Bible.
"I always start my day with Scripture. The
story is found in Matthew."

The words Ted read of Jesus calming the
Sea and Peter walking to Him on the water
were spoken with a reverence that stabbed
at her conscience and filled her with longing for more.

When he'd finished, Ted met her gaze.
"The words Jesus spoke to Peter came to
me at the parsonage, not audibly, but just
as real. 'O Thou of little faith, wherefore
didst thou doubt?' And I knew no matter
how bad it looked, I wasn't to doubt that
you were the one . . . the answer to my
prayers."

Elizabeth had never connected stories in
the Bible with her life. She could identify

with Peter sinking beneath those waves. But how she could be the answer to anyone's prayers baffled her.

"Walking on the water isn't comfortable. May even feel like lunacy," Ted said.

Tears filled her eyes and she glanced away.

He cupped her chin with his palm and turned her face to his. "You and I are out of our boats, Elizabeth. Two very different boats, I might add." He smiled at her. "No matter how afraid we feel, God's help is only a 'Save me' prayer away. He'll stretch out His hand and never let us sink."

If only Elizabeth shared Ted's confidence. God might save him, but God didn't listen to her. If He did, surely He could have found an easier way to give Robby a home.

Ted laid the Bible aside and rose to get his boots. "I gathered the eggs for you this morning."

Relief swished through her. "Thank you."

"The egg money is yours. You can keep whatever Sorenson's paying."

"Really?"

"Tomorrow morning I'll introduce you to the chickens, give them a chance to get used to you."

"Get used to me?"

"They can peck your fingers if they're nervous. Or worse, stop laying." He grabbed his coat. "I appreciate the meal. A man has to eat to work."

But the words he didn't say, the words Elizabeth discerned — that her cooking didn't measure up to Rose's — hung between them. Most likely chafing against that peace he had about their marriage. How could Ted believe she was the answer to his prayers?

He buttoned his denim jacket. "I'll get more wood for the box," he said, then left the kitchen in a rush.

Elizabeth took another bite, choked it down then shoved her plate away, tears springing to her eyes.

She didn't blame him.

She'd leave, too . . . if she had somewhere to go.

Stomach rolling in protest at the meal grinding away inside, Ted gathered up an armload of firewood from the huge mound he'd stacked in even rows against the shed. From Elizabeth's expression earlier, Ted suspected she remained unconvinced that their marriage was God's plan.

He suspected she didn't know much about The Word and even less about listening for God's quiet voice. But she'd soaked up the Scriptures he'd read like a woman hungry for their comfort.

Probably desperate for reassurance that she hadn't made the biggest mistake of her life. If so, he couldn't blame her disquiet. She had far more adjustments to make than him.

Back in the kitchen, he found Elizabeth at the sink, doing dishes. She might be slower than sorghum, but he found her jaunty profile appealing. And when she wasn't scowling at him, her smile warmed a man better than a hot brick at the foot of a bed on a cold winter night.

He dumped the wood into the bin then stepped outside for another load. Elizabeth followed behind, broom at his heels, sending flour, straw and dirt onto the stoop. Hustling back inside, she returned with a dustpan. Using one hand to hold the pan and the other the broom, she swept the debris into the dustpan, looked around, then shrugged and tossed the contents into the lilac bushes alongside the stoop.

He chuckled. His wife had a way of making the simplest task an ordeal . . . and life a whole lot more interesting.

Next thing he knew she strode toward him, stopping mere inches away, and folded her arms across her chest, the dustpan aimed skyward. And thankfully not at him.

She must have heard him laugh. Appeared he was in for it now.

"From here on," she said, "please take off your boots before you enter the house."

"Seems to me that mess in the kitchen was your doing."

"I couldn't help that the flour exploded, but you and those boots you wear *in the barn* need to part company before you take a step inside."

He smiled, enjoying her rosy-cheeked snit. An urge to pull her into his arms crashed through him. But in her mood, she'd likely crown him with that dustpan. "Is this that teeny temper you warned me about?"

"You haven't seen anything yet, if you don't cooperate." She wagged a finger at him.

"In that case, yes, ma'am. From now on I'll remove my boots." He doffed his hat and bit back a chuckle, then another bubbling inside him. If he laughed, she might get all teary on him as she had last night. The prospect squelched his mirth faster than a hailstorm could destroy a crop in the fields.

She nodded curtly. "Thank you."

Without a word, she turned toward the house. Unable to take his eyes off his bride, he watched her sniff the lilacs, putting her pert face in profile. Upturned nose, slender neck . . .

He shook his head. This dawdling wasn't getting the sheep moved to the north pasture. He whistled for Tippy. From the porch, the dog rose from his nap in the sun and trotted over, his tail wagging. Ted leaned down and scratched the canine's ears, rewarded by a lick on the hand.

On the way to the barn, Ted took one last glance toward the house. Elizabeth was nowhere in sight. A peculiar sense of disappointment plowed through him and pushed against his lungs.

"Come on, Tippy," he said, grouchier than he'd intended.

In the barn, he gave the ewe he'd bottle-fed as a lamb a pat on the nose. Tame as a dog, Suzie followed him everywhere, as she did now, out of the barn with the rest of the small flock falling in line behind like baby ducks trailing their mama. Tippy hung back, nipping at the heels of stragglers daring to stop and graze along the way.

At the north pasture, Ted lifted the wire loop then swung open the gate. His neighbors poked fun at him for raising sheep. But he liked the reminder they provided of the Good Shepherd and His wandering lost sheep.

A robin swooped from a tree, hopping across the grass, and then stopped, cocking his head toward the ground, listening. Suzie and Tippy did their jobs and Ted returned to the barn, which, from the odor, was badly in need of mucking. He could use more hours in the day. With Elizabeth here, he hoped to get caught up with the chores.

His gaze lifted to the haymow overhead. Not exactly pleasant accommodations, but Anna and Henry would be back in their room tonight. He needed to talk to Elizabeth about the sleeping arrangements. He'd compared their marriage to a business deal, though he doubted God approved his assessment. Still, a wise man wouldn't push a woman into intimacy. Time would solve the issue. Or so he hoped.

As he strode into the yard, Elizabeth emerged from the back door, carrying a dress in her arms, her hair tied back with a length of twine. Water sluiced off the heavy fabric, dripping down the front of *his* shirt. The flannel plaid hung to her knees, making her look like a skinny sack, while *his* denims ended in rolled cuffs resembling feather-filled bolsters sagging at her ankles.

He stopped, dumbstruck at the sight. Rose might've worn pants under her dress on the coldest days, but this —

125

His pulse tripped in his chest at this woman standing before him.

Cocking her head, she met his gaze, all innocent-eyed while at her bare feet a puddle formed on the slab of concrete outside the kitchen door. One of her little toes was crooked. For some unknowable reason he found the slight imperfection endearing.

He chuffed at his silliness. He'd have to find those boots today.

"I washed my dress."

As if he needed an explanation with all that dripping going on. "So I see."

"I had to put on something. Knowing you weren't too happy about me wearing Rose's robe, I made do with these."

He opened his mouth to argue the point, but couldn't. Seeing Elizabeth in that robe had been a sucker punch to the gut. His resistance to Elizabeth using whatever she needed had not been fair.

How was she holding up his pants, anyway, with those slim hips and tiny waist? "Can't figure how my pants would fit you."

"Twine works for a belt." She raised her chin. "I can improvise."

"Which would explain your hair."

"You don't like how I look?" She parked a fist on her hip.

He liked how she looked, all right. "I didn't say that."

Lugging the dress, she headed for the clothesline, barefoot like a tot barely out of nappies. Didn't she know she could pick up a nail or a thistle or get bit by a spider?

She heaved the bodice of the dress over the line and it hung from the waist, the skirt almost touching the ground. She turned back to him, a self-satisfied smile on her face. Behind her, the weight of the wet skirts pulled her freshly washed dress over the cord and onto the grass.

His expression must've alerted her. She spun around. "Oh, no!"

"Clothespins might help."

He walked to the bag hanging on the line, pulled out a handful of wooden pins and sauntered to her. He took the dress from her clutches and pinned it in place by the hem as he'd seen Rose do countless times. Then he took the rod leaning against the post, raised and propped the line.

She grabbed a pin from the bag and stuck it in between two of his. "Five might work but six is better."

Her gaze locked with his and her wide blue eyes dared him to disagree, setting off something that coiled in his stomach. This turmoil didn't have a thing to do with breakfast and everything to do with the woman before him.

Well, he wouldn't let those eyes make him lose sight of what he wanted from Elizabeth — a mother for his children — and help getting a grip on his off-kilter world.

He'd better remember, if he let this woman get close, she'd unearth his secrets and the open wounds he'd sealed.

"My children are coming home today." He looked toward the barn. "I've rigged a bed in the loft."

Color dotted her cheeks. "I appreciate it."

Nodding, he glanced at the sun rising in the sky. "As soon as I haul my things to the barn and finish the morning chores, I'll pick Henry and Anna up at the Harpers'. We'll be back in time for dinner."

She smiled. "That gives me plenty of time."

"Dinner is at noon in these parts."

"In Chicago we call that lunch."

"Call it whatever you like but make it big — I'm plowing this afternoon. You'll find canned food in the root cellar outside the front door. Oh, and don't forget to ladle off the cream, then put the milk and cream in the icebox."

She shot him a glare. "You're good at barking orders, Mr. Logan. Have you forgot-

128

ten I'm not so good at obeying?"

"How could I forget?" He ran a hand through his hair then plopped his hat in place. "Well, the children and I'll see you at noon."

A parade of emotions marched across her face. Apprehension. Uncertainty. Not that he could blame her for feeling nervous. He shared her qualms. The biggest — would his strong-willed daughter accept Elizabeth's presence in the house?

By the time Ted drove the wagon down the lane, he whistled a tune. His relationship with his wife might be fragile, but at least he'd given his son and daughter a mother, a huge step toward returning their lives to normal.

Elizabeth pulled open the slanted cellar door and ambled down the stone steps, thankful a stream of sunlight lit her way. Bushel baskets of potatoes, wrinkly apples, onions — some growing roots — lined the walls. Dried herbs hung from the ceiling, little upside-down bouquets. Elizabeth inhaled those fragrances mingled with the cellar's musty smell. Not perfume, but not unpleasant.

Crude wooden shelves lined one wall and contained row upon row of filled glass jars of green beans, applesauce, tomatoes, corn and grape juice. Many with homemade tags hanging from the necks, identifying the friend or neighbor who'd sent it, wishing Ted peace, giving Bible verses or even a recipe. Apparently, friends and neighbors continued to look after Ted's family. Elizabeth remembered how her family's friends in Chicago had looked away, whispering behind their hands. Her heart squeezed. No doubt that was the difference between squandering wealth and losing a loved one.

She plopped four potatoes and an onion in the wide pockets of her apron, grabbed a glass jar of tomatoes and a crock of canned beef, ingredients for the soup she intended to make for lunch, and carried them up the steps.

Inside the kitchen, she added more wood to the red embers and got the fire going again. Following directions, she chopped the ingredients, regretting the onion the minute the tears started. Other than one cut on her index finger, preparing the soup went smoothly and it soon bubbled away on the stove, releasing a mouthwatering aroma.

From what she'd seen Ted consume at breakfast, he had a voracious appetite. Yet he didn't have an ounce of fat on his solid, muscular frame. A man built for the work he did.

With the meal under way, she rushed outside to check her dress. The dog rose from the covered porch and ambled over for a scratch. A beautiful animal, he had a gentle disposition and eyes that settled on her with the warmth of an old friend.

Robby would love Tippy. How long before she could bring her brother here? Already she'd prepared two meals. Cleaned up the kitchen twice. Tomorrow she'd gather the eggs. Why, she'd practically completed her list of chores. A week of egg money would surely pay for their train tickets. Wouldn't it?

Soon she'd tell Ted about Robby. Her smile faded. How would a man short on cash react to the news that he'd have another mouth to feed?

At the line, Elizabeth found her dress still damp. Perhaps that would make it easier to iron. She carried it inside. The quiet of the house had her beckoning the dog to follow. Tippy hesitated, but only for a moment.

Elizabeth found the flatirons and the padded ironing board where Ted said they'd be. She placed both irons on the stove and wrestled the board upright. She didn't know the first thing about ironing. If only she'd paid attention to the running of the Manning household. But she'd only thought about parties, fancy dresses and the latest hairstyle. Of late, that life had seemed meaningless and her friendships shallow.

Life on the farm provided food, an existence forcing people to rely on the basics, to look out for one another. But it had taken less than a day to discover the work was pure drudgery. How could she survive the endless tedium?

By remembering Robby would love the farm.

But would Ted's children take to him? To her?

Elizabeth tightened her jaw until her teeth ached. What if she couldn't manage to care for Anna and Henry? What if they resented her? What if her inexperience brought them harm?

Perhaps if she prayed about it, God would give her some of that peace Ted had talked about.

Well, she wouldn't meet Ted's children wearing anything but a proper dress. She picked up an iron and laid it on the collar, which had bunched up on one side. As she smoothed the fabric, a little hissing sound startled her into moving the iron. When she did, a scorch remained in the exact shape of the tip. "Oh, no!"

Elizabeth propped the flatiron and raced to the sink for a cloth, but no amount of scrubbing erased the scorch. Well, who needed a collar, anyway? A collarless dress would be unique.

This time she kept the iron moving. When one iron lost its heat, she exchanged it for the other. Pressing the yards and yards of fabric made her arms ache. Ted had called them sadirons. Good name for the heavy, ugly instruments of torture. Just when she thought she couldn't stand the discomfort another minute, she met up with the pressed side of her dress.

Except for the collar, she'd done a fine job. She laid the garment over a chair while she set the table for four. When she'd finished, she grabbed up the dress, took the shears from the pantry and hauled them to the bedroom.

The waist was still dampish, but her dress smelled like sunshine. With endless stitches holding the collar in place, she didn't have time to remove the seam. Using the shears, she trimmed away the lapel, slipped into her undergarments, and then donned the dress. From her reflection in the mirror she decided even with the missing collar, she looked presentable, except for her hair. She untied the twine, brushed and then twisted her tresses into a chignon. Now prepared to meet Ted's children. Or so she told herself.

In the kitchen, Elizabeth stirred the soup. Some of the vegetables had stuck to the bottom. Well, it couldn't be helped. How could she watch the soup and get ready? In an attempt to disguise the taste, she added pepper and salt. When she ladled up the soup, she'd avoid the bottom of the pan.

Suddenly exhausted, she flopped into the kitchen rocker. Tippy laid his head on her lap. She gave his nose a pat, and then leaned back against the chair, closing her eyes.

A sense of exhilaration slid through her, odd considering her fatigue. She'd never accomplished this much, never experienced this satisfaction.

In Chicago she'd lived like a sailboat without a rudder, without a compass, blown to and fro, getting nowhere.

Now as Ted's wife, she had a ready-made purpose. A job. Responsibilities.

The weight of those responsibilities sat heavy on her shoulders. Yet they also gave her a new view of her life. One where waking up in the morning meant hard work, yes, but also . . .

Fulfillment. That was the word.

Elizabeth giggled. All that insight from

preparing a bowl of soup.

But then reality reared its disagreeable head and the joy drained out of her faster than a bottomless jug.

Could she really do this? She knew nothing about motherhood, about anything outside of teas and balls.

Like a dress off the rack, she suspected the role wouldn't quite fit. Well, when the job got too big, she'd pin a section here and there. Squeeze into the confining areas that chafed. Though the garb would surely feel more suitable for a costume ball than for her.

Regardless, she'd find a way. Do whatever she must to ensure her brother had a happy life.

But at what price?

CHAPTER EIGHT

"I don't like you." The pale blue eyes staring at Elizabeth were defiant, strong, so like her father's, and not about to be dissuaded by a scorched bowl of soup.

No matter how hard she tried to pretend otherwise, Ted's daughter's declaration squeezed against Elizabeth's heart. For a second she wanted to rush in with words, to find a way to soothe the waters between them. But really, what could she say that would change Anna's mind? Why wouldn't Anna dislike the woman she'd see as her mother's replacement?

As if Elizabeth held any such aspiration.

She wouldn't get attached to anyone in this house. Opening her heart might lead her down a risky road she dared not travel.

Elizabeth gave a bright, friendly, let's-work-together smile. "Well, Anna," she began, seeking a truce between them. "We both live in this house so what do you say we try to make the best of it?"

Anna shoved folded arms across her chest. "I don't want to."

"Let's try." Elizabeth bit back a smile at the all-too-familiar stance she'd used as a child. "We can start by —"

"You're not my mommy. I don't have to do anything you say." Anna's eyes narrowed to icy slits. "Why are you here?"

Good question.

No, Elizabeth had an important motive for marrying Ted. Her brother.

"Ahem." Ted stood in the doorway. From the wary look on his face he'd heard her exchange with Anna.

He shot her a smile, then another to Anna, trying to ease the standoff between them. How long could he sustain that resolute smile plastered on his face before it cracked?

Anna streaked to her father's side. Solid, well muscled with thick blond hair and a stubborn jaw, she was a replica of her father. "My, it's good to have you home, sweet pea," Ted said, giving his daughter a kiss, then hoisting Henry in his arms. "You, too, big boy."

The toddler planted his chubby hands on his father's cheeks as Ted nuzzled Henry's nose. His son let out a squeal then lunged closer, every ounce of his body bouncing with joy.

A pang rose in Elizabeth, a deep yearning for her family — for Papa, Robby and Martha. Not that the nanny was her mother, but she was a substitute of sorts. Perhaps, with thought, Elizabeth would see how Martha managed to walk that line. Then she could do the same with Anna.

Ted crossed to the stove. "Hmm, soup. Your favorite, Anna."

Leaning against her father's leg, Anna screwed up her face at Elizabeth then brightened as she faced her father. "Sit, Daddy. I'll get it for you. Like I always do."

Ted tugged his daughter's braid. "Yes, pumpkin, you've been a big help, but Elizabeth should serve since she made the soup."

Anna's face flattened. The spark in her eyes faded to a vacant stare.

"You can put milk in the glasses." Ted slipped Henry into the high chair. He tucked a towel around his son's middle, securing the ends to the back, and then tied a bib around the boy's neck. "Try to keep your food on this, my boy."

His hand lingered on Henry's shoulder, a fatherly, most likely absentminded connection Ted didn't realize he made, Henry probably barely felt and Anna didn't see.

But Elizabeth noticed. She saw the love

that simple contact embodied, and almost felt it.

How often had she wiggled free from her mother's touch because of some silly irritation with Mama? Now those opportunities were gone, along with her mother. Gone too soon. Gone before Elizabeth appreciated the simple gift of her mother's touch.

She shook off the loneliness that threatened to unravel her. The past couldn't be undone. She had a job to do here. She'd focus on that. And be extra patient with Anna, who'd lost her mother years before Elizabeth had hers.

She crossed to the counter to load a plate with cheese sandwiches, bringing her near Anna. The child carefully balanced the pitcher of milk as she poured it into four glasses. Though the container was heavy, she didn't spill a drop.

"Nice of you to help," Elizabeth said. Anna rewarded her with a frosty stare.

Well, apparently Elizabeth had a lot more trying to do if she wanted peace between her and Anna. The only trouble was she had no idea how to create harmony with a seven-year-old hurting child. For now she'd concentrate on ladling up the soup, something she could manage.

As she stood at the stove, Ted came up

behind her, filling the narrow space with his overpowering presence. She caught the scent of his soap, clean and fresh, as crisp as a March breeze. Like a doomed moth drawn to a flame, she turned to him. The heat from his skin, from the intensity of that silver-blue gaze burned in her cheeks, muddling her thoughts.

Determined to sever the connection, she whipped back to the stove. But her hands shook and she slopped soup over the brim of the stoneware like an old lady with tremors.

"I know this has to be hard," he said near her ear, his breath drifting along her jaw. "I'll do what I can to make it easier, but . . ."

Unable to resist, she faced him, took in his expression now shadowed with worry, darkened by uncertainty. Evidence he held the same doubts as her. A comfort Elizabeth hadn't expected, but held close to her heart.

"But you're as new at this mail-order-bride thing as I am," she said, then grinned. "Sally's not the only one with cold feet."

He laughed — a deep, hearty sound, dissolving her concern faster than the cookstove melted butter. "Anna will put the fire to our toes, that's for sure," he whispered, then asked her to put only vegetables in

Henry's bowl, the moment over.

Ted struck up a conversation with his children about nothing, really, but enough for Elizabeth to feel like an outsider peering in the window of a family home. She clutched her bowl. Well, she lived here, too, and soon —

Soon she would feel like she belonged.

A part of her whispered belonging meant joining. Belonging meant being part of a family in all ways, not just cooking for them. Belonging meant opening her heart.

Her stomach dipped. She knew how much it could hurt if . . . if things didn't work out. Time and time again, she'd learned by watching her parents that what a spouse gave could easily be withdrawn. Better to keep her distance than try to join an already complete circle.

While she served the soup, Ted scooted the high chair closer to the corner of the table then took the seat at the head with the children on either side of him. As she had at breakfast, Elizabeth sat to his right, close to the stove.

Anna pointed an accusing finger. "She's sitting in Mama's chair. She's not s'posed to."

Ted nodded slowly. "I know, pumpkin, but women sit where they can keep an eye on the food."

Mama's chair.

Elizabeth's mind rocketed back, far from this simple kitchen to the elaborate dining room, to the ornate, massive chair where her delicate mother had always sat. Now empty. Her eyes stung, remembering a hundred meals spent with her guilt-ridden, grieving father filling his place at the other end of the table while she and Robby avoided looking at that chair. Or tried to.

No other woman had claimed her mother's place. In that chair. Or in Elizabeth's heart.

A wave of sympathy crashed through Elizabeth. How would she have felt if someone had taken her mother's place at the table? Probably much like Anna. Anna wanted Rose, not a stranger. Not just in this chair, but here, in this house.

Elizabeth searched for the right thing to say. The words Robby must've craved at Anna's age. None came. But there was something she could do. She picked up her bowl. "Would you like to trade seats, Anna? You should sit in your mother's chair."

Tears welled in the little girl's eyes. She nodded and then, carrying her bowl, took Rose's seat at the table. Now Anna would fill it. No one would look at that empty chair. A good solution or so Elizabeth hoped as she took Anna's place.

If Elizabeth had expected gratitude she didn't get it. Well, one small step at a time might bring peace. Eventually.

Sending her a nod of thanks, his eyes misty, Ted clasped his hands together. "Let's bow our heads."

Both children folded their hands. Elizabeth glanced at Henry. From behind his fist, the toddler peeked at her, sporting a drooly grin and guileless, sparkling eyes.

The small flame of Henry's friendly face melted a tiny portion of Elizabeth's frozen heart. She grinned back.

After the prayer, Ted cut up one half of a cheese sandwich for Henry, then gave the other half to Anna. He dumped the cooled vegetables on Henry's tray and chopped them into manageable pieces. The little boy dug right in, picking up a piece of corn with amazing agility and popping it in his mouth.

Anna slurped the soup from her spoon. "This doesn't taste good like Mama's soup."

"Well, it tastes better than mine." As if to prove it, Ted ate heartily.

Elizabeth detected the faintest hint of scorch. Still, the soup fared better than her collar, better than breakfast, and gave her hope she'd wrestle a measure of control over the cooking.

When he finished, as he had that morning, Ted thanked her for the meal, but this time Elizabeth heard a ring of sincerity in his voice. Close to praise. Perhaps she could handle this job of wife. But then she remembered he'd called their marriage a business arrangement. Exactly how she wanted it. Or so she told herself, as the truth sank inside her like a stone.

Anna dawdled over her food then pushed her chair back. "Can I be excused?"

Ted shook his head. "Not until we're all finished."

Anna frowned then slipped into her seat. "Are you going to read me a story after dinner, Daddy?"

"I can't, pumpkin. I have to plow." His gaze settled on Elizabeth. "But I'm sure if you're nice, Elizabeth would be glad to read you a story."

Anna's gaze darted to Elizabeth, then away. "That's okay. I'm too old for stories."

Apparently the price of nice was too steep for Anna to pay.

Ted ruffled her hair. "We're never too old for a good book."

A few minutes later, when Henry had finished, leaving his tray and the floor a disgusting mess, Ted excused himself from the table and headed back to the fields.

Leaving Elizabeth alone with his children.

Anna stared at her, eyes shooting daggers. Henry gave her a curious look like he would a new toy. All around the kitchen dirty dishes sat . . . waiting.

Every muscle in Elizabeth's body ached. A few feet away, the open bedroom door beckoned. She'd done enough for one day and wanted nothing more than a nap.

"You gonna wash the dishes?" Anna's eyes narrowed. "Like you're supposed to?"

"Oh, yes, the dishes." Elizabeth sighed. The work never ended. "You're a big girl. Want to help?"

"No." Anna gave her a small smile. "No thank you," she qualified then headed up the steps to the living room.

Elizabeth pursed her lips. A brat, plain and simple. Well, she'd practiced the art most of her life. Miss Anna might not know it, but she'd met her match in Elizabeth Manning . . . er, Logan.

Elizabeth pulled herself to her feet with fresh determination, picking up a bowl as she did and affecting an I-don't-care pose. "I'm glad you don't want to help."

Anna stopped cold in her tracks.

"That means I don't have to share."

Anna pivoted back. "Share what?"

Elizabeth swished a bar of soap around in the pan. "Why, the bubbles, of course."

"I'm too old for bubbles, too," Anna said, then stomped out of the room.

Elizabeth dropped her focus to her sudsy hands. Had she made the biggest mistake of her life yesterday? Not only for her, but also for Anna, a little girl who didn't want her here.

She'd done it for Robby, but . . . what if being here among all this unrest made Robby's life miserable? Once again he'd be living in a house of turmoil. Not a good solution for him.

Or for her.

But what choice did she have?

Across the way, Henry, red faced and bellowing, jerked against the towel anchoring him to the high chair. Elizabeth rushed over, freed his tether and picked him up. Legs pumping, arms flailing, he resembled a windup toy gone berserk. She held him at arm's length until at last his spring wound down. Yawning, he rubbed his eyes with dimpled fists.

"You look like you could use a nap. Well, so could I." Not that she'd get the luxury.

After washing him up, Elizabeth carried Henry into the living room. She stood there uncertain what to do, while the boy

146

squirmed in her arms. At this rate, he'd never fall asleep.

She thought of the quiet moments in the nursery she'd witnessed as a fourteen-year-old girl, moments between her mother and Robby. Mama held Robby close, rocking him back and forth, told him one story after another. By the second tale, Robby's eyes would close, but Mama kept rocking, holding him tight. In those moments, even as she held herself aloof from her mother, Elizabeth wished she could turn back the clock, be that child in her mother's arms.

Henry arched backward, nearly falling to the floor. She tightened her hold and hurried to the rocker near the window. Here, she had a view of the fields. In the distance, she could see Ted walking behind his team under the scorching sun.

With Henry on her lap, she rocked, but he stiffened his legs, refusing to settle. Why would he fight a nap when she'd love nothing better? She needed a story. *Children's Bible Storybook* lay open on the table beside the chair. Perfect. Elizabeth turned to the middle. "Oh, look, Henry. Noah and the Ark. That should be a good story for you." As Elizabeth read the first page, Henry climbed over her like a monkey at the zoo. "You'll never get sleepy if you don't sit still, you little octopus."

Anna marched in from her room. "He wants me, not you," she said with seven-year-old disgust, then plucked the book from Elizabeth's hands and stuck it under her arm. She raised her hands to Henry. Her brother tumbled into them, looking as content as a debutant with a full dance card.

Apparently Elizabeth would sit this one out. Well, she couldn't be happier. Her feet hurt, anyway.

Without a word exchanged between them, Elizabeth rose from the chair. A terrible heaviness pressed against her lungs, weighing down her movements. This wasn't the nursery at home. This wasn't her family. She couldn't even get a toddler to accept her in this house. She was failing as a homemaker. Failing as a mother. She blinked hard against the tears welling in her eyes, refusing to care.

Plopping Henry on the cushion, Anna quickly took Elizabeth's place, pointing to the picture. Two blond heads merged as one over the page, as close as Mama had held Robby. Just like then, Elizabeth stood watching. If she'd known how to forge the breach separating her and Mama — the stubbornness of a teen too young to under-stand her mother's need to put a happy spin on Papa's gambling trips, though Elizabeth had known what was going on — maybe she'd know how to connect with Anna.

Or might she have to face the unfaceable herself? That Ted's daughter might never accept her. Now Elizabeth understood her mother's dilemma. Bringing something into the open didn't change it. And might make it worse.

"What does a duck say, Henry?" Anna said.

"Quack, quack!" Henry settled against his sister.

"That's right." Anna shot Elizabeth a smug smile.

Well.

Anna had established her territory, making it clear she considered herself the lady of the house and Elizabeth an interloper to be ignored like a fly on the ceiling of her life.

Back in the kitchen, Elizabeth attacked the dirty dishes, a lump tightening in her throat. Why hadn't she realized this wouldn't work before she married Ted? She didn't belong here.

She sighed. But Robby did. He needed this. No matter what, for him, she'd make this work. But how?

As a small child, she and Mama had been

close. They'd shared many happy times playing dress-up and with dolls, reading, drawing and performing at the piano. She'd recapture those moments and give them to Anna and Henry and, in time, her brother.

Her mind wrapped around a fresh resolve. Elizabeth Manning Logan wasn't going anywhere. Wasn't giving up. Not that easily. Not until she had given Robby the one thing all children deserved. Security.

Her lungs expanded until she felt light, almost buoyant. Once Robby joined them, she'd have an ally in this house, someone who'd look at her with acceptance, with love. Then she'd be content.

She would.

From the living room, in a sweet voice Elizabeth barely recognized, Anna sang a lullaby. Elizabeth dried her hands on her apron and slipped to the doorway. Anna cradled her brother on her lap. Henry's eyes closed, yawning around the thumb in his mouth. In no time, the tot's head drooped.

Anna looked up and found Elizabeth watching her. "Daddy says I can't lift him into his bed." Pink dusted her cheeks, as if embarrassed by the admission.

Perhaps sharing this moment could be the first brace in building a bridge between them. "Glad to help, Anna." Elizabeth gathered Henry from his sister's arms. He curled against her body, his wispy hair soft against her chin as she carried him into his bedroom and lowered him in his crib. Lying there asleep, he looked angelic.

But looks were deceiving. She mustn't get caught in this trap. Her parents' love for each other had ran the gamut from high hopes to despondency, as Papa let his family down time and time again. The pain of it all settled inside her, adding to her resolve. She wouldn't make the mistake of opening her heart to Ted and his children, only to get it stomped on.

She tiptoed out of the room. Anna sat on the top step leading down to the kitchen, sucking her thumb. The little girl looked tired — or maybe sad. Seeing Elizabeth, she jerked her thumb away.

"You're a hard worker, Anna."

Anna's expression revealed the battle going on inside her, fighting between accepting recognition for her efforts and the desire to shut out Elizabeth. "Thank you," she said finally.

"Your mother would be proud of you."

Anna's face clouded. She rose and slipped out onto the porch, letting the screen door slap behind her. Elizabeth heard the squeak of the swing, then a soft sob followed by another.

Her breath caught in her lungs. Though she hadn't meant to, she'd added to Anna's pain. Unsure what to do, Elizabeth stood there, thinking of all the times she'd wept since Mama died. Perhaps a good cry would help Anna. If she tried to comfort her, Anna would most likely resent her efforts.

The sobbing stopped. Elizabeth tiptoed to the door. Anna lay curled on the swing, sound asleep, her breathing even, her little-girl face tranquil.

Elizabeth swallowed against the sudden tightness in her throat, then turned toward the kitchen to finish cleaning up and make preparations for the evening meal.

Later, the chore behind her, she dropped onto a living room chair, relieved to get off her feet. Earlier Ted had popped in with the excuse of refilling his water jug, when he could've easily gotten it at the pump. He was no doubt making sure neither she nor Anna had drawn blood. He'd smiled when he'd seen Anna snoozing on the swing.

Whatever the reason for Ted's appearance, she'd welcomed his presence. The walls had begun to close in on her. Those few minutes of conversation with an adult had kept her going.

She yawned. Closing her eyes, she leaned

her head against the back, so tired her body molded into the chair.

A soft babbling from his bedroom announced the end of Henry's nap. Elizabeth groaned as Anna raced past on her way to her brother. She pulled herself to her weary feet and followed, expecting to lift Henry from his crib. Instead she found Anna tugging the toddler over the bars. Evidently house rules changed with Henry awake.

Elizabeth watched while the little girl deftly changed Henry's diaper. She obeyed Anna's orders — handing her a diaper and disposing of the wet one in the lidded pail Anna indicated. An odor of ammonia smacked her in the face. Elizabeth's stomach tumbled. She dropped the diaper inside and slapped the lid on after it. What would her stomach have done if the diaper had been more than wet?

Was motherhood, even to Robby, a role too big for her to handle? So much to do — the stories, the naps, the meals, the dishes, the diapers, the laundry — the list was endless.

"Don't forget to wash them. I'm not doing it," Anna announced.

Elizabeth fought the urge to stick out her tongue at the little girl's bossy face. Instead she glanced at Henry, now exploring his nose with a finger. My, babies had the manners of Reginald Parks.

She scrubbed Henry's hands then followed the toddler out of the room. As he staggered about the living room, darting from one thing to another, she held her breath, hovering, arms out, ready to grab him.

Barely missing hitting his head on the corner of the end table, he kept going and tripped over the rocker of a chair, landing hard on his bottom. Immediately he pulled himself to his feet then almost crashed into the desk. He yanked at the knob on the desk drawer. Her heart lodged in her throat as she made a grab for him.

When the drawer didn't open, he tugged the corner of a magazine, pulling the entire pile to the floor, then plopped down to tear the cover from an issue of *Prairie Farmer.* Drool dripping on the pages of the magazine he ripped to shreds, Henry remained in one spot. That was well worth the sacrifice of a magazine. Elizabeth heaved a sigh of relief.

Then as if she'd conjured him up out of sheer panic, Ted appeared. Hair and forearms damp from washing up at the pump. Elizabeth could've hugged him. Finally, someone in the house who'd know what to do with a mischievous toddler.

Looking at his son, Ted gave a gentle smile, his face tender. "Hi, my boy."

Squealing with joy, Henry scrambled on all fours to his father. Ted gathered his son in his strong arms and kissed his cheek, then turned to Elizabeth. "Where's Anna?"

"She was here a minute ago." Elizabeth looked around the room for Anna, her heart skittering like a crab. Had she run off somewhere? Was she hiding? Hurt?

"I'll find her," Ted said calmly.

Hinges creaked. Anna stood in the doorway of the living room, her face pinched, hands hanging limp at her sides, her soft blue eyes bleak, like the sky before a rain.

"I was about to look for you, Anna," Ted said.

"I was in your bedroom." In her fist, she clutched a handkerchief. "Was this Mama's, Daddy?"

Ted passed Henry to Elizabeth then walked to Anna, knelt before his daughter and touched the corner of the hankie. "Yes, pumpkin."

"Can I . . . can I have it?"

Ted tucked a curl behind his daughter's ear. "Of course you can. Your mama would've liked you to have it."

He pressed the linen to Anna's hands, then kissed his daughter on the cheek.

Anna's lips trembled in an attempt to smile that failed, tearing at Elizabeth's resolve to remain detached. Without a word, Anna carried the hanky into the bedroom she and Henry shared and closed the door.

Ted remained where he crouched, head bent, shoulders slumped, as if in prayer. The sight of that hurting child, this strong man's dejection, seized Elizabeth's throat. She choked back tears. She knew grief, had felt that blanket of pain. But she didn't know what to do.

Finally Ted rose and turned toward Elizabeth, his forehead etched with worry. "Anna hasn't been herself since Rose died. She loved her mother, misses her terribly," he said, his voice hoarse, raw with emotion.

"I know how she feels," Elizabeth said softly. "My mother died two years ago. I ached for her. Wanted her back, for one more talk, one more hug." For one more chance to make amends.

Ted's worried expression softened. "I'm sorry you lost your mom."

How little they knew about each other. Yet the desire to help Anna united them. Ted's daughter needed their support and compassion.

"I thought by now . . ." His words trailed off.

"It's . . . something you never get over. Not really." She cleared her throat. "Anna's young to lose her mother. She misses her touch, her smile, her scent. Her very essence. No one else will do."

Ted nodded. "Not even me." Swallowing hard, he took the chair beside her, propping his forearms on his knees and hunching forward with his attention on the floor.

"You're wrong. She loves you, Ted, so much she can't stand sharing you."

"When I decided to marry, all I could think about was keeping the children near, making sure they had good care. I didn't consider how that would affect Anna." He ran a hand through his hair. "That's not true. I did, but I chose to ignore it. I thought I had a good reason, but —"

"What choice did you have, really?"

He lifted his gaze to hers, holding it as if the link was a lifeline. "You see that I never wanted to hurt Anna or you?"

She gave his hand a squeeze. "Of course."

"I'm sorry the brunt of her anger falls on you." His expression turned wary. "How did it go this afternoon?"

Elizabeth refused to add to his load. "Good," she said brightly.

The grim smile he gave suggested he knew she'd tempered her response. "Once she's gotten used to you . . ."

"My presence upsets Anna. She sees me as trying to take her mother's place."

"But only for a while, until she feels more comfortable."

His words might ring with confidence, but his eyes held the unspoken fear he might be wrong. Ted was a good father. He did all he could to meet his children's needs, even marrying a stranger to give them a mother.

The truth settled around Elizabeth's shoulders, as heavy as chain mail. That solution had blown up in his face.

So why did Ted keep looking at her with such hope in his eyes? He'd have about as much success with pinning his hopes on her as seeing rain in a fleeting, fluffy cloud during a drought.

She couldn't fix the unfixable. She wouldn't even try.

CHAPTER NINE

Ted tucked his children in for the night. Not easy with Anna clinging to him, tattling about Elizabeth's every move, no doubt hoping he'd toss his wife out like a busted toy. He'd tried talking to his daughter about her attitude, but the stubborn tilt of her chin told him he'd wasted his breath.

At last Anna's eyelids drooped and she slept, still hanging on to Rose's handkerchief. Ted tucked the sheet under her chin, then rested his elbows on his thighs and lowered his head to his hands.

Had he made a mistake remarrying? Had he misread the freedom of choice God gave His children, seeing Elizabeth as God's will for them? And added to Anna's unhappiness? Made Elizabeth's life miserable? The fear of failing his children and his new wife weighed him down, all but crushing him.

"Lord, mend Anna's broken heart. Help my children accept Elizabeth," he whispered. "Bless this marriage."

As he laid his burdens at the foot of the Throne, several Scriptures came to mind, precious promises of God's gift of wisdom, of His provision. The Father could bring good out of bad. Buoyed by renewed hope, the burden on his shoulders lifted.

God would help them, was helping them even now. He'd expected too much too soon. Establishing harmony in his house would take time. Adjustments had to be made. He'd keep his expectations on an even plane, his usual course, and the wisest.

He and Elizabeth might not be the typical couple, might never fall in love, but with God's help, they could make this family work.

With one last glance at his children, their faces peaceful in slumber, Ted left the room, prepared by his time with God to bolster his wife. This surely had been a difficult day for her.

In the living room, he found Elizabeth at the desk, leafing through a cookbook. Her hair had pulled loose from the pins and curled around her face. At odd moments like this, he'd glance her way and that beauty would sock him in the gut.

The dejected look on her face now tore at him. Anna wasn't the only miserable person

160

in this house. He hoped, in time, Elizabeth would find contentment.

But life had taught him happiness wasn't a guarantee in this world. He'd give anything if he'd been able to protect his children from that truth, but Rose's passing had introduced them to the harsh reality of death. He'd explained to Anna that her mother now resided in Heaven, but that assurance didn't stop her from missing Rose on earth.

Time. Healing would take time. Accord would take time.

He dropped into a rocker near the potbelly stove, stretching out his legs toward the warmth of the fire. As he stared into the window at the flames, thinking how difficult childhood could be sometimes, his mind catapulted back.

Fire and brimstone. Exactly what his father had preached at those revivals. Men and women rushed to the altar to lay down the load of their sins. But behind his father's fiery demeanor lived a liar. Even as young as five, Ted had known his dad pocketed the offering, laughing at the stupidity of those he bilked. Not a preacher at all, but a charlatan who stole money to gamble.

When the gaming tables had taken his last dime, he'd put down the cards and pick up the garb of a preacher again, until he'd swindled another stake from trusting souls in another town.

The flames flickered, but Ted barely noticed the dancing oranges and yellows. He saw an endless parade of towns, filled with faces his father had betrayed. Ted had sat on the front row, throat tight with shame, and waited . . . fear crawling up his spine, sure God would strike his father dead on the spot. But God never did.

The flames began to ebb, but the heat remained. Much like God's love. God didn't kill sinners — He loved them. Even men like his father.

Even men like him.

"Ted."

"I'm sorry, what?"

"How long . . . since Rose . . . ?" Elizabeth glanced away, evidently too uncomfortable with her question to finish it.

"Rose died thirteen months ago, one month after Henry's birth."

"I'm sorry. I can't imagine the joy of a baby shattered by his mother's death."

"Rose had one goal, to give our baby life." He swallowed hard. "If only we hadn't decided to have another child —"

He refused to finish. Elizabeth had enough to deal with, without taking on Rose's death and the guilt he'd felt but had finally released to God.

He got up from the chair and walked to the side door, eager to change the subject, searching for a way to lighten the mood. "Clear sky tonight. Lots of stars. A full moon."

Keeping her distance, Elizabeth peered out. "It's serene."

He turned toward her. Her eyes widened, filling with uncertainty. "More serene than you."

"Why would you say that?"

"You tiptoe around me like you're afraid I'll bite."

She lifted her chin. "I do no such thing. I'm not the tiptoeing sort."

"Is that right?" To prove his point, he reached out a hand and she jumped. He grinned then sobered. "Things are difficult now, but once Anna adjusts, we'll find an even keel, a way to coexist amicably."

Elizabeth's brow wrinkled. "Is that your goal, Ted? To just coexist?"

She made accord sound dull, boring. But to him, a tranquil life sounded perfect. His father's example of Bible-thumping preaching, his zeal for gambling, had taught Ted to shun fiery passion. When he'd left the riverboat and his "Hold 'Em" Logan existence,

163

he'd promised God he'd make a new start. From that point on, he based his life on God's Word, not on unreliable feelings and bursts of emotion.

"Calm waters, a cool head, looking to God for wisdom — that makes for a happy home."

She gave him a wan smile. "If so, we're failing."

"Don't underestimate God's authority in this, Elizabeth. Give it time. Pray about it. God is faithful."

"No doubt God listens to you, a church-going man."

The words she didn't say spoke volumes. "You don't believe He's listening to you."

"I don't rely on God to solve my problems."

If God intended Ted to heed His call, why had He given him a wife with shaky faith? Or was that somehow part of God's plan? "Perhaps He already has," he said, studying her.

Looking unconvinced, Elizabeth merely shrugged.

Somehow Ted suspected his wife's problems referred to more than Anna. Was she talking about him or something else? "No one besides God is worth relying on."

Their eyes locked. All those unnamed

problems fell away, leaving just the two of them. Something wounded and raw in Elizabeth called to him. He wanted to protect her. To give her whatever he possessed. Whatever she needed. But he dared not push her. Though he'd pray for her daily, she'd have to find her way. With Anna. With him. With God.

Standing this close, alone in the quiet house, sent his skittish wife to the couch. "Where did Anna and Henry stay last year during planting and harvest season?" she said, deftly changing the subject.

"After Rose's parents returned home, the children stayed at the Harpers' during the day and here in the evening. Anna hated being separated from me." He sighed. "She'd like to follow me around the place while I'm doing the chores. It's not safe."

"Anna's lost one parent. Naturally she wants to keep an eye on you."

He rubbed the back of his neck, stiff from hours behind the plow. If only he could soothe his hurting daughter as easily. "I'm sure you're right."

"How long have you lived in New Harmony?"

"Nine years." She looked at him expectantly, clearly fishing for information. Maybe if he gave her some, she'd be satisfied. "We moved here right after Rose and I married."

"That's when you bought the farm."

He nodded. Rose had desired nothing beyond a simple existence living off the land. Exactly what he wanted . . . or so he told himself every day. Though at times the life chafed against him like new wool long johns in winter.

"The work is endless, but I'd appreciate it if you found time to read and play with the children each day. That was Rose's way. They're used to some attention."

"Anna's the little mother around here." Elizabeth laughed but Ted didn't miss the lack of humor in the sound. "Not me."

Ted cringed. He hadn't missed his precious daughter's bossy, belligerent behavior with Elizabeth. "Anna's conduct will improve once she gets to know you," he said with all the assurance he could muster.

"Are you trying to convince me or yourself?" She smiled. "Don't worry. I can handle Anna. I wasn't an easy child. I know all the tricks."

"Why doesn't that surprise me?" He chuckled, and then sat beside her on the sofa.

Close enough to notice the curve of her cheek, the length of her lashes and the silky texture of her skin. Though she'd tried to

166

tease about her behavior as a child, the pain of her admittance clouded her pretty blue eyes.

Lord, please free Elizabeth from whatever's bothering her. Help me to make her feel at home here.

Though, surely his stinginess at the mercantile yesterday hadn't helped matters. "If I acted like I begrudged you the fabric and garments, I apologize. I hate to go into debt but that's the way of life for farmers. If the harvest's good, the bills get paid. If not . . ."

"If not, you work harder the next year."

"That's farming."

"It's honest work," she said. The admiration in his citified wife surprised him.

"Yes, and that's what matters. But some days I feel like a mule pulling a plow through the mud, that I'll never reach the other side of the field." He paused, forcing a laugh, then sobered. "But I do. I have to."

"What did you do before you took up farming?"

The kitchen clock struck the hour. "This and that," he said, rising. "It's late. If Anna or Henry wakes, don't hesitate to fetch me."

Elizabeth hugged the armrest like a long-lost friend. "My presence is inconvenient. You probably won't sleep well in that drafty barn."

167

"No, your being here means I can plant and keep my children with me. That's all that matters."

A flash of something he couldn't read streaked across her face. She quickly smoothed her expression. Had he hurt her? If so, he hadn't meant to, but even if the truth hurt, it didn't change the facts. Anna and Henry were his priorities.

He hadn't lied when he'd called their marriage a business arrangement. Perhaps in time, they'd come to mean more to each other. Ted felt far more comfortable in the world of friendly coexistence — two people living together, working toward a common goal — than in strong attraction. Though every time Elizabeth came near, she made him question that opinion.

Worse, she questioned him. Tried to figure out what made him tick. He couldn't let her unearth his past and risk his children's future.

He ambled toward the door. "Before I turn in, I'll find those boots. Can't have you working in your party best."

"Even a mule deserves to be well shod." Elizabeth's steely eyes held not one shred of humor.

"I hoped you knew that taking care of my household wouldn't be easy. I didn't try to mislead you."

She glared at him. "Just once, try putting yourself in my place, Ted Logan. Stick your feet in those boots you promised and see if the fit's comfortable." She left the room in a huff.

He'd intended to mend the fences his daughter had broken, but instead he'd driven a wider wedge between him and Elizabeth.

Perhaps that was for the best.

If they got close, she might discover the truth about him, and soon the whole town would know. All havoc would break loose.

And destroy the way of life he'd made for his children.

Ted must be feeding his hens molasses or something equally sticky. Their eggs stuck to a pan like shy debutants wedged together at a ball. When Elizabeth tried to turn one over, half the white stayed behind while the yolk spewed out, a yellow stream navigating the cast iron, as if two hens went to war in the pan.

So much for her plan to start the morning off on a good note, thinking a well-cooked meal would be a way to ease into the "Oh, by the way, I have a brother" discussion. Instead, once Ted saw the meal, she'd be fortunate if he stayed at the table, much less let Robby join them there.

"Bam! Bam!" Henry beat his spoon on the tray of the high chair. Oatmeal flew, landing on the floor with a splat.

"Henry Logan, I don't have time to clean up the mess you're making. So stop that. Please."

"Bam! Bam! Bam!" He did it again, this time laughing at his cleverness. The last bang sent the spoon clanging to the planks.

If he knew the trouble she'd had making that oatmeal, he'd treat the meal with more respect. Elizabeth bent to retrieve the utensil. "I asked you nicely. Flipping oatmeal is nasty."

No sooner had the words left her mouth, than something plopped on her head. She reached up and grabbed hold of one oatmeal-coated, chubby hand and looked into Henry's grinning face. "Good thing you're as cute as a bug's ear, young man."

"Bug!"

"You're a boy, not a bug."

"Bug," he said, then whacked her square on the nose with an oatmeal-loaded fist.

"Ouch." No wonder Mama had taken her breakfast in bed. The kitchen was a hazardous place. A woman could languish under a mountain of oatmeal and pasty eggs. She wanted to be mad, but found herself running a finger along his cheek.

Henry giggled, ducking his head.

Whenever she saw the mischief in his eyes, part of her softened like butter on a sultry summer day. "I won't be swayed by those dancing eyes, young man."

She walked to the door and whistled Tippy inside. He gobbled the oatmeal and licked Henry's extended hand for dessert before Elizabeth herded him back outside. If Tippy could master a dust mop, he could get a job as a maid.

The smell of smoke brought her nose up in the air. Something was burning. "The toast!"

She raced to the oven. Using a towel, she flung it open and yanked out the pan. Their closest neighbor to the south had sent over a loaf of fresh-baked bread with her oldest son and she'd destroyed the gift. Her eyes stung. She'd been counting on the toast, at least, to be edible.

How would she ever convince Ted to allow her to bring Robby here if she couldn't handle the work she already had?

The back door opened and closed. Anna wrinkled her nose. "I smell smoke."

"How's breakfast coming?" Ted asked.

From across the kitchen, Elizabeth shot

him a scowl.

A crooked grin tugged at the corner of his mouth. "Guess I don't have to ask."

He washed his hands and asked Anna to do the same, then took the toast from Elizabeth's hands. "Better check your hair before that lump of oatmeal dries." He scrapped the burned crumbs into the sink.

"That lump is a gift from your son."

Ted chuckled. "He's a generous boy, like his father."

Rolling her eyes, she whirled toward the mirror hanging near the sink and plucked at the oatmeal, shaking it off her fingers into the slop jar, then dabbed at the gooey spot with a damp towel, avoiding Ted's gaze.

"You, ah, missed some." Ted came around her, took the towel and with a gentle touch, wiped at the mess. He stood facing her, mere inches away, close enough she could feel the heat emanating from his skin. She remained motionless, for surely if she took a step, she'd find herself in the comfort of his arms.

"Your hair is beautiful." Husky and quiet, his tone rumbled with something intimate. "Like sun-kissed wheat." His gaze locked with hers, sending a shiver down her spine.

Elizabeth had received dozens of compliments over the years, but never had one left her reeling. She pressed a palm to the mass of curls she hadn't had time to tuck into a chignon. "My hair's a mess. I'll put it up later —"

"Don't. I mean, you needn't worry. You look . . . good as new."

"I do?" She ran her fingers through her hair, searching for another chunk of Henry's breakfast, while her wayward heart hammered in her chest. "I doubt that."

"Never doubt a man's compliment. They don't come easy for most of us."

Across the way, Anna watched Elizabeth and Ted with narrowed eyes, her mouth thinned in disapproval. Hadn't Elizabeth watched her parents as Anna watched them now? Not out of jealousy or pain as Anna surely did, but with hope.

Time and time again, she'd seen Papa sweet-talk his way back into the good graces of his disgruntled wife. Those moments of affection between her parents hadn't lasted. The inevitable letdowns had sent her mother to bed and her father to the gambling tables.

Elizabeth fingered her mother's cameo, the only piece of jewelry that hadn't been sold to pay the bills.

Her thumb roamed the face of the cameo as she thought of another necklace. A strand of shimmering pearls. Papa had swooped in at breakfast and draped them around Mama's neck. "Happy anniversary! You get prettier with every year, Amanda. As young as the day we married."

Mama had giggled at the claim.

"You don't believe me." He pointed to the mirror hanging over the buffet. "Look at yourself."

With her cheeks flushed with pleasure and her eyes sparkling, Mama was beautiful, regal like a queen. Standing at her side, Papa was her crown prince, tall and imposing. The perfect couple — or so they appeared.

Then Papa danced Mama around the room. She'd thrown back her head laughing, her face glowing like the morning sun.

"I've made reservations for dinner," he said. "Afterward we'll stop at the club."

Mama paled. "Not the club. Not tonight."

He kissed her cheek. "I'll win enough to buy the matching bracelet and earrings. Wouldn't you like that?"

Watching them leave, Elizabeth had never seen a more enchanting couple, looking as if they'd stepped out of a fairy tale. She'd waited up to see them come home. A little after midnight, Mama came in alone. The next day Papa arrived home, and rushed back out again to sell a painting and Mama's pearls to pay a debt.

As always, Mama had smiled, but that smile was a little dimmer, her face a little more shadowed. She and Papa never danced in the breakfast room again.

Her mother might've pretended the Mannings lived in a rosy world, but she hadn't fooled Elizabeth. A hundred times over in her parents' lives, she'd witnessed Papa charm his way into Mama's heart one minute, then break it the next.

Their happiness had been as fleeting as a shooting star. Love led to shattered dreams and broken hearts. Elizabeth's throat tightened as her hand fell away from the cameo.

Don't. Don't get close.

Don't get wrapped up in Ted and his compliments.

She needed to forget about her parents, forget about Ted's flattering and concentrate on finding a way to ease into the subject of Robby.

Resolute, she turned to the stove. Oh, my, now all the eggs were cooked hard, the river of yellow solid. She sighed and scrapped three of them on a plate, added four slices of bacon and set the dish in front of Ted, who gifted her with a smile.

Ignoring that smile, she returned with a

bowl of oatmeal and a glass of milk for Anna. Last she brought the toast, slapped it down at Ted's elbow and then filled his coffee cup.

Ted waited for her to sit, and then bowed his head for prayer. When he'd blessed the food, he grabbed a spoon and scooped oatmeal into his son's open-like-a-baby-bird mouth. Henry grabbed the spoon, playing tug-of-war, and then gave up on the contest and fed himself with his fingers.

Elizabeth should rush over to wash Henry's hands, but that meant tattling on Tippy and on her. Besides, a little dog-lick wouldn't hurt a perpetually grubby boy like Henry. Would it?

"Daddy lets me milk Nellie and Bessie on Saturday," Anna said between bites of oatmeal.

"You're Daddy's helper." Ted tugged one of Anna's braids, and then dove into the hard-cooked eggs.

"Me and Daddy saw you let Tippy inside," Anna said in an accusing tone.

Elizabeth smiled. "Tippy is better at mopping than I am."

"She said Tippy mops." Anna chuffed. "He can't hold a mop, can he, Daddy?"

"Well, evidently he has other ways of cleaning up." He motioned to Henry. "With this guy around, I can see the advantages of bringing Tippy inside upon occasion." Ted's eyes roamed over her face, sending Elizabeth's pulse skittering. "Wish I'd thought of it."

He reached out and brushed a crumb from her lip. Elizabeth gulped as heat flushed her cheeks. This man did strange things to her insides that she wouldn't trust.

She shot up from the table and grabbed a cloth to wipe up Henry. The little boy wailed in protest, shaking his head back and forth with a speed Elizabeth couldn't match.

Anna slipped in between them, took the cloth out of Elizabeth's grasp. Trapping Henry's chin in one hand, Anna sang a tune about scrubbing in a tub and cleaned the cereal from her brother's face. Then, smirking at Elizabeth, she strolled toward the back door.

"Anna, you need to ask to be excused," Elizabeth said without thinking.

"I don't have to, do I, Daddy?"

"Yes, that's the polite thing to do. I've been negligent about our table manners."

With her lower lip protruding, Anna returned to her seat, eyeing Elizabeth. "Can I go, Daddy?"

"Yes, you may."

Anna walked past Elizabeth. "Was your

mama as mean as you?" She raced out the door, letting it slap behind her.

Ted sighed.

Elizabeth swallowed hard. She'd tired of her mother's focus on etiquette, while under that facade of perfection their world tumbled out of control.

Did Anna feel the same?

She forced a laugh, but even she could hear the wobbly hurt in it. "Maybe I was too tough on Anna."

"I'm sorry about Anna's behavior. Since Rose died, I haven't had the heart to discipline her. It shows."

"I understand that." She was very aware of the ramifications of losing a mother.

To smooth her relationship with Anna, she'd overlook the small things that didn't matter to children. And leave the training of his daughter to Ted.

She glanced at her husband. Ted's attention had drifted away. He'd gone somewhere else, somewhere far from his kitchen. "It can't be easy, stepping into another woman's shoes," he said at last. "It's not easy for me, either. I try to be a good father, but I'm failing Anna when she needs me most."

The anguish in his tone banged against Elizabeth's heart. "I'm not sure men occupy the same role as women. Some women are born mothers." She didn't bother to add she was not one of them. Ted already knew.

He brought his gaze back to her. "True. My mother . . . wasn't."

That pause said a lot. Elizabeth wanted to ask, to probe, but she wasn't here to be Ted Logan's confidant. She was here for Robby.

"What kind of a mother was yours?" Ted asked.

"Loving." She sighed. "I was strong willed and she didn't know what to make of me." Amanda Manning could no more stand up to her daughter than she had her husband. "Martha arrived when I was five and laid down the rules."

"You must've been more like your father."

His assessment stung. But she couldn't deny it. "Papa laughed at the antics that put Mama in a tizzy. He'd say, 'Leave her alone, Amanda. She'll never be bedridden by life.' " Elizabeth swallowed hard. "I realized later they were talking about each other, not about me." She clasped her hands in her lap. "It was never about me."

"I'm sorry." Ted brushed his fingers along her cheek. "You're a precious child of God. Don't let anyone's assessment, even your own, determine your worth."

Tears brimmed in her eyes. She turned her face away. "I'm sorry I was too young

179

to understand her. To understand the battles she fought every day. If only I could ask her forgiveness."

"Nothing Anna and Henry could do would stop me from forgiving them. I'm sure your mother felt the same."

Could Ted be right? Could Mama have forgiven her, even without Elizabeth asking for absolution? "I hope so."

Ted stretched out a hand, taking hers in his firm grip. "If you ask Him, God will forgive you anything. And give you the peace about your mistakes that you need. That we all need."

She gave a wry smile. "You sound like a preacher."

Disquiet flitted across his face. He withdrew his hand. "I'm glad you're in here fixing breakfast when I'm out at the barn. I can't thank you enough for taking care of us and for watching my children."

She shrugged as if it was nothing. But in truth just making eggs was a formidable task. Yet nothing compared to the demands of taking care of Ted's children.

"Maybe some women aren't born to be mothers," Ted said. "But they can *become* good mothers."

"If you're thinking of me that would take a miracle."

He studied her, his eyes dark, penetrating, as if he wanted something from her that she couldn't give.

Elizabeth rose, gathering the dishes and carrying them to the sink, but for the life of her, she couldn't remember what to do with them.

Behind her she heard the scrape of a chair, then felt the heat of Ted's body as he closed the gap between them. "I hope . . ."

She turned toward him, waiting. "Hope what?"

He leaned nearer until he stood mere inches away. The solid comfort of his presence slid through her. With his cupped hand, he lifted her chin. Her pulse kicked up.

Would he . . . ?

Would he kiss her?

"I hope in time you'll be happy here," he said. "In every way."

Then he turned and left.

They'd opened up to each other, given a peek into their worlds. And she'd gotten sidetracked from raising the subject of her brother.

Instead of planning her next step toward accomplishing that goal, she slumped onto a chair, reliving that almost kiss.

Feeling the oddest sense of relief.
And disappointment.

CHAPTER TEN

Even from yards away, the odor of the place hit Elizabeth harder than a belch from Reginald Parks. She shoved the egg basket at Ted. "I'll, ah, wait out here."

He arched a brow. "You're afraid of a few chickens?"

"I didn't say I was afraid." Elizabeth put her hand over her nose. "It's just . . . they stink."

He bent down and chucked her under the chin. "You *are* afraid." He laughed. "I can see it in your eyes."

She couldn't let him know he was right, not with those teasing eyes daring her to act. These smelly birds would pay for her and Robby's tickets. She dared not refuse to gather their eggs. "Fine, I'll do it . . . if you go with me."

"I'll show you how it's done." He touched her scarf looped around her head. "If you plan on getting along with the hens, you

183

might want to remove that red kerchief."

"I can't go into that nasty coop without covering my hair."

"Still, you'd better —"

She fisted her hands on her hips. "Ted Logan, you're always telling me what to do."

"Fine. Do it your way."

He opened the door and she slapped a hand over her mouth and nose and stepped inside with Ted on her heels. As the door closed, the henhouse exploded with activity — squawking hens, flapping wings. Chickens streaked across the wooden floor. Flew to perch on the rafters.

Heart pounding, Elizabeth turned to Ted. "These birds are wild! And you suggested I come in here without a kerchief. My hair could be caked with lots more than oatmeal."

He opened his mouth, but she shot him a look and he clamped it shut. *Good.* He'd gotten the message. Finally.

She turned back to the peevish hens, determined not to let her disquiet show. "Haven't you seen a lady in pants before?" she crooned. "Only difference — your pants are made of feathers."

The chickens clucked. Ted joined in with a soft chuckle. Finally the henhouse quieted. Elizabeth inched farther into the coop, letting her eyes adjust to the dim interior.

Two chickens, unruffled and serene, remained in their straw-stuffed boxes. They didn't look all that scary.

She approached the first box on her left, overflowing with a fat, white hen. "Can I have your egg?" The hen blinked at her and squatted farther into the straw. "Please?" She shooed the bird but the stubborn creature didn't budge.

"Slip your hand beneath the hen, real easy like, and pull out the egg," Ted said.

But when she reached, the hen turned one beady, ferocious eye on her, a warning she'd heed. She took a step back. "Keep it, if it means that much to you."

"Here, I'll get it." Ted retrieved the egg without incident. He met her gaze and shrugged. "They know me."

"Too bad I left my calling cards in Chicago." Gripping the egg basket, she ignored Ted's laugh and edged down the row, plucking eggs from the vacant nests. As she approached the next sitting hen, the bird hopped aside to reveal a pristine egg.

Elizabeth smiled. "Now, that's more like it." She stretched out a hand. In a flash, the hen pecked the top. "Ouch! You'd better watch it or you'll end up as Sunday's dinner."

Not that she could kill that bird . . . unless looks could kill.

"Let me." Ted tried to step between the hen and her, but Elizabeth would not give way.

She reached again. The hen pecked again — harder. Elizabeth let out a shriek. A bird flew from its perch on the rafter into her face. Blinded, her heart lurching against her chest, Elizabeth jerked away, stepped into a water pan and staggered backward, dropping the basket.

Ted caught her before she hit the floor. "Are you all right?"

"I'm fine." But she wasn't. She fought back angry tears. She loathed this farm and all the smelly, scary, noisy beasts living on it. Right now that included Ted.

But in truth, she wanted him to put those strong arms of his around her. Make her feel safe. Secure. Tell her everything would be okay, even though it wouldn't.

"I'm sure you have more to do than watch me make an idiot of myself," she said.

"I tried to tell —"

"I'm tired of you telling me what to do and how to do it." Her eyes stung. She would not let Ted see how overwhelmed she felt. "I'll learn. Maybe the hard way, but I'll learn."

"Fine with me." Ted stomped off in the direction of the barn.

Fine with her, too. She didn't need Ted. Or his help.

By the time Elizabeth reached the pump, the tally favored the hens. Twelve eggs broken, four intact and one very rattled egg gatherer badly in need of a bath.

At this rate, she'd never get Robby here.

As she turned to rinse out the mess in the basket, she caught sight of a wagon pulling into the barnyard. A little girl cuddled against the woman driver. She had company. Until that moment, Elizabeth hadn't realized how lonely she was for female companionship.

From the other side of the screen door, Anna came running.

Elizabeth looked down at her attire. Men's pants and a castoff, frayed shirt. Too late now. This woman had seen her unusual outfit and still waved a greeting.

By the time she reached the wagon the girls chattered away. Holding a tiny bundle, the visitor dropped her gaze to Elizabeth's attire but the smile never left her face. "I'm Rebecca Harper, your nearest neighbor. Hope you don't mind us dropping in."

Elizabeth smiled. "I'm glad for the company."

"This is our Grace." Rebecca nudged her daughter forward. "Say hello to Mrs. Logan." Grace mumbled a greeting. Rebecca motioned to the baby. "And this is our Faith — eight weeks today."

"How nice of you to pay a visit." Elizabeth reached out a hand, spotted the slime from the broken eggs and pulled it back. "Sorry. The hens and I got off on the wrong foot."

Rebecca grinned, leaned over and pulled a piece of straw out of Elizabeth's hair. "They can be nasty little boogers. Though I'm sure that red head scarf didn't help."

Elizabeth's gaze darted to the barn. "What?"

"Chickens are easily frightened. Red promotes turmoil."

Ted had warned her to not wear the scarf. If only she wasn't as easily riled as the hens whenever he gave her an order, maybe more eggs would've survived.

Anna scooted to her side and peered into the basket. "You broke the eggs? Papa's going to be mad."

"A hen flew right into my face and I dropped the basket."

"You musta upset the hens. I'm going to tell —"

Elizabeth sighed. "Your father knows. He

was with me."

"No point in tattling, now is there?" Rebecca gave Ted's daughter a stern look. "I would've expected better of you."

Anna toed the ground with her shoe. "Sorry."

Rebecca turned back to Elizabeth. They exchanged the smiles of conspirators and Elizabeth knew she'd found a friend.

"You're forgiven." Rebecca ruffled Anna's hair. "Now you girls go play while we have a visit."

"Do I still have to watch Henry?" Anna tugged at Elizabeth's shirt. "Me and Grace wanna make a clothespin doll."

Two days ago Elizabeth didn't even know what clothespins were. "Go ahead. I'll listen for Henry."

The girls raced across the yard to the line.

Rebecca smiled. "I'm embarrassed I didn't get over sooner, but Dan didn't finish planting until yesterday. He agreed to keep the boys so we could chat in peace. That is, if you've got the time."

Elizabeth glanced down at her clothes. "Being caught wearing these, I'm the one who's red faced."

"Are those Ted's pants?" Rebecca asked.

Elizabeth hitched up the rolled waistline. "I'm afraid so."

"Are they comfortable?"

"They're too long and wide but until I get something else to wear, I'm stuck with them."

Rebecca chuckled. "Since I had Faith, I can't even button my dress at the middle." She flapped the skirt of her apron. "This covers the worst of it."

"Oh, I think you look beautiful." And she did. Rebecca all but glowed with happiness. "Go on in. I'll just be a minute."

Elizabeth pumped water over the eggs, picked out the broken shells and tossed them behind the lilac bush, her thoughts scrambling like crabs at the beach.

What should she do to entertain a visitor? Martha served tea and scones. Tea would be an easy task. Scones she didn't have. But maybe she had something else Rebecca would find palatable. Biscuits. She had plenty of those.

Inside, Elizabeth set the egg basket on the floor and scrubbed her hands. "Henry is down for a nap so we can have some peace and quiet. Would you care for tea?"

"Love some." Rebecca laid the sleeping baby in the rocker, pulling back the blanket from around her tiny face.

Elizabeth supposed it wouldn't be polite to ignore the baby, not with her mother

190

standing over her, proud and smiling. She walked over to take a peek. And promptly fell in love. Such a sweet little thing. With lots of dark hair, long black lashes and a bow-shaped mouth.

Elizabeth reached out a finger and traced a line along the sleeping baby's cheek. "She's gorgeous."

How could she feel mushy over a baby when she knew perfectly well babies grew into messy toddlers who exhausted you, then older children who defied you?

No, babies weren't for her. Nor marriage, either, and yet here she was married and drooling over a baby. She'd been cooped up too long. A feather drifted off her clothes to the floor. Cooped up in more ways than one.

Rebecca took a seat at the table. Elizabeth got out the teapot and prepared tea. "Would you care for a biscuit? There's a few left from breakfast."

"Thanks, I'd love one."

"Really? That's so nice of you."

"And here I was thinking how nice it was of you to offer."

"This batch is crumbly," Elizabeth apologized as she set out a plate of biscuits and compote of jam.

Rebecca spread a layer of strawberry jam on top. Though a chunk of the biscuit fell away, she managed to take a bite. "This is delicious."

Elizabeth beamed her thanks. Maybe she was making progress. She returned to the table with cups and saucers.

"So, has Anna declared war yet?"

"Well, if not war, definitely a skirmish." Elizabeth went back for the pot, set it on a hot pad to steep then plopped down in her seat. "Anna resents me for usurping her mother's place. Or so she sees it. She's taken the role of little mommy to Henry and helper to Ted with no intention of giving up her territory."

"Anna's one determined little girl."

Elizabeth poured the steaming amber liquid into their cups. "Kind of like me." Her gaze slid beyond the living room to the children's bedroom door. "Now Henry, he's like a windup toy. Keeping up with him wears me out until he slows down. Thank goodness he takes a three-hour nap and goes to bed early. It's the only time I can cook and clean."

"Boys are more rambunctious, but all three of mine together are less trouble than Grace."

Elizabeth added sugar to her tea. "How old are your boys?"

"Jason's the oldest. He's seven. Mark is

four and Calvin, two. Enough about my children. I'm here to get to know you." She took a sip from her cup. "So why did you give up dresses for pants? Is this some new French fashion that hasn't made it to the cornfields?"

Elizabeth grinned. "The one dress I have isn't comfortable to work in."

"One dress? Shame on Ted."

"It's a long story and not at all Ted's fault. He bought material to make three, but . . ."

"Let me guess. Between the baking, egg gathering and laundry, you haven't had time to make them?"

Avoiding Rebecca's eyes, Elizabeth toyed with her cup. "Truth is I don't know how to make a dress."

"Oh. Sounds like you could use some help."

"I doubt Ted's thrilled with me wearing his clothes."

Rebecca grinned. "From the way you look in those pants, I suspect Ted doesn't mind."

Glancing at Ted's old jeans, all Elizabeth could see was rolled waist and cuffs, frayed ends of twine dangling from her makeshift belt and pieces of straw sticking here and there.

She plucked them off and tossed them into the stove. "I look like an old faded scarecrow."

"Not from behind." Rebecca laughed. "But, before you fall on your face, let's cut some length off those pants."

Ted might not like that, but then the hems were worn and he had more, so why not? In minutes, Rebecca had whacked the jeans down to fit using the large shears she'd found hanging in the pantry.

"There, now we can get started sewing up a dress."

"I can't let you do that." Then Elizabeth held her breath, hoping Rebecca would do that very thing.

Rebecca drained her cup. "It'll be fun. I haven't made anything new in ages."

Elizabeth sent a sidelong glance at Rebecca's dress. The cuffs at her wrists had frayed, but it was pressed and clean. "All right, but only if you'll accept material for making it."

"Oh, no, I couldn't." Rebecca blushed. "I'm glad to help." She carried her dishes to the sink. "I can't let a neighbor of mine wear pants to the ice cream social."

"A social?" Elizabeth clasped a hand to her chest. "Oh, that sounds like fun."

"We hold sack races and horseshoe contests. The men crank freezers of ice cream. The women bring a favorite cake to share."

Favorite cake? She had to bake a cake?

194

Wouldn't biscuits do? Oh my, she'd better get practicing.

Rebecca checked the baby, sleeping peacefully. "Time's a-wastin'. Let's make that dress while the younguns nap."

In no time, Rebecca devised a pattern from newspaper. Satisfied it would fit, she cut out a dress and then ran it up on the sewing machine. As Rebecca guided the fabric beneath the metal foot, the soft whir of the wheel accompanied the thump of the treadle.

Hoping to learn something about sewing and her new husband, Elizabeth pulled up a chair. "How well do you know Ted?"

"The way he cared for Rose when she took sick and his kids tells me all I need to know about Ted."

But Elizabeth had questions.

"Why do you ask?"

"No special reason. Ted doesn't say much about his life before he came to New Harmony. Almost like he has no past."

Or one he's hiding.

"All I know is he and Rose showed up at church the Sunday after they moved in. We were mighty glad to see them bring life to this house."

"Were you and Rose friends?"

Rebecca nodded. "She was a sweet

woman. Quiet. Thoughtful."

The exact opposite of Elizabeth.

"I recall Rose saying they married in her home church about twelve miles west of here. Their search for a farm brought them to New Harmony."

"Wonder why New Harmony?"

"The Martin place sat empty after Paul died. Reckon the price was right. And close enough for Rose's parents to visit. Often."

Something about Rebecca's tone didn't flatter Rose's parents. But that wasn't her priority. "Does Ted have family?"

"None of his people came to the funeral. Why not ask him?"

Elizabeth forced a laugh. "Now why didn't I think of that?"

Rebecca stopped pedaling and snipped the thread. "What about you? You got any family?"

The question ended her speculation about Ted. She couldn't lie, exactly . . . "Yes. My father lives in Chicago."

"You must miss him."

Elizabeth swallowed against the sudden knot in her throat, a result of her deceit. "Yes, I do."

Rebecca lifted the skirt from the machine and held it and the bodice against Elizabeth. A dress. Something Elizabeth had taken for granted but now seemed a monumental achievement.

As Rebecca pinned the skirt to the bodice, she glanced at the clock. "Feel free to start supper. I'll have to feed the baby soon."

Perhaps Rebecca's presence in the house renewed her energy or maybe she had finally figured out how to handle that black monster of a stove, but Elizabeth fried up a slab of pork with a minimum of difficulty, peeled potatoes, only nicking her finger once, and put on a pan of sauerkraut. The food bubbled away on the stove, filling the house with heady scents. For the first time, she felt optimistic about the meal.

Back in the bedroom, Rebecca still hunched over the sewing machine. She nodded toward a packet of buttons. "Found those in one of the sewing drawers. They're perfect for this dress."

Lovely mother-of-pearl buttons gleamed in the afternoon sun streaming in the window. Probably Rose had planned to put them on a dress. The thought dampened Elizabeth's mood.

"How did you know how much material to buy?" Rebecca asked.

"Mrs. Sorenson told me."

"The Sorensons are good-hearted. The best. Allow farmers to run up a bill till harvest. Poor Hubert can't keep up with his accounts and his wife has no head for figures."

"I love math."

"Really! Well, God knows what He's doing when He passes out our gifts."

Elizabeth had never thought of her skill in math as a gift from God. How often had she ignored what God had done for her and instead focused on the disappointments?

Rebecca grinned. "I'd sooner eat grubs than face the Sorenson ledger."

"I'd rather swallow earthworms than take shears to fabric."

Giggling, Rebecca taught Elizabeth how to do a blind hemstitch, the topic of math forgotten.

For the second time Elizabeth had heard the Sorensons needed help with their books. Soon as she could, she'd talk to Mr. Sorenson about a job.

Once she'd mastered the hemstitch, Rebecca showed her how to attach the buttons to the bodice. "I'll come back to make the other dress," she promised.

Elizabeth didn't know why Rebecca had done all this for her, but her new friend waved away her thanks, saying it was the Christian thing to do. Elizabeth didn't know much about Christians, but one wore the name Rebecca Harper.

After much convincing, Rebecca had agreed to take the fabric in exchange for making two dresses. When Rebecca, Grace and Faith pulled out the lane, the pink twill stretched across Grace's lap.

Elizabeth hoped Ted wouldn't be angry with her for giving away the material.

"Smells good in here." Ted scooted past Elizabeth as she stood at the stove. Apparently his wife had gotten over the run-in with the hens, by the refreshed, even happy look on her face. "Did I see some familiar fabric in the living room? In the shape of a dress?"

Elizabeth's eyes lit. "Rebecca made a pattern, cut out a dress and seamed it up all in one afternoon. It fits perfectly."

"Rebecca's a generous woman."

"She is. I don't know how she managed to get away from her brood long enough to help, but she did."

"Probably has to be fast with five children under seven."

"I like her."

"Figured you would. She helped me out with Henry and Anna more times than I can count."

"Ted, I gave Rebecca the pink material in

exchange for making two dresses."

He touched her cheek, smiling into her troubled eyes. "I'm glad."

"I thought you might be upset."

"For being generous? Never." His hand fell away. "Rebecca and Dan are struggling right now. Keep them in your prayers."

"I will."

"Are two dresses enough?"

"Yes." She cocked her head at him, a saucy look in her eyes. "I've decided I like wearing pants."

"Now that, dear wife, is very good news." He pulled her close, inhaled the scent of soap with the faintest hint of roses. Sweet Elizabeth.

Face flushed, she pulled away. "We had a good visit."

Ted put himself in her line of vision. "So what did you two talk about?"

"Nothing really. Just the usual lady talk."

But the wariness in her eyes told Ted the topic had likely been about him. Or perhaps Rose. Had she pumped Rebecca for information about his past? If so, she'd been disappointed.

No one knew his secrets.

CHAPTER ELEVEN

Sunday morning Pastor Sumner welcomed Elizabeth from the pulpit. The topic of his sermon wasn't deceit, as she'd feared. He never mentioned she'd switched places with Ted's mail-order bride and the lies that entailed. For that kindness Elizabeth paid close attention as he spoke on God's love.

One verse in particular stuck in her mind. *Love is not easily angered. It keeps no record of wrongs.*

A love Elizabeth lacked.

Deep inside, she harbored a terrible anger toward her father. Papa only cared about gambling, putting his family at risk. Killing Mama. Not with a weapon, perhaps not even intentionally, but Elizabeth didn't doubt for a moment that Papa had caused her mother's death.

Her heart squeezed. Truth was she'd even been angry with Mama. For pretending all was well while their lives fell apart. For hiding in her bedroom rather than taking a stand with Papa. On the surface her family appeared typical, but Papa's gambling whipped up wild waves of misery while underneath the surface, strong currents carried them further and further apart. All the while Mama never lost her smile. Papa never lost his bravado.

Until Mama's failing health kept them home, Elizabeth had accompanied her mother to church. But most of Elizabeth's attention centered on the latest fashions and liaisons of her peers, not on the sermon. Except for an occasional stab of fear that Papa would wind up in hell, Elizabeth had given little thought to pleasing God.

But now, during the altar call, a deep longing for such a love brought a lump to Elizabeth's throat. A lump formed by the memories of withholding affection from her mother.

She wouldn't find this Biblical love with Ted. Not when keeping up her end of the bargain they called their marriage was all that mattered.

But maybe here in this church, in the Bible Ted shared with her in the pew and at home, she'd find the answer for the empty ache she carried and the anger devouring her peace.

One final song and the service ended, leaving Elizabeth with an odd sense of loss. But she didn't have time to examine her feelings. Parishioners flooded the aisles, greeting her like a long-lost friend instead of a newcomer.

Outside the wind had come up, blowing the women's skirts and lifting Anna's bangs off her forehead. Spying Grace Harper across the way, Anna took off at a run.

"Did you enjoy the service?" Ted asked.

"Yes, very much."

The pleased expression on his face revealed his desire for a wife with strong faith instead of a backslider like her. He leaned close. "Henry only called out twice during the sermon. Anna created a racket kicking the back of the pew only once. A good service all in all." He winked. "If we swapped the kitchen chairs for pews, maybe Anna would behave better."

Ted's attempt at humor told Elizabeth he didn't blame her for Anna's attitude. But he'd blame her for keeping Robby's existence from him. If only she had the courage to inform him about her brother. She would, as soon as she earned money for their tickets. This morning, she'd look for an opportunity to speak to Mr. Sorenson about a job.

Rebecca caught up to them with Faith draped over her arm like a rag doll. "Have you finished hemming your dress?"

"Not yet, but when I do, I'll wear it to church."

Before Elizabeth could ask if Rebecca had found time to make her own dress, the womenfolk of the church surrounded them.

Lydia Sumner and Lucille Sorenson greeted her warmly while Elizabeth scrambled to keep the names straight of the women she'd met inside. Gertrude Wyatt — buxom with flawless skin; Ruth Johnson — tall, willowy, wearing jet bead earbobs; Carolyn Radcliff — petite with sun-streaked hair.

"Why, I'd heard Ted got himself a wife," Ruth Johnson said, giving her wide-brimmed, bow-bedecked hat an adjustment, setting her earbobs in motion.

"Is that a new hat?"

Ruth beamed. "It arrived yesterday from the Montgomery Ward Catalog."

"It's lovely," Elizabeth said. "Perfect for the shape of your face."

"Ted's new wife's a dear," Lucille Sorenson interrupted. "Bought all her niceties from me." She flashed a look at Ruth. "Not like some folks who feel the need to order from the catalog."

Mrs. Radcliff frowned. "You really should stop broadcasting people's shopping lists, Lucille."

A blush dotted the proprietor's cheeks. "It's good for business."

"The Sorenson Mercantile stocks everything a farm wife could want," Elizabeth said, trying to ease the sudden tension.

Ted shot her an amused glance; he then leaned close and murmured in her ear, "The hens are clucking their approval. Appears they've welcomed you into the coop."

Elizabeth coughed to cover a burst of laughter. Someone patted her on the back.

"Mrs. Logan, are you from these parts?" Gertrude said.

"I'm from Chicago."

"Chicago!" Gertrude clasped her hands. "Such a grand city. Will's cousin, Mary Beth, lives there. She's married to a slaughterhouse man name of O'Sullivan. Wouldn't it be something if the two of you knew each other?"

"O'Sullivan? Uh . . ."

"Oh, you could hardly miss noticing Mary Beth." Gertrude waved a palm. "Red hair, freckles, a pretty girl, but she's let herself go since the babies started arriving."

Carolyn patted her friend's arm. "Chicago's a big place, Gertie. You can't expect

Elizabeth to remember Will's cousin even if she's the size of Orville's prize Angus."

Gertrude's face fell like an underdone cake. Martha's only cooking disaster, according to her nanny. "I thought it would've been lovely if they'd met."

Elizabeth pursed her lips. "I bumped into a woman once with more freckles than a hive has bees, but the only words we shared were an apology."

"That's gotta be her!" Gertrude exclaimed. "Imagine that. Why, we're practically family."

Across the way a knot of young ladies giggled. A few days ago, Elizabeth would've fit that group. Now she mingled with married women. Odd how she didn't fit anywhere.

"Where did you and Ted meet?" Ruth took up the slack. "Far as I know he hasn't left town."

Ted shifted the weight of his sleeping son and widened his stance, obviously uncomfortable with the question, but Elizabeth saw no point in hiding the truth. "At the depot."

"Well, of course, but when was the *first* time you met?"

"That was the first time."

Lydia Sumner beamed. "Isn't that romantic? She and Ted married in our parlor the day she arrived."

"You're saying you never laid eyes on Ted before that day?" Carolyn Radcliff's eyes went wide with shock.

"Elizabeth is what I've heard called a mail-order bride," Lydia Sumner explained.

Gertrude gaped. "Well, I do declare. I'm speechless!"

"Well, however you two met, congratulations, Elizabeth. You've accomplished something the single women of New Harmony hadn't been able to do," Rebecca said with a wink.

Ruth Johnson frowned. "Why would you marry a stranger?"

"Ted never seemed like a stranger, not from the minute we met. Why, his greeting nearly swept me off my feet." True enough. Ted's talk about milking cows and strangling chickens had all but made her swoon.

Ruth Johnson waved a finger Ted's way. "As the saying goes — still waters run deep."

Ted coughed, amusement dancing in his eyes.

Rebecca laid a palm over her baby's face and took a step back. "I hope you two aren't coming down with something."

"Your dress is lovely, Mrs. Logan," Ruth said. "A collarless dress must be new."

"Ah, quite new."

A puzzled look came over Lydia Sumner's face. "I distinctly remember that dress having a collar."

"I'll have to remove the collars from my dresses." Ruth fingered the lapel on the front of her frock. "I can't keep up with fashion."

A dark-haired woman, her bonnet covering her face, walked past, herding four children in front of her, glancing neither right nor left.

"I'll be right back." Lydia Sumner hustled after her.

Elizabeth watched the pastor's wife put an arm around the woman. The two put their heads together. "Who is that?"

Gertrude frowned. "Lois Lessman. Most likely her husband Joe's over at the saloon. His gambling's going to put his family in the poorhouse."

"I hate gambling," Elizabeth whispered, her voice trembling with emotion. "Can't you close down the saloon?"

All eyes filled with speculation and darted to Elizabeth.

Mumbling something about finding Anna, Ted trudged toward the group of girls playing on the lawn.

Elizabeth's heart thudded in her chest.

She'd revealed too much, raising the ladies' suspicions. How would they feel — worse, how would a religious man like Ted feel, if he discovered her father was a gambler?

"It's a dirty shame. Lois takes in ironing and laundry, cleans for the Moore brothers. Does everything she can to see to it that her boys don't go to bed hungry."

The attention of the group turned back to the Lessman family and off her, easing the tension between Elizabeth's shoulder blades. Perhaps here in this town, she could find a way to ensure gambling split no family apart.

"So how do you like New Harmony, Elizabeth?" Gertrude asked as Lydia Sumner returned to the circle.

"This is only my first trip to town since our wedding."

"It's a good place to live." Rebecca's gaze dropped to the ground. "Just hope we can stay."

Lydia Sumner slipped an arm around Rebecca. The pastor's wife must wear herself out ministering to the women of the congregation. "Are you thinking of moving?"

"We don't want to, but if this drought doesn't end, the decision may be out of our hands."

Her new friend's struggles pinched at Elizabeth's mood.

"Let's not borrow trouble," Lydia advised. "Remember God's in control and we've got His ear."

"Well, it's April. We normally have had lots of rain by now," Rebecca said softly.

The group grew quiet. Elizabeth supposed everyone had a stake in the weather. If the farmers did poorly, the whole town suffered. "Perhaps we should all wash our windows. That always brought rain in Chicago," Elizabeth said brightly.

Five troubled faces turned to her then eased into smiles.

"Yes, and we could keep our laundry on the line," Gertrude declared with a chuckle.

"Or plan a picnic," Carolyn offered.

Lydia patted Elizabeth's arm. "You're good for us, my dear."

"In the meantime," Elizabeth said, "we can work on getting the streets ready for all that rain. From what Ted told me they'll turn into a muddy river."

"What a good idea! What do you suggest?"

Mrs. Radcliff waved a hand at a group of boys tumbling in the yard. "Before we solve all the problems of New Harmony, our youngsters are getting restless."

The ladies broke up, moving off to gather their children.

Gertrude turned to Elizabeth. "I can't wait to hear more about your life in Chicago. I've never been to a big city."

A rocklike weight settled to the bottom of Elizabeth's stomach. What if these women really knew her? Uncovered her secrets? They wouldn't think much of her then. Suddenly the privacy of the farm sounded good.

Elizabeth hustled to the wagon. Across the way, Mr. Sorenson stood talking. Asking him about keeping his books would have to wait until the next time she came to town.

Ted helped her onto the seat, handed the still-sleeping Henry into her arms, then swung Anna aboard and scrambled up beside her. His humor-filled gaze met hers over Anna's head. "I'll be the laughingstock once the men hear I nearly made you swoon at the depot."

Elizabeth squirmed. "Well, at least the men won't be removing their collars merely because I scorched mine," she said, eliciting a chuckle from Ted.

Her heart skipped a beat. And the women won't be quizzing you about your life in Chicago the next time you meet.

Elizabeth stood on a chair in the kitchen, trying not to fidget, while Ted held a yardstick against the skirt of her new dress and pinned the fabric for a hem. To keep from giving in to a crazy urge to run her fingers through the golden hair on his bowed head, she clasped her hands tightly in front of her.

Perhaps Ted prayed as he pinned. The man talked to God at every opportunity.

She couldn't shake the feelings of remorse the pastor's sermon had surfaced that morning. She'd tried to lay all her regret for hurting Mama at Papa's feet.

"You're awfully quiet," Ted said. "Something wrong?"

Everything. "Nothing."

"You sound like something's bothering you."

She sighed. "I've made a lot of mistakes."

"Haven't we all." He rose to his feet and dropped the packet of pins on the table. "I hope I didn't make a mess of this. I measured every few inches and it looks straight, but —"

One look at her face and he lifted her off the chair. "You're not talking about housekeeping, are you?"

"No." Tears filled her eyes.

He tilted her face up to his. His tender expression tore at her. "We all have regrets, Elizabeth." He motioned toward the yardstick. "God doesn't love us according to a measure of our goodness. Or withhold His love by calculating the number of our sins. Whatever we've done, He'll forgive us. All we have to do is ask." He squeezed her hand. "Have you asked Him?"

Unable to speak, she nodded. Countless times she'd asked God for His forgiveness.

"Then He has. Psalm 103:12 says, 'As far as the east is from the west, so far hath he removed our transgressions from us.' "

If only she could share Ted's confidence, his strong faith. But she didn't feel forgiven.

"Trust God, Elizabeth. He'll never let you down."

Perhaps she could trust God. But could she trust Ted? What would he do when he learned she had a brother and intended for Robby to live here? Would he forgive her for keeping the truth from him the way he promised God would?

Ted took her hand in his, his firm grip warm, soothing. "You're my wife. I don't want to let you down, either." His callused thumb slid over the top of her hand.

She fought the comfort of his touch. "I'm a housekeeper, not a wife, with two children to care for and every imaginable chore to do."

"Being a wife is hard work." His attention dropped to her lips. She forgot to breathe. He leaned closer and closer still, until she could see every eyelash. She'd never noticed that narrow circle of silver, stunning against the black of his pupils. "But I could name some benefits of the job."

Before she could ask for a list of those benefits, his hand encircled the back of her neck. With gentle fingers, he tilted her face to his. She got lost in his intense gaze, asking permission. As with a will all their own, her eyelids fluttered closed. A feathery touch of his lips, gentler than butterfly wings, caressed her lips. The kiss grew, deepened, sending tremors to the core of her.

And a sense of rightness she refused to accept.

Love had destroyed Mama.

She clasped his hand and removed it. "Let's get one thing straight. You were the one who called our marriage a business deal. I may be a substitute bride, but a business deal doesn't include love." She took a step back. "Or kisses."

His eyes turned stormy. "What do you have against affection? I'd hate to live the next forty years without it."

"I'd rather be hitched to a team of oxen than yoked by that burden."

"That can be arranged, wife," he muttered.

Elizabeth spun on her heel and raced to

her room, matching the speed of her pounding heart, taking with her a void she didn't know how to fill.

She closed the door and leaned against it, sliding her fingertips over her lips, reliving his kiss.

Her demonstrative father had kissed Mama as often as she'd let him. Elizabeth had always known Mama loved Papa. Loved him to *death*. Kisses meant nothing. She'd put no trust in Ted's.

Elizabeth was grateful for the time alone while Ted drove Anna and Jason Harper to school. Well, not exactly alone with Henry in the house, but somehow she managed to read the Bible for a few minutes, hungry for words to guide her. She'd just breathed a prayer to God to help her handle each day when behind her the door creaked open.

Ted's gaze lit on the Bible, then her. "I'll set up the laundry for you," he said.

"I'd appreciate it."

She took Henry from his high chair and plopped him in the pen Ted had fashioned from chicken wire while Ted lugged laundry tubs and carried water to fill them. All the while he avoided her eyes, obviously still angry over last night's stalemate. Having fulfilled the role of a good husband, he said goodbye and then walked to the barn.

Watching his retreating back, Elizabeth sighed. Except for providing the roof over her head and the food on his table, she dared not count on Ted. He needed a mother for his children. The reason he'd married her. She needed to give Robby a home. The reason she'd married him. Assuming Ted agreed to bring Robby here, they'd both get what they wanted.

So why did she feel so hollow?

Sleeves rolled up to the elbows, Elizabeth pushed the first load of clothes under the sudsy water. An hour passed, maybe more. Elizabeth arched her back, then blew out a puff of air and once again bent over the washtub. Ted had called this warm, sunny, breezy weather a perfect laundry day. She couldn't imagine doing this chore when the weather turned cold.

Lois Lessman washed clothes and took in ironing to pay the family's bills. If only Elizabeth could help her. Surely if the proprietor of the saloon understood that gambling was damaging a family in town, he'd put a stop to it.

She chuffed. How likely was that when it came to bringing in business? But even if it were, Joe Lessman would find a game somewhere else. Hadn't Papa?

Her sore knuckles struck the ridge of the scrub board. Elizabeth grimaced. Washing Henry's diapers had rubbed them raw. "I hope you're grateful, young man."

Henry hung over the fence, gnawing on a wooden spoon, showing no appreciation for the pain he'd caused. Poor tyke probably had enough of his own with those teeth pushing through.

She boiled the diapers, and then dropped them with a stick into the rinse water. At the line, she used one clothespin to fasten the diapers together, saving time and pins. Anna had made a family of clothespin dolls, decreasing her supply. Flapping in her face, the diapers smelled fresh, clean.

She refilled the tub with clean water for another load. The time dragged by as she stirred, scrubbed, pinned. She fished in the tub and pulled up Ted's white shirt, his Sunday best.

Now pink!

Something was definitely wrong. But what?

With all her might, she scrubbed the shirt on the board but the new color remained.

Heat zipped through her veins. Her dress. Her *only* good dress! She shot a hand into the washtub and yanked it out.

Her beautiful dress was streaked with

shades of maroon. She moaned, dropping it into the rinse water, then brought up her head scarf, now faded. Under the suds, the water was red.

Tears stung her eyes. She had to get far away from all this hated work.

"What happened to my shirt?"

Elizabeth jumped.

Ted stood across from her, arms folded across his chest, staring at the pink garment draped over the washboard.

If she'd had the strength, she'd have thrown her dress at him. Right now, she wanted nothing more than to use that return ticket to Chicago. Even Reginald Parks sounded good.

Ted surveyed the damage to their clothing then the world of hurt on Elizabeth's face. He loped to the house. Nothing could be done about her dress, but perhaps he could save his shirt. He returned with the blueing mixture Rose kept on hand. Gradually the garment lost its pink hue, giving him optimism he'd be able to wear it on Sunday.

Elizabeth whirled to him. "Will that concoction fix my dress?"

"It would ruin the delicate fabric. Next time sort the clothes, darks in one pile, whites in another."

"You've got all the answers, Ted Logan." Her anger at Papa, her concern for Lois Lessman, all of it rolled inside her. She thrust her hands on her hips. "How about figuring out a way to get gambling out of New Harmony? I can't stand the idea of Mrs. Lessman doing this chore every day."

After hearing Elizabeth's emotional remark on Sunday, Ted had no doubt of her hatred of the gambling lifestyle. Not that he approved. He'd seen what compulsive gambling had done to others — the desperation, the lack of any human emotion other than greed. What it had done to him, a man who earned his living at the expense of others. Now Joe's family suffered because he couldn't pass up a game.

He'd try to talk to Joe on his next trip to town. "Cleaning up a man isn't like cleaning up New Harmony's streets, Elizabeth. Shutting down a saloon won't put a stop to what a man's determined to do. The only way for Joe to control his gambling is to repent and seek God's help."

Elizabeth eyed him. "You know a lot about the subject."

Ted's stomach knotted. "I'm speaking about what the Bible teaches, no matter what issue is taking over a person's life." He rinsed his shirt. "I'll talk to him, but if you

219

want to help Lois, help her find a better-paying job."

Elizabeth returned to the line. From here, he could practically see her mind working. His suggestion seemed to pacify her. But what would she do if she found out about his gambling past? His chest squeezed. Most likely leave him.

Not that he blamed Rose for dying, but losing her hurt. He and Anna still grieved. For different reasons. Rose had been the center of Anna's world. Meeting Rose had been a turning point in his.

But he somehow knew that if he and Elizabeth ever found their way in this marriage, they'd share a bliss he and Rose never had. He couldn't forget the experience of holding Elizabeth in his arms, of the feel of her lips moving under his.

Yet she'd shown not one whit of reaction since. What man knew what went on in a woman's mind? If Elizabeth wanted his touch, wouldn't she give him a smile or say something that would tell him which way the wind blew?

He suspected she kept things from him. How could he condemn her? He lived his life doing the same. One day the secrets would come out. What would happen then?

CHAPTER TWELVE

The days rolled by, until one week had passed since Elizabeth had arrived in New Harmony. Each day during Henry's nap, she made those mainstay biscuits. The cookbook had promised that "good biscuits had saved the day for many a housewife."

The *good* had been the tricky part but practice made perfect, or so Papa used to say, so she always made one batch, sometimes two. Much to her surprise, the batch she pulled from the oven was flaky, golden — perfection. She smiled, anticipating Ted's reaction to her success.

At dinner, she carried the bread plate to the table with her head held high like one of the Magi bearing gifts.

Ted took one look at the pile of biscuits and shook his head. "Biscuits. Again?"

"What do you mean *again?*"

"Nothing, I'm just . . . full."

"How can you be full? You haven't eaten yet."

He looked at Anna, then at Henry, but neither of his children said a word, leaving Ted on his own. Whether he knew it or not, he was heading into dangerous territory.

"I'm full of biscuits," he said, ducking his head.

"These are perfect. Really. They're not burned on the bottom or hard or bitter or crumbly. Try one." She thrust one at him, but he held up his palm.

"I'm up to here with biscuits," he said, indicating his throat. "Sorry, I can't face another one, no matter how good."

"What do you mean, you're sick of biscuits? You said you had hollow legs that needed filling three times a day."

He had the grace to look sheepish. "I do, but you've given me biscuits for breakfast, dinner and supper for a week."

"Well, that takes the cake!"

"Now, cake, that I could eat."

She swatted at him. "I slaved over perfecting the biscuits you're so fond of and now you won't eat one? Not even a bite?"

"I'm sure in a few days, I'll get over it and —"

"Get over it? Well, see if you can get over this!" She dumped three biscuits on top of the mound of meat and potatoes on his plate. "At this table we're having biscuits."

Ted closed his eyes then rose. "I learned long ago when a woman gets in a snit, a man better head for the hills. In my case, the barn works fine." With that, he walked out the door.

Elizabeth folded her arms across her chest. No one appreciated anything she did around here. She opened her palms and rubbed a finger across a callus. Her hands were a mess. Her feet ached from hours at the stove, sink or washtub. She slaved from dawn to dusk — and for what? To be unappreciated and criticized? To give her brother a good life, she'd tried to mold herself into the perfect housewife. But the apron didn't fit.

She didn't fit.

She walked to the mirror and peered at her reflection. A smudge marred her cheek. Tendrils of her hair drooped at her neck. She never had time to primp. She turned away from the face in the mirror, so different from her own that she almost didn't recognize it.

Returning to the table, she grabbed one morsel of perfection and buttered it, but when she took a bite and tried to swallow, it stuck in her throat. Her shoulders slumped.

Why not admit it? She was sick of biscuits, too.

Grabbing a couple, she walked outside to the stoop and whistled for Tippy. He came loping from the barn. She dropped the biscuits into the iron skillet that served as his dish. He walked up, sniffed at them and backed away, tail tucked between his legs.

"Traitor."

Back in the kitchen, she found one biscuit lover. Henry. He'd stuffed half a biscuit into his mouth, flinging crumbs on the floor. Of course, Martha had once said babies would eat dirt and drink kerosene; not much of a recommendation.

She plopped into her seat with a sigh.

Across from her, Anna leaned on her elbows, a glum look in her eyes. "Mommy didn't shout at Daddy."

Rose, the saint. Well, Elizabeth was no saint and not the mommy, never would be. Still, she'd grown tired of hearing about the perfect Rose.

Anna turned those light blue eyes on her. "You made Daddy's ears hurt."

Elizabeth guessed Daddy's tummy was empty, too. Just because Ted didn't want biscuits didn't mean he didn't want to eat. She'd riled him into leaving the house without his supper. "I guess I'll have to say

224

I'm sorry."

"Yep," Anna said, then went back to her meal.

Another thing Elizabeth didn't do well. But since she'd been reading the Bible regularly, she no longer could cling to her old habits. And for some reason she couldn't fathom, she cared what Ted thought of her, cared if he forgave her.

Why? She'd never apologized that much to Mama and Papa.

As she forced down her food, never tasting a bite, the realization dawned — every day she lived with regret for not having apologized to Mama. Once she got the chance, she'd apologize to Papa for disobeying him, even though he'd been wrong to try to marry her off for profit.

But Ted was different. Ted was . . .

Well, she wouldn't think about that now. He was her husband. She'd leave it at that. They needed peace. Peace that came with the price of one gritted out *I'm sorry.*

Elizabeth plopped some blocks on the tray of the high chair then grabbed Ted's plate. "Will you watch Henry for a few minutes, Anna?"

Amazingly, Anna nodded her agreement.

Elizabeth dumped the biscuits on Ted's plate into the slop jar and headed out the door. A man who liked harmony must find living with her unsettling. She met Ted halfway between the house and the barn.

His troubled eyes collided with hers. "I forgot —"

"Your dinner." She motioned to the towel-covered plate. "I'm bringing it to you."

"Thank you." His eyes darkened. "Sorry about the fuss I made over the biscuits."

"I tossed them in the bucket for the pigs. If *they* dare to reject my biscuits, I'll pull their tails."

He peered over his shoulder, craning his neck as if looking at his backside. "In that case, I'll eat whatever you say."

She laughed. "Your food's getting cold. Come on inside."

Stepping around her, he held the door. "You look tired. Get off your feet while I put the children to bed."

Elizabeth *was* tired. Tired to the bone.

Still, she didn't have to make all those pointless calls on people she didn't like. Or wear a tightly cinched corset every single day of her life or feel so bored her skin crawled.

Or sit across from Reginald Parks.

Elizabeth set Ted's plate on top of the cookstove to keep it warm, and then cleaned up the dishes. When Ted returned to the kitchen, she and his dinner sat at the table waiting on him.

"I'm saying it right out. I'm sorry I got mad." She plopped her chin on her hands. "I *have* made a lot of biscuits. Truth is I'm sick of biscuits, too. Even Tippy wouldn't touch them and he usually wolfs down every scrap I give him. Sort of like you."

Ted took his place at the table and smiled. "Was this another example of that teeny temper you warned me about?"

She bit her lip and nodded.

"Seems it's less teeny than you promised."

"Seems you're less of a biscuit fan than you said."

He laughed. "That's what I like about you — you're never at a loss for words." A crooked grin eased the tension between them. "I accept your apology. And offer one of my own." Taking her hand, he ran a finger over her reddened palm. "You've worked hard taking care of us and I appreciate it. I should have eaten the biscuits, even if it gagged me." He chuckled, then sobered, regret filling his eyes. "I've been expecting too much."

She pulled away from his touch, studying the chipped nails on her left hand and the narrow gold band still shiny and new — a symbol of promise. "I'm not one bit like Rose."

"No, you're you — Elizabeth Manning Logan. My wife. And I'm proud of you."

Ted's words slid into the lonely emptiness inside her, balm to regrets she didn't know she carried. What if she started to care about this man?

A chill slid down her spine, an icy reminder not to foolishly put her heart in Ted's hands.

She leaped to her feet and poured a cup of coffee she didn't want, putting distance between her and Ted, vowing not to let her husband get close.

Elizabeth glanced at the clock. Half past four and Henry still slept. Home from school, Anna played on the porch with her clothespin dolls, dressing them with scraps from Elizabeth's new dress. Potatoes bubbled on the stove. A jar of beef and noodles from the cellar simmered away. Peace reigned.

She had time to rearrange the kitchen. The upper shelves were mostly empty, but well within Elizabeth's reach. She cleared the table, putting all the clutter away, and then organized the cabinet and cupboard to suit her.

From the bedroom, Henry set up a howl. Smiling with satisfaction at her newly arranged kitchen, Elizabeth hustled to his crib. For once, Anna didn't beat her. Apparently she hadn't heard her brother.

Arms outstretched, Henry leaned against the rail, grinning at her.

"What a long nap you had, little man." She swung him into the air. He squealed, releasing a dribble of drool onto the bodice of Elizabeth's new dress. Ah, babies. Nasty little creatures. The reason God made them cute.

She changed his diaper, then gathered Henry to her chest. One plump arm cradled her neck, his soft baby face nuzzling her cheek. The feel and scent of him filled her nostrils, putting an odd hitch in her breathing.

"Mama."

Her breath caught.

He said "Mama" again.

Elizabeth carried Henry to the dresser. "*This* is your mama, Henry," she told him, holding up the picture of Rose and Ted.

"Dada." He pointed to Ted with a wide grin revealing six tiny teeth. Raring back, Henry patted her cheek. "Mama."

Elizabeth shook her head. Surely Ted would set Henry straight.

Only a month old when Rose died, Henry wouldn't remember his mother. Still, Elizabeth didn't want the toddler to forget the woman who gave him birth, probably destroying her health with the effort. She replaced the picture, promising to show Henry his mother's likeness every day.

In the kitchen, she put Henry on the floor to play with some wooden spoons and a pan. But within a matter of seconds, he'd crawled to a chair and pulled up, then toddled toward her.

Ted appeared at the door for dinner in his stocking feet, dewy and fresh from cleaning up at the pump. Sniffing the air, he swept Henry into his arms. "Mmm, smells good."

"Better than smoke and burned biscuits." She grinned, moving to the stove. "As soon as I mash the potatoes, we'll eat."

"You're looking mighty cheerful."

"Well, I am. I had a good afternoon."

"Here, let me do that." He walked to the stove, exchanged Henry for the potato masher and went after the lumps, biceps bulging with each stroke.

She swallowed hard. Those potatoes didn't have a chance.

Ted glanced up, catching her watching him, and winked at her. "Tell me about your day."

Anna dashed in the door, and before Elizabeth could tell Ted anything, she prattled on about school, proudly showing him her growing family of clothespin dolls.

"Using straw for hair's clever of you, Anna. Why don't you lay them down and set the table for supper."

Anna put a pout on her face but did as Ted said. He looked over his daughter's head at Elizabeth. "Looks like you finished that hem." His gaze roamed over her. Something about his expression made her insides flutter. "Does this mean you won't be wearing my pants anymore?"

"Only in the chicken coop and garden."

Ted paused in the mashing and gave her a searing look that had nothing to do with fashion. "Pity."

Heat filled her cheeks. She ran a finger around her buttoned-up collar. Gracious, the kitchen was warm.

"Where's the spoons?" Anna asked.

For a moment, Elizabeth had forgotten about Anna. She dragged herself back to reality. "Oh, I put the flatware in the drawer over there."

"Mama kept them in the spooner."

"Well, with everything put away, I don't have to cover the table in case flies sneak in."

Anna folded her arms across her chest. "Put them back."

Elizabeth looked at Ted for support, but his lips had thinned. He took Henry from her arms. "After you add salt and butter, they're ready to eat."

Ted sat in the rocker with Henry on one knee and Anna leaning against the other, explaining how much ground he'd planted in oats, and taking Anna's mind off the argument.

Recalling the disapproving set of his mouth, all the joy of the day slid out of Elizabeth. She'd worked her fingers to the bone taking care of Ted's house, meals and children, but she had no say in anything.

Ignoring Anna's lack of obedience, Elizabeth set the table herself. Why hadn't Ted taken her side with Anna? Was she merely some maid? Well, if so, she should earn a wage.

At dinner, the food was good, and without a single biscuit, but Ted said very little except a polite, "Will you pass the potatoes?" or "Anna, eat your meat."

Anna chattered away while the meal churned in Elizabeth's stomach.

After dinner, Ted told Anna to wash the dishes then went out to the barn to milk and bed down the animals. Elizabeth prepared the dishwater, and then moved aside for Anna. Surprisingly she pulled over a chair and set to work.

"This water is too hot," she complained.

"Put in a dipper of cold."

"You do it," she said in a bossy tone. "My hands are drippy."

Elizabeth added the cold water without comment, too tired to deal with Anna's attitude.

Ted hadn't supported her attempt to make things more convenient, as if she had no right to make changes. Rose lived in the house with them. Elizabeth understood Ted and Anna still mourned her. She felt bad herself about Rose's early death and all she missed, but how long would it be before what she wanted mattered? Five, ten years? Maybe when Rose's children were grown and gone?

Maybe never.

She slumped against the sink. Ted made promises as easily as her silver-tongued father. Empty promises. Why had she believed him?

Everyone should be quick to listen, slow to speak, and slow to anger. She'd read the verse in the Book of James that morning. But didn't that Scripture include Ted?

A moan pushed past her lips. She'd done

all she could to make this marriage work. She shouldn't have to feel like an intruder in this house. She'd had it with the chickens and the biscuits. With Anna's belligerence. And her so-called husband's lack of consideration.

Tears stung her eyes. What choice did she have? Robby needed a home. He would love this farm. He would love Ted, would probably follow Ted around like his shadow.

In her entire life, she'd never felt so trapped.

Finished with the chores, Ted returned to the house, put the children to bed and then came into the kitchen, unable to meet Elizabeth's gaze as she wiped the dinner dishes. He could feel the annoyance radiating off her from here.

He rummaged in the cupboard and then slammed the door shut. "I don't know where anything is anymore."

"What are you looking for?"

"My stomach's in an uproar. I'm looking for a peppermint."

Her steely expression said he had only himself to blame. "They're in the pantry." Her tone could freeze the pond in June.

"Why?"

"Peppermints are edible. Everything ed-

234

ible is in the pantry." A smug expression rode her face.

"You've moved things around, taken things off the table —" His gaze swept the kitchen. "Couldn't you leave it like it was?"

"Don't you mean the way Rose had it?"

Hurt pinged off each syllable. Still Ted held his ground, refusing to relent. If he did, before he knew it, she'd change everything. The furniture. The routine. Him.

He crossed his arms across his chest and leaned toward her. "What's wrong with the way Rose had it?"

"I'm taller. I can reach higher in the cabinets. I moved things up, making room for what hid under that tent on the table." She threw a hand out toward the table. "I'm not used to living in a pigsty."

He threw up his hands. "Pigsty?"

"I'm sorry. But burying condiments and flatware under a pyramid made of cloth is just . . . well, strange."

Ted ran a hand through his hair. In his chest a battle warred. Part wanted to let her fill that hole inside him, the hole left vacant by more than a few changes in the kitchen. And part was tired of dealing with the trouble in this house.

"Put them back."

"You sound like Anna. Why? It's not like

you can't learn where things are." She tossed down the dish towel, her icy blue eyes flashing. "It's not Rose's kitchen anymore."

"You may be my wife, but are you forgetting this is *my* house?"

"Yes, I guess I am," she said, her voice shaking. "Before we married, you claimed all you had would be mine." She crossed the room. "But you've made it clear. Nothing's mine here. And never will be."

She stabbed a finger at his midsection. "Well, I've got news for you, Ted Logan. I've got an eight-year-old brother. As soon as I can, I'm bringing him here. Then I'll finally have an ally in this house!"

Ted felt he'd been sucker punched. "What are you talking about?"

"You heard me. My father will lose our house in a couple weeks. I want Robby to live with us."

He glared at her. "You kept the existence of a brother from me? Why would you do that?"

"I was afraid of your reaction." She stepped closer until they stood toe to toe. "But I no longer care. Robby's my responsibility. I won't let him end up living on the streets." Her voice broke. "He wants to live on a farm. That's why I married you! The only reason."

Ted stomped toward the door.

"You're always running."

He stopped and pivoted toward her. "What do you mean?"

"You'd rather run than deal with our problems."

"That's not true." Was it? He ran his fingers through his hair. "I've learned it's better to calm down."

"Ah, yes, anything to keep that even-keel nature you're so proud of."

His long strides swallowed the distance between them. She eyed him like an angry bull, head down, hands planted on her hips, looking ready to go for his midsection.

"Did you stop to consider how bringing your brother here would affect Anna? You're not just changing the cupboards. You intend to change the number of people living under this roof."

"I'm sorry if it upsets Anna, but I have no choice."

Why had he thought he could marry a substitute bride, a total stranger, and make the marriage work? "What we have doesn't fit anyone's idea of marriage. I see no loving or obeying, even *trying* to obey, in this union."

"You were the one who called our marriage a business arrangement."

Ted's shoulders slumped. That agreement favored him and his children. Truth was, he'd expected Elizabeth to take a backseat to his daughter. "When we married, I believed your desperation stemmed from a lack of money, but now I know you switched places with Sally to give your brother a happy home on a farm. This home can hardly be called happy."

"And whose fault is that?"

A weight settled in his chest, squeezing against his lungs. God probably wasn't pleased with him. Much of that lack of contentment in their marriage could be traced to him.

He better spit out his apology. "First off, I was wrong to give the impression that the kitchen doesn't belong to you."

"It doesn't. Nothing belongs to me. You spoke the truth."

"No, I reacted without thinking. As my wife, this house, this farm, everything, belongs to you as much as it does me." He leaned against the counter, searching for words to make her understand. "Rearrange anything that makes your life simpler. Anna will get used to it and . . . and I will, too."

"You saw the changes as my trying to wipe out Rose."

He grimaced. "I can't expect you to understand — I don't understand it myself." He took a deep breath. "That's not sensible. Maybe not even sane."

"It's like Anna hanging on to her mother's handkerchief." She swallowed hard. "You both still love her."

He dragged in a breath and looked away. "Rose and I weren't a great love match." He hastened to add, "But we were content."

"If you weren't in love, why did you marry?"

"The timing was right for both of us. I knew a good woman like Rose would make a wonderful mother. I wanted my future kids to have that."

"Unlike your home growing up?"

Ted didn't answer. He couldn't get into his home life. He cleared his throat. "We still need to talk about bringing your brother here."

By the look in Elizabeth's eyes, he'd hurt her by avoiding the question, but when he pulled out a chair, she sat in it. He grabbed another and joined her. "To hear about Robby's existence in the heat of an argument, well, it threw me. I apologize for that. I'm sure you're worried about him and he misses you."

239

Tears welled in her eyes and she looked away.

He cupped her chin and turned her to face him. "I have some money for emergencies. We'll use it to buy two train tickets back." She would come back, wouldn't she?

She raised a palm. "I won't add to your burdens. I'll use the egg money to pay for the tickets."

Another child in the house would complicate everything. Cost more, too. Not that Ted could refuse a home to Elizabeth's brother. Poor kid probably waited in Chicago, wondering when his sister would come for him, afraid of what the future held.

Hadn't he done the same as a boy?

"With the way the hens are laying and the price of eggs, it'll take forever to save that much. You're my wife. You and your brother aren't burdens."

She laid a hand on his face, her touch gentle on the rough bristle of his beard. "Robby can help around the place." Her expression brightened. "He's a good boy . . . nothing like me."

He chuckled. "It'll all work out."

"What about Anna? How will you tell her?"

"She'll love a big brother." Ted doubted he spoke the truth, but he couldn't consider the alternative. "You know, I think Anna's softening toward you." He met her incredulous gaze. "No, really, I do. You're making a difference around here, in the children . . . and in me."

Her hands fell limp at her sides. A look of despair took over her face.

It pinched at his pride that she didn't care about him. Like it or not, he had feelings for her. Not that he'd let her know. She'd made it abundantly clear she didn't want a real marriage.

Where would this end? How long could he go on this way? He wanted peace, not this constant upheaval. A wife to share his life, not fight him at every turn. A man couldn't bed down in the barn forever.

If he didn't know it before, he knew it now. Elizabeth battled their connection.

Perhaps he was wrong.

Perhaps she didn't even feel it.

CHAPTER THIRTEEN

At the noon meal, Elizabeth had avoided Ted's gaze, keeping things impersonal. He thought they'd gotten close last night, but then she'd pulled away, running as she'd accused him of doing.

He'd dropped Anna at the Harpers' to play with Grace on this blustery Saturday afternoon then walked the mile back to his house. By now Elizabeth had put Henry down for his nap.

A perfect opportunity to show an interest in his wife.

He found Elizabeth in the kitchen, putting on an apron over his pants, which she still wore from gathering eggs that morning. "Planning on making those delicious biscuits of yours?"

Her mouth gaped. "You want biscuits?"

No point in admitting the thought put a knot in his stomach. "I'm hungry for a batch." He gave her his most innocent look.

"Want some help?"

"And you want to help?" She cocked her head at him, a smile tugging at her lips. "In the middle of your workday?"

With one field to plant with corn, he should hitch up King and Queen, but his suggestion appeared to cheer her. "If you don't mind."

She examined his palms. "Only if you wash those hands."

Well, at least she was touching him. A good sign peace had been restored. He headed for the sink. "Yes, ma'am."

Suspicion clouded her dazzling blue eyes, as if she didn't believe a word he said, but Elizabeth handed him an apron. He didn't hanker to wear it but no point in making a fuss and take a chance of ruining the harmony between them.

She reached for a crock then opened the door that hid the flour bin. "Measure out two cupfuls of flour." She handed him a knife. "Use this to level it."

He fumbled with the cup and knife.

"Do it like this," she said, showing him how, then handing the knife back to him. "Add another cup of flour."

With her standing so near, he could barely absorb her directions but somehow managed to dump the flour into the bowl. By the sparkle in her eye and the smile playing around her lips, she enjoyed bossing him. She looked . . . happy. Why hadn't he tried harder to give her joy? Why had he expected her to fall into his arms? With the planting and all the chores to do, he'd neglected his wife. He wouldn't make that mistake again.

She thrust a spoon at him. "Add four teaspoons of baking powder."

And so it went with her giving orders and him following directions until he was wrist high in dough, his hands a mucky mess. He shot her a grin. "This is fun, kind of like playing in the mud. Care to join me?"

She rolled up her sleeves and dove in, squishing the dough between her fingers.

"A nice way to take out your frustrations," Ted said.

"Why do you think I've gotten so good at biscuits?"

He chuckled. Within minutes, they were battling with their fingers over territory in the bowl. When she tried to shove him out of the way, he raised dough-globbed fingers at her in a sinister pose sending her into peals of laughter.

Next thing Ted knew, Elizabeth streaked a doughy finger across his cheek then stepped back, grinning at him. Well, he couldn't let that go without a fight. He grabbed her wrist. She ducked and tried to pull away, but he managed to draw a circle on her forehead.

She retaliated with a batter-smeared mustache above his lip. "You look ever so handsome," she teased.

"You'd look mighty good with one yourself." She scrambled out of reach, but he lunged for her waist, twisted her around and smeared the dough above her lip. "Now your face matches those pants you're wearing."

Things went downhill from there, giggling and making a mess even Tippy wouldn't touch.

Trapping his bride in his arms, Ted lowered his head and planted a gooey kiss on her lips. Amazingly she kissed him back, dissipating the humor like shadows on a cloudy day. Leaving them both breathing deep and staring into each other's eyes with the beat of Ted's heart thumping in his ears.

"I had no idea you were so fond of biscuits, Mr. Logan."

"From now on, I'll take my biscuits raw."

She laid her head on his chest, shaking with laughter. Even covered with dough, he relished having her near.

"Anybody home?" a male voice called through the screen door.

The Stevenses. His in-laws. This wacky scene wouldn't improve their already strained relationship. He walked to the door, stepping aside to let them in. "Lily. Richard. What a surprise."

Lily's hand shot to her mouth, her eyes wide with alarm. "Whatever are you . . . doing?"

"Making biscuits," Elizabeth spoke up.

Lily, all four feet eleven inches of her, continued to gawk at Ted as though she'd never seen a man in the kitchen before. But then she probably hadn't, especially wearing an apron and a dough mustache. "You're looking well, Lily. A little pale. The trip probably tired you."

He scrubbed a hand across his upper lip, then tore off the apron and hung it on the hook.

Wearing a frown, Lily turned her focus on Elizabeth. "Who are you and why are you wearing —"

"The pants in the family?" Elizabeth winked. "Just teasing." She smiled. "I'm Ted's wife."

Lily swayed on her feet. "Richard, get me a chair."

Taking a firm hold of his wife, Richard eased her into the rocker and fanned her face with a section of the newspaper he'd plucked from the armrest.

Ted should've written Rose's parents about his marriage, but he'd suspected the news he'd taken a mail-order bride would give Lily one more reason to question his fitness as a parent.

He turned to Elizabeth and made introductions.

"Nice to meet you," she said, then scurried to the sink to clean her hands and face. "You'll have to forgive our appearance. We weren't expecting company."

"Sorry for . . . intruding." Richard glanced at his wife, now pressing a hand to her bosom. "We just got into town and hoped to see our grandchildren."

"Anna's visiting a friend and Henry's down for his nap."

Lily slumped back in the chair. "Thank goodness." Tears sprang to her eyes. "So this is the replacement for our Rose."

"Lily, there's no call for that," Richard said. "The children need a mother."

"They wouldn't need one if Ted would let us raise them!"

Ted planted his feet wide, ready for battle. "I'll never —"

Eyes blazing, Elizabeth stepped forward. "Ted loves his children more than any man I've ever met. He's a wonderful father."

Ted had been about to rehash the familiar argument with Lily until Elizabeth had stepped in.

And defended him.

Described him as a good father.

A loving father.

His gaze connected with his wife's and something new sprang between them. As if she understood how it felt to be judged by a biased jury.

A heavy silence fell over the room. Richard mopped his forehead with a handkerchief. "So, how did you two meet?"

Ted and Elizabeth's gazes collided, but she quickly averted her eyes. Since the day she'd arrived, he'd never known Elizabeth to be quiet, but now, when he needed her most, she had her mouth nailed shut.

He cleared his throat. "Ah, Elizabeth came out on the train for the wedding."

"But when did you meet?" Richard asked.

Ted swallowed. "Well, we didn't actually meet first —"

"You sent for one of those mail-order brides?" Lily shrieked as if he'd made the faux pas of the century. "Married a stranger and brought her in to care for our grandchildren?"

"I couldn't very well bring Elizabeth into my home unless we married first."

Lily eyed Elizabeth again. "We'll have to extend our visit. See how you and the children are getting on."

How dare Lily question their parenting or their marriage! "They're getting on just fine," Ted said. Though in truth, Anna and Elizabeth mixed like oil and water.

One look at the scowl on his face sent Elizabeth to the stove. "Would you like some tea and biscuits?"

Richard smiled. "Sounds like a good idea."

Lily glanced at the mess and shuddered.

"I made this batch yesterday," Elizabeth said.

"Well, in that case, I will try your cooking."

No doubt to criticize it, but if so, Lily would be disappointed. Elizabeth had perfected the art of making biscuits.

He ushered his in-laws to the parlor then helped his wife clean the kitchen that looked as if pigs had wallowed in muck. Come to think of it, he and Elizabeth looked the part of the pigs.

"They said they were extending their visit. How long do you think they'll stay?" Elizabeth whispered as she corralled her tousled hair into a bun.

He grimaced. "They usually stay a week."

"Oh. My." Elizabeth lifted a stash of

biscuits from the glass jar and set out jam and butter. "Once I serve biscuits breakfast, lunch and dinner, they'll cut their visit short."

Ted grinned. "I like the way you think, Mrs. Logan." He laid a hand on her arm. "I want to thank you."

"For what?"

"For trying to make me look good with Rose's parents."

She lowered her eyes, dark lashes brushing against her cheeks. "I didn't do anything."

"Oh, but you did." He came closer, reaching for her, but she turned away, out of his grasp.

"I — I — better get the jam."

"It's on the table."

"Oh, of course." Her cheeks flushed as rosy as the preserves. "I'm sorry I had to meet Rose's parents looking like a mess."

He tapped her playfully on the nose. "Their opinion of you can only go uphill from here." But he didn't care what the Stevenses thought of his wife. Though he'd been upset with her last night, he knew she was exactly the right mother for his children. Her patience with Anna astounded him.

He called Richard and Lily to the kitchen. They all gathered at the table and sipped the tea and sampled the biscuits, easing the stiff mood.

Richard wiped his mouth on a napkin. "Your biscuits are delicious, Elizabeth."

Beaming, she flashed Ted an "I told you so" smirk before turning back to Rose's father. "Why thank you, Mr. Stevens. That's one of the nicest things you could say to me."

He smiled, obviously warming to Ted's wife. "Please, we're family. Call us Richard and Lily."

"She's not a member of our family, Richard. And never will be."

"You might want to reconsider that, Lily," Ted warned affably enough, but he saw in Lily's eyes that she'd caught his meaning.

"When will Anna return from the neighbor's?" Lily asked.

"She should be home soon."

No more had the words left his mouth, than Rebecca knocked at the back door and peeked through the screen. "Well, hello, Mr. and Mrs. Stevens." The door opened, Anna entered. "Have a nice visit," Rebecca called through the screen, practically running to the wagon, tugging Grace along after her. The coward.

Lily flung out her hands. "Anna, darling! Grandma and Grandpa are here for a visit."

Anna stepped into the circle of her grandmother's arms, accepting her hugs and kisses, giving a hearty embrace in return. "Who fixed your braids, sweetheart? They've almost come undone."

"Come here, sweetkins. Grandpa's got a nickel for you." He dug in his pockets, coming up with the coin.

Beaming, Anna took the money then kissed Richard's cheek. "Thank you, Grandpa. I can buy some candy at the mercantile."

"Just don't ruin those pretty teeth."

Having her grandparents near had put a sparkle in Anna's eyes. Their presence appeared to comfort her.

A wail sounded from the children's bedroom. Ted rose from his chair. "I'll get him." He changed Henry's diaper in record time and returned to the kitchen.

Lily rose and took Ted's son out of his arms. "Big precious boy!" she cooed. "Oh, look at your shirt. What is that? Oatmeal?" Her accusing gaze traveled to Elizabeth.

Henry wiggled out of Lily's arms to the floor.

As he toddled away, Richard grinned. "My goodness, look at that, will you? Henry's walking."

"Come to Grandma!" Lily called.

Arms stretched out for balance, Henry tottered over to Elizabeth, throwing his arms around her legs.

Lily buried her face in her hands. "Oh, how I wish Rose could see this. She'd be so proud of her little boy." Her eyes brimmed with tears. "And of you," she said, blowing Anna a kiss.

His eyes misty, Richard cleared his throat. "So, Anna, what do you think of your baby brother's walking?"

"He gets into my stuff," Anna groused.

As Henry sailed past Ted's chair, he made a grab for his son. "He's starting to climb."

"Be careful he doesn't fall out of his crib," Lily said.

"So . . . how long will you be staying?" Ted asked.

Lily's gaze never left Henry. "Long enough to spoil our grandbabies." She bit her lip. "We've been at loose ends of late."

Across from him, Elizabeth's eyes brightened, a smile curving her face. He could almost see an idea plant itself in her mind. What was she —

"I'm glad you're here," Elizabeth said, turning to his in-laws. "You can help Ted look after the children while I return to Chicago . . . for my brother."

Without a word to Ted, Elizabeth had set

her plan in motion. Would she remain in Chicago? No, she'd return for her brother's sake and in obedience to those vows she'd taken. He couldn't delude himself. He was not the draw.

"Richard and Lily, you can take, ah, our room while Elizabeth's away." He cleared his cup to the sink. "I'll sleep in the barn."

Lily clapped her hands. "A change will do us good. Richard can help with the chores and I'll help with the children and the cooking. It'll be fun!"

Elizabeth gave a huge smile. Obviously pleased by the turn of events. While he'd have to deal with Lily alone. And deal with his daughter's reaction to having a big brother.

Elizabeth's plan had nearly come full circle. In a matter of days she'd give Robby the dream she'd promised — a home. On a farm. With a dog. And her open, dependable arms.

As she walked toward the barn in search of Ted, she pictured Robby hugging Tippy, feeding the livestock and trailing after Ted. So why did she feel a twinge of doubt nip at her stomach? Why did she feel this icy shiver slither through her veins?

She tamped down her silly reaction.

Everything would be fine. She was sure of it. Things had worked together beautifully so she could go to Chicago, knowing with Lily and Richard in the house, Ted could finish planting without uprooting his children.

Whether Ted would agree or not, the Stevenses' arrival today was the answer to her prayers.

In the west, the sun had dropped to the horizon, the sky awash with soft pink and peach. As if God had dipped a long rag mop into paint and streaked it across the heavens. The quiet, the stillness of the farm enveloped her, filling her with peace. For a moment, she felt happy. At home.

Then from the barn, she heard a cow low and the soft bleat of the sheep, a reminder of all the work left undone.

The sweet scent of hay mingling with the pungent odor of manure drifted through the door. She paused, waiting for her eyes to adjust to the dim interior. Ted was bent over some kind of metal contraption, tinkering with it then pushing a lever. Nothing happened. He tried it again. Again nothing happened. He paced in front of the machine, muttering in disgust, and then gave it a good kick.

Alone in the barn, or so he no doubt

thought, Ted had relaxed the tight rein he kept on his emotions. In his hunched shoulders, she saw tension, even hostility.

"That thing causing you trouble?" Elizabeth said.

Ted whirled to her, then he tried a smile that fell flat. "Yeah."

"Looks like you're having a hard day."

A sigh whistled out of him. "Farming's hard work," he said then went back to the machine. "It doesn't help that this planter's clogged."

She watched him fiddle with that lever, his frustration mounting with every passing second. "Hard work wouldn't deter you. It's something else." She laid a hand on his back. Beneath her palm, his muscles bunched. She blinked, startled by sudden insight. "You hate all this."

"If you mean this planter, well, I think I do right now." But he didn't turn around when he said it.

"No, Ted, that's not what I mean." She stepped back. "Why can't you be honest about what you feel? About this life, this farm?"

He stepped away from the planter and leaned against a rough-hewn support post, his gaze roaming the barn. "Maybe I don't have time to feel. I do the work, pray for rain, sun and warm nights. I don't examine my feelings about the job."

His relaxed posture and matter-of-fact tone didn't conceal the rigid lines around his mouth, his lack of eye contact, as if . . .

As if he had something to hide.

Why would he deny emotions — anger, joy, sorrow, all the feelings she struggled with daily? "You hate relying on something you can't control."

"If that were true, I wouldn't be married to you."

Though a smile turned up her lips, she refused to credit his comment with a reply.

"The Bible teaches God is in control, not man."

Had Ted used the Bible to avoid her questions? Hadn't she read that believers were to share one another's burdens? That should definitely be true of husbands and wives.

Elizabeth looked around her at the sturdy barn, the cows munching in their stalls and sheep curled up in their pen for the night. "What is it about farming that you don't like, then?"

He shifted under her steady gaze. "Reckon you're determined to make me open a vein and bleed my innermost thoughts." He removed his straw ranch hat, swiped his sleeve over his forehead. "I hate breaking my back planting the crop and then a hailstorm, too much or like now, too little rain, undoes it all." He slapped his hat on his thigh. "Not because of the need for control, but for the risk farming is for my family."

"So why do you stay?"

His eyes lost their focus. "I've had a thought . . . nothing I'm ready to talk about now."

"Well, if I could, I'd leave."

He took a step closer. "Would you? Really?" he said, his voice soft, his eyes compelling as he searched her face.

Had her declaration hurt his male pride? If so, why? He didn't love her. He wanted to coexist amicably, to give Anna and Henry a mother, a good home. Exactly as she wanted to do for her brother. Yet the lump in her throat said she'd miss Ted if she left. Not that she could. The ring on her finger tethered her to a world she didn't fit.

How had he managed to put the focus on her? "Why do you stay?" she persisted, ignoring his question.

"I'm a man who sticks with things. I stick with this farm. And I stick with this town."

"Well, that's just silly. You should like what you do."

"I'm a father, Elizabeth. Fathers don't run

off to pursue whatever whim or urge they get."

She looked away, at the hay cascading over the haymow, at the rafters where owls roosted. At anything but Ted. "Sometimes," she whispered, "they do."

Ted cupped her jaw with his hand. "Good fathers don't. I'm sorry if you had a childhood filled with uncertainty."

She jerked away from his touch. "I didn't. It was . . . fine. Everything was fine."

But it hadn't been. She was playing the game she'd been taught, the one her mother always played. Put on a brave face, pretend everything was all right and eventually Papa would come back home and make it so. For a while.

Oh, why had she asked the question? Why couldn't she have come in here and said goodbye and been done with it?

He frowned. "When will you be back?"

"I'll return with Robby by the end of the week."

"I'll miss you." He raised a hand toward her then let it drop to his side. "This afternoon . . . making biscuits . . . I had the most fun I've had in my entire life."

His admission rocked her back on her heels, but she wouldn't let him know how much his words meant. "I liked telling you what to do."

"Never a doubt in my mind about that."
He tweaked her under the chin.

She headed to the door.

"Elizabeth."

She circled back.

"I want to thank you."

"For what?"

"For filling a bit of the emptiness this
house had."

His words squeezed against her lungs.
"I'm glad," she said, her admission a whisper.

He took a step toward her, but Elizabeth
strode to the house, eager to get away from
Ted and the feelings he brought alive in her
heart.

CHAPTER FOURTEEN

Ted dropped Anna and Jason at school, and then drove to the parsonage. Holding Henry in the crook of his arm, he knocked at the door, every muscle as tightly strung as a new fiddle. Perhaps talking to Jacob would set him back on his even-keel course.

Lydia ushered them inside, snatching his son from his arms before they made it to the living room. "Jacob's in his study. Go on in." She ran a fingertip down Henry's neck and he giggled. "I'll watch this precious little boy."

Sitting across from Jacob's desk, Ted told his pastor he'd experienced another verification of God's Call. Three different people had told Ted he sounded like a preacher. "But I'm certain I've misinterpreted God." To prove his assertion, he shared every ugly part of his past. When he finished, he said, "No church is going to accept an ex-gambler for a pastor, Jacob, especially this

261

one. Not when my father swindled our church out of the remodeling fund."

Jacob's brow wrinkled. "Though the debt wasn't yours, you made restitution for that swindle." He rose and walked to the window, pointing in the direction of the saloon on down the street. "I believe you're the right pastor for Joe Lessman. He might actually listen to you."

If only Ted could believe that. Whether he believed it or not, The Call got stronger every day. And so did his resistance. For reasons God must surely approve. He had to protect his family. "I've made too many mistakes."

"The Bible's packed with stories of men who failed, yet God used those men in a mighty way."

A few of those men paraded through Ted's mind. Moses killed a man before God spoke from a burning bush and commanded him to save his people from Pharaoh. To hide his sin with Bathsheba, David arranged for Uriah to die in battle, yet David was God's man. Saul persecuted the early Christians, but God gave him a new name and the task of taking the Good News to the Gentiles.

Ted didn't doubt God had used these men and countless others to do His will. Could Jacob be right? Could men like Joe be the reason God wanted him, of all people, to pastor a church?

Jacob perched on the corner of his desk. "I have a story I want to tell you, Ted. About a young man who didn't believe in God. This man made a point of using God's Holy Name in vain. This man snorted in derision at others' attempts to tell him about the love of God. This man committed every sin in the book and then some. I'll spare you the details.

"And he was miserable." Jacob's voice cracked. "One night he met God. Not in some miraculous way, but in the deeds and love of a godly woman." He smiled. "I was that young man, Ted. That woman is Lydia." His brow crinkled. "I'm no squeaky-clean pastor. And yet, God forgave me. For every sin I committed. For every foul word out of my mouth. For every time I jeered His name. After receiving that pardon, I wanted to devote my life to serving and leading others to Him."

Tears filled his eyes. "Amazingly I've had the privilege of sharing with others the joy I've found in the Lord. Not to judge them, but to love them, as Jesus did the sinners in the gospels. As Lydia did in my life. As I know you will here one day."

Ted was speechless, barely able to take in

that this scholarly pastor had lived such a life.

Jacob took a deep breath. "I haven't shared that story often. Conversion isn't about me. But upon occasion someone needs to hear that nothing he's done puts him on a list of untouchables, of spiritual lepers. Because of God's perfect love, we all have hope."

Ted stared into Jacob's eyes and saw the humility, saw the awareness of missed years, missed opportunities. But he also saw a man who valued the gift God had freely given him — forgiveness.

"Ted, Lydia's parents are getting old. They need us. And Lydia's home church needs a pastor." He smiled. "I'd be amazed except I've seen God provide time and time again. We'll miss the good folks here, but we've decided to move back home." He studied Ted. "God is calling you to fill the pulpit here. Not because you're righteous. No one is." He smiled. "Though I can name a few who believe they are. But because you've experienced the incredible pardon of Jesus, and you want to lead others to that precious freedom."

Ted shook his head. "It's too big a risk. I'd have to tell Elizabeth and this town about my past. I could lose my wife." *If I haven't already.* "Once people know about my past, they won't allow me to fill the pulpit. I can't blame them."

"God doesn't call a man to a task without giving him what he needs to accomplish it and that includes an open door. You're never on your own when you're obedient."

In his humanness, Ted couldn't see how his past and God's Call could mesh without bringing harm to those he loved. "Don't you see? I can't let Anna and Henry suffer the ostracism I faced as a child."

"Secrets have a way of coming out, Ted."

As easily as a hot knife slid through butter, Jacob's words sliced through Ted's arrogant assumption that he had the authority to protect his family.

"God's in control, Ted. We aren't. He's opened the door. Will you walk through it?"

Elizabeth pushed through the crowd of travelers moving pell-mell across the platform and spotted Robby, riding her father's shoulders and waving wildly to get her attention. Papa's big welcoming smile eased her concern that he'd still be angry at her defiance. By the time she reached them, he'd swung Robby to his feet.

"Hello, princess," he said, wrapping her in a hug then releasing his hold.

Dropping her satchel at her feet, she tugged her brother close, smothering his upturned face with kisses. "You've grown a foot!"

Robby giggled and puffed out his chest. "Papa says I'm his little man."

"Yes, you are." She turned back to her father, noting for the first time that his suit hung on his large frame; lines grooved his once-smooth face. "You've lost weight, Papa."

"About time," he said. "You look wonderful."

She smiled her thanks. "I've gained a few muscles working on the farm." She ruffled her brother's hair. "Oh, Robby, you're going to love all the animals, one shaggy black-and-white dog in particular."

Robby leaped up and down like a tightly coiled spring. "Really, Lizzie? A dog for me?"

"Tippy belongs to Ted, but —"

Papa's brow knitted. "Who's Ted?"

"I'll explain later. Right now, I can't wait to see Martha."

"She asked that I hurry you home." Papa picked up her bag and they moved toward the street where he hailed a hack. Once they'd settled inside, Robby plied her with questions about the farm the entire way.

266

The hack stopped in front of the imposing portico. Ted's two-bedroom farmhouse would surely fit into the third-floor ballroom. She dug in her purse, but Papa paid the driver. Where had he gotten the money?

They hadn't reached the front door before it opened. Martha stood waiting, a smile as wide as her open arms and a dusting of silver softening her fiery red hair. Trim, tall, with an iron will and a no-nonsense demeanor, Martha let her hazel eyes skim over her, sizing her up in one swift glance.

Elizabeth slipped into the comfort of those arms and gave the nanny a fierce hug. "I've missed you." A few weeks in Ted's household had given Elizabeth new appreciation for all Martha handled.

"This house isn't the same with you gone," Martha declared, leading her inside. "I want to hear all about what's happened since you left."

As they walked through the main hall, their footsteps echoing in the all but empty house, Elizabeth's heart dipped. Even more of the furnishings were gone.

In the kitchen, they enjoyed a simple, delicious meal while Elizabeth regaled her family with stories of her life on the farm. Catastrophes that had hurt her now brought laughter.

After dinner that night, Martha packed Robby's clothes, books and favorite possessions. Elizabeth kissed her brother goodnight, then left Martha and Papa to tuck him in one last time.

In her room, she glanced out the window onto the lawn where she'd made her escape a few weeks ago. Though it felt like a lifetime. She filled a trunk with books, shoes and clothing. She'd donate the ball gowns and frivolous things that would be out of place in New Harmony.

On her way downstairs, Elizabeth noticed a light on in her father's study. She rapped on the door then let herself in.

Papa and a stranger had their heads together. From the expression on her father's face, the conversation had taken an unpleasant turn.

"This must be your daughter, Manning."

Her father paled. "Yes."

The stranger strode to her. "Your father and I go way back. I'm Victor Hammer. Most people call me Vic."

That scar, those eyes, her father's demeanor put Elizabeth on alert. Who was this man?

"I understand you've recently married."

"Yes."

"Seymour said you live on a farm. Big

268

change, I'd imagine." When she merely nodded, he turned to her father. "I'm sure you
want to spend time with your daughter. I'll
show myself out."

Papa walked him to the door. "I'll find a
solution."

The man's smile didn't reach his eyes.
"I'm counting on it," he said, then left.

Waiting until the outside door opened
then closed. Elizabeth released a gust of air.
"Who is that man, Papa?"

"No one of importance."

Elizabeth knew her father. He'd avoided
her questions about that man. Why? As if
an icy finger slid down her spine, Elizabeth
shivered.

Papa motioned to chairs near the fire. "Sit.
Tell me more about this husband of yours
and his children." He grinned. "Guess this
means I'm a grandpa."

"I hadn't thought of that, but you are."
The streaks of silver in his hair only made
her father appear more distinguished. "You
don't look like one."

He smiled. "With two ready-made children and your brother, you're going to have
your hands full."

A log tumbled forward, shooting sparks
up the chimney. Elizabeth jumped. "I'll
admit Anna's a handful." No point in

disclosing how much. "Taking care of Henry's a full-time job, but Ted's good to me. It'll work out." Amazingly, she believed what she'd said. "Robby won't be any trouble."

"A small farm can't provide much money." He frowned. "Can your husband give you what you've been accustomed to?"

Elizabeth looked around the barren study, stopping at the spot where Papa's desk and chair once sat. Bookcases crammed with leather-bound books now stood empty. What an irony that Papa was concerned Ted couldn't provide for her when his gambling had almost put them in the poorhouse.

But possessions didn't bring happiness. Another lesson she'd learned.

"Don't fret about me, Papa." She squeezed his hand. "I'm living a rich life. I have all I need and more."

Her father jerked toward the sound of a clearing throat.

Vic stood in the open doorway, his eyes bright like a hawk. "Sorry for the interruption. I forgot my hat." He motioned to the wide window ledge. "Ah, there it is."

Papa ushered Vic out, then returned, his composure shaken though he tried to hide the fact under a wide smile. "So tell me more about the farm."

"It's the perfect place for Robby," she said. "He'll love playing with Ted's dog."

A flash of pain crossed Papa's face, probably guilt over the puppy he'd given then taken away. "Take Robby and leave tomorrow on the first train. I'll see to the arrangements."

"I'd planned to leave after lunch." Alarm traveled her spine. "What's wrong?"

"Nothing new. I'm about to lose the house. I want Robby settled with you as soon as possible." Out of his pocket, he pulled a slip of paper and a pen. "Write down your address in Iowa so I can reach you."

Elizabeth did as he asked, then handed it to him. "What will happen to you? Where will you go?"

"I got a job. Imagine that?"

She smiled. "Doing what?"

"A sales opportunity. I'll be fine, as long as I know my children are safe."

Her stomach turned over, a queasy reminder of Vic. "Safe? What do you mean?"

Papa smoothed the lines on his forehead. "You know, taken care of. Content." He looked deep into her eyes. "Are you happy, princess?"

"I'm fine. All that matters is Robby."

Papa had changed. How much she didn't

271

know, but she couldn't bring herself to broach the subject of his gambling.

"I'm sorry I insisted you marry Reginald. I only wanted what I thought was best for you."

"I'll never understand how you could've promised me to Reginald in exchange for the payment of your debts."

He studied his hands. "I did what I had to do to take care of my family."

"I don't agree with what you did, but I forgive you."

"I can't tell you what that means to me." He met her gaze. "I'm sorry about losing the house. It should've been yours and Robby's."

"The house doesn't matter. Robby and you and Martha, that's what matters."

Papa's charming smile firmly in place, he rose and tugged her to him. "I hope your husband knows what a treasure he married."

No need to tell her father that she and Ted didn't have a real marriage. "Treasure or booby prize." She forced up the corners of her mouth. "I'm not much of a farm wife."

He chuckled. "I have trouble picturing that, as well. Is Ted a patient man?"

"Remarkably."

Suddenly tired, Elizabeth stifled a yawn. "I'm going up to bed. We'll talk more in the morning."

Her father wrapped her in a hug and kissed her cheek. "I love you. Sweet dreams, princess."

"I love you, too, Papa."

That night Elizabeth dreamed of her and Ted climbing an endless hill. She wanted to rest, but he towed her along, insisting they'd make it. An odd dream, but perhaps they would.

The next morning, Elizabeth went down to breakfast. Martha gave her a big hug. "You just missed your father. He left for work."

Elizabeth hurried to the window. Papa stood outside talking to a man. The same man she'd met in his study. Vic. Perhaps Martha could give her some insight into the man. "Who's that talking to Papa?"

Martha glanced out, then shrugged. As Elizabeth watched the men go their separate ways, the nanny bustled around the kitchen, making small talk, but Martha's frenzied behavior only increased Elizabeth's uneasiness.

Robby appeared, rumpled from sleep and ready for breakfast.

"I'll never stop missing you two," Martha

said, putting out a breakfast fit for a king.

"I wish you could come to Iowa. I could sure use your help with Ted's children." She sighed. "But there's no room in the house and no money to pay you."

"From what you said last night, your struggles with Anna can't be fixed with good meals and fair rules, though those things are important." She took Elizabeth's hand. "Anna needs you to open your heart to her. To love her. Even when she's unlovable. That's what all children need." She smiled. "That's what I gave you."

At Martha's advice, Elizabeth released a shaky breath, knowing getting close to Ted and his children meant inevitable heartache.

She took Martha's callused hand, now much like her own. "When do you leave for your sister's?"

"I've changed my mind about that." Her eyes filled with tears. "I can't let Seymour go through this alone."

Elizabeth noted the use of her father's first name. What had transpired between Martha and Papa? "What are you saying?"

"I've taken a position as a cook in the same boardinghouse where your father's taken a room."

Elizabeth studied Martha's damp eyes, the lines etched in her brow. Never once had she seen anything improper between her and Papa. But the misery in Martha's eyes reminded her of an expression she'd seen in her own. "Are you in love with —"

Nodding, Martha squeezed her hand. "Is that all right with you?"

"Yes." Why hadn't Papa mentioned their relationship? Perhaps she'd been too focused on her own life to notice the attraction between them.

"But I won't marry a man who's set on destroying himself. And those he claims to love. I'm praying for him. For you. For all of us."

"Papa broke Mama's heart. Don't let him do that to you."

"I'm not your mother, God bless her. I've lived in this house since you were five. I never once saw her oppose Seymour."

"Are you saying if she had, things would've been different?"

"Who's to say? Seymour and I have talked. He knows where I stand when it comes to gambling, to what he's done to his family. He wants to change, but whether he can . . . well, that's why I'm staying in Chicago, for now."

Maybe this woman had made a change in Papa. Or perhaps he'd reached the bottom of the abyss and had found the courage to climb out. Or maybe God was working in Papa's life. Whatever the reason, hope latched onto her heart. Maybe God would perform a miracle where Papa was concerned.

Martha accompanied her and Robby to the depot, and waved goodbye from the platform, tears streaming down her cheeks.

Elizabeth wiped Robby's tears as the train pulled away, tugging him close. "You're going to love the farm."

Her brother would find happiness in Iowa. She hoped Martha and her father would find happiness with each other in Chicago. Without a doubt, Martha was a good influence on Papa.

That Martha and Papa had found something she and Ted might never possess squeezed against her heart.

At least, by marrying Ted, she could give Robby his dream.

Anna blocked the doorway into her room, her arms folded across her chest, her chin thrust to the ceiling. "He's not coming in here."

"Mind your manners, young lady." Ted's stern tone issued a warning, but Anna stood her ground.

"My brother will share my room, Anna,"

Elizabeth said, wishing she'd thought to settle this before she'd left for Chicago.

Anna smirked. "Daddy doesn't like you and Robby."

"Anna! That's not true." Ted exhaled. "Why would you say such a thing?"

" 'Cause you sleep in the barn."

Crimson climbed Ted's neck. "Never mind where I sleep. Elizabeth and I are the adults here. We make the decisions."

Ted's harsh tone crumbled Anna's bravado. Tears filled her eyes. She spun into her room, slamming the door.

The three of them stood mute. At their feet, Henry clapped his hands, as if he'd witnessed a stunning performance.

Robby leaned into her. "I want to go home." Elizabeth dropped to her knees and drew her brother close. He buried his face against her shoulder. *"Please,* Lizzie, take me *home."*

How could she tell her brother he had no house to go home to? "It'll be all right, sweet boy. You'll love the farm."

Ted laid a hand on Robby's shoulder. "Do you want to watch me milk the cows?"

Robby shook his head. Tears stung Elizabeth's eyes. Ted was a good man and did what he could to keep things on an even keel. But Robby wasn't some ship passing through rough waters. He was hurting.

"Robby," Ted said, "there are cookies on a plate in the kitchen. Why don't you have a couple before bed."

Robby looked to her. She nodded. "I'll be right there."

Her brother shuffled across the living room and down the steps to the kitchen.

Ted tugged her to the sofa and leaned close. "You're trying too hard, Elizabeth."

"What do you mean?"

"You can't force the children to get along. Give it time. They've just met."

"Would it have hurt Anna to show Robby her room?" she whispered. "She wouldn't even let him look at it."

"She's acting like . . . Anna." He smiled. "I'll talk to her. But you and I need to relax and give the children time to get used to the idea of being a family. We need to be careful not to pick sides. In the meantime, we'll ask for God's help, then leave it in His hands."

"I'll try."

"I know how disappointing this is for you. Give Robby time to adjust." He patted her hand. "I'm going out to milk."

She walked Ted to the kitchen door. He turned to Robby. "Good night, Robby. Sleep well."

Robby had finished his snack. As Elizabeth led him to her room, she felt a prickle down her back. She'd married Ted to give her brother a home, to give Robby the security he lacked. Never once had she considered that he wouldn't be happy here.

But Anna wasn't about to accept Robby any more than she'd accepted Elizabeth. And her brother missed Martha and Papa more than she'd expected.

But then she remembered Ted's words. She needed to pray. To give it time.

Please, Lord. Work this out for Robby's sake. For Anna's sake. For all of us.

With Tippy loping alongside him, Ted wrestled the slop jar while Robby gripped the pail, not much help, but doing what Ted had asked. His gaze lifted to the sky. Not a cloud in sight. "Looks like another dry day."

Robby nodded.

"Not good for the crops. We need rain."

Robby nodded again, looking jumpy, as though he wanted to hightail it back to Elizabeth.

"You like pigs?"

"I dunno."

From the sad expression on his face, the poor kid must think he was heading to the gallows instead of the pigpen. Earlier Ted practically had to hogtie the youngster to get him to release his hold on Elizabeth's apron strings.

Ted stopped and waited until Robby looked up at him. "Way I see it, you have two choices. You can keep on saying no more than two words to me or you can try and enjoy yourself here."

Robby toed the ground. "I'm probably not gonna stay, anyway."

His words pretty much summarized Ted's childhood. Sympathy rose in his chest. He'd find the same patience he had with Anna. His daughter chose to fight while Robby chose to shrink from connection. He'd do all he could to bring this boy to life.

"My family went from place to place and I know how hard it is to fit in."

Robby glanced up at him, then quickly away.

"I know how difficult it must've been for you to leave your life and family in Chicago to come to an unfamiliar place. I'd like to help you feel at home here . . . if you'll let me."

Robby didn't say a word, but his eyes glimmered with tears.

He'd no doubt been the pet of the family. Having to share Elizabeth's attention must hurt. But sitting on the sidelines, feeling edgy, lonely and overwhelmed only made things worse. He'd involve Robby in the work on the farm. The best remedy for what ailed him. Time in the fresh air and sunshine wouldn't hurt, either. He'd run the boy ragged.

"This morning, you and I are going to feed this slop to the pigs. By the time we're done, breakfast will be waiting for us. And we'll give those pigs a run for their money." He chucked Robby under the chin. "Now don't you go telling your sister I mentioned slop and her breakfast in the same breath, or we'll both find ourselves in the dog-house."

As if against his will, the corners of Robby's mouth twisted up. "Yes, sir." He cocked his head at him. "Slop?"

"That's what we call what's in this pail. The pigs get the potato skins, eggshells, every scrap of edible food left from our table. They love us for it. And we love them for using our leftovers to grow side meat and chops."

The boy looked puzzled. Better to leave him in the dark for now. "God knew what He was doing with every creature He made. Not that we always appreciate them all. Any animal or bug you could do without?"

Robby shrugged.

At the pigpen, Ted hauled the bucket over the fence, hopped it and then helped Robby scramble over the slats. Tippy sat on his haunches, watching. With Robby's help, Ted dumped the slop into the trough, then stepped back and called the pigs. "Suey! Suey, pig, pig!"

Ted heard them before he saw them. They left their foraging in the woods and trotted toward them, snorting, grunting and shoving toward the trough. Noses plowed through the mixture, fighting their neighbors for a share. "They're not much for table manners," Ted said.

"No, sir."

"They remind me of Henry going after your sister's biscuits."

Robby almost smiled.

"Sometimes you've got to be like those pigs, Robby, and push your way in." Especially with a girl like Anna.

Ted motioned to the nearby pen. "Never climb that fence. That old boar isn't above adding boy to the menu."

"Yes, sir."

Back at the house, they washed their hands at the pump. "Better take your shoes off. If you don't, your sister will tan my hide."

Inside, Henry sat in his high chair, smearing oatmeal on his hair. Ted glanced at Robby. "Does my son remind you of anybody?"

"Yes, sir," Robby said, and his eyes almost twinkled.

The boy's conversational skills could use work, but the amused expression on his face looked promising.

Whereas his daughter eyed him warily, her mouth turned down as she finished laying out the flatware.

Elizabeth poured the milk. Her questioning gaze met Ted's.

"Your brother was a big help, Elizabeth." Ted glanced at Anna. "With two children to lend a hand around here, the work will get done a lot faster. Perhaps Anna and Robby could handle the egg gathering." Maybe they'd find a way to get past all this timidity and hostility.

Anna crossed her arms across her chest. "I can do it by myself. I don't want his help."

"We all need to rely on others, Anna," Ted said.

"I don't."

Robby's face flattened, his gaze throwing up a wall between him and Ted's family. In the blink of an eye, Anna had undone what little progress Ted had made.

CHAPTER FIFTEEN

A vanilla cream cake. What should have been a simple creation. Elizabeth had fretted over the layers as if they were newborn babes. That morning when she'd examined her handiwork, she'd realized she'd created a cake not merely for the Sumner's silver anniversary party, but for her husband.

To show Ted she could master more than biscuits. That she was a wife he could admire. Her heart skipped a beat. If she could, she'd have tossed the cake into the slop jar. Because no matter what that adage said about the way to a man's heart —

She had no intention of letting one vanilla cream cake take her any closer to Ted Logan.

The entire town had been invited to the ice cream social, including Richard and Lily, who'd moved into the boardinghouse and showed no signs of leaving. Elizabeth had been practicing her cake baking on Rose's parents, even learned a few tips from Lily, who delighted in being the superior cook. She and Lily had gotten off on shaky footing, but Lily's willingness to pitch in and her kindhearted treatment of Robby had eased the tension between them.

With the fields planted, the men crouched before ice cream freezers, wearing smiles on their faces, hats shoved back on their heads, eagerly cranking the handles that transformed the glob of eggs, cream and sugar into a luscious treat. Around them, children played kickball, marbles and jacks and giggled their breathless way up and down the hills.

"Looks like everyone is having a good time," Elizabeth said to Ted.

"You look mighty happy yourself."

She gave him a smile, surprised to realize she was. "I love parties. And I'm hoping Robby will make a friend."

With Henry in his arms, Ted reached up to help her out of the wagon. "I'll have to remember your love of parties."

Looking into that handsome smiling face, she marveled that Ted wanted to please her and strived to help Robby feel at home. As he helped her down, the warmth of his touch shot through her. Her insides felt like a cup poured full to the brim, ready to spill over.

Surely this couldn't last.

Anna joined the other children while Robby plodded along with Ted and slouched nearby as Ted set up then cranked his own freezer, with Henry perched on his knee.

Elizabeth carried her basket to a long table covered with a white cloth flapping in the gentle breeze. Women gathered around it, putting out their cakes.

"Hello, Elizabeth." Gertie Wyatt squinted up into the sky. "Not a cloud in sight. All this sunshine gives me the willies."

Ruth Johnson set out a cake frosted with a burnt-sugar icing. "It'll rain, Gertie. Always has." She raised her eyes to the heavens. "Though sooner's better than later, Lord."

Gertie opened her basket, lifted a cake sprinkled with coconut. "Remember when that evangelist came here for a prayer meeting? We had terrible storms all week. But all that rain didn't douse his fire-and-brimstone sermons."

"Yeah, that podium pounding cost us our building fund besides."

"It's the Sumners' anniversary. Let's enjoy the party." Rebecca Harper shifted Faith in her arms. "I hear enough dreary talk at home."

Elizabeth put her basket beside the others and lifted the lid. Inside rested her masterpiece, a towering cake with peaks of white frosting gleaming in the afternoon sun.

Rebecca peeked inside. "What a beautiful cake. You've outshone all of us."

"Don't be silly." Elizabeth looked around at all the marvelous cakes, secretly pleased by Rebecca's appraisal.

Ted came up behind her just as she lifted the cake plate from the picnic basket. The top layer slid toward her. Elizabeth tipped the platter to reverse the momentum, but that only sent the layer toward the ground. She yanked it back and the top layer slid across the bottom, coming to a stop against the front of her dress. "Oh!"

"Let me get a knife," Rebecca said, handing Faith to Ted, then turning to her own basket. Rebecca slipped the spatula under the wayward half and lifted it back in place, then smoothed the frosting over the crack in the top. "There."

Ted eyed Elizabeth's dress. "You look mighty delicious covered with frosting, Mrs. Logan."

The women chuckled.

He stepped closer. "Better even than wearing biscuit dough," he murmured in Elizabeth's ear.

Scrubbing at her dress, Elizabeth's hand stilled. She didn't want her husband drooling over her like she was a confection made only for him.

Winking at her, Ted handed Faith over to Rebecca then wandered back to the men.

Rebecca grinned. "You're perfect for Ted."

"A perfect wife wouldn't be covered with frosting."

"You must not have seen the look in his eye. He's smitten."

Elizabeth's gaze followed Ted. Her heart took a little dive. Did he care about her? What did it matter, really? She wasn't perfect for Ted. She couldn't fill Rose's shoes and was a sorry substitute for Sally. She'd married to give Robby a good home and now that he'd arrived, her brother wasn't happy the way she'd expected. She had no idea why. Or what to do about it.

"Elizabeth Logan, you'd better do something with this girl!" Cynthia Atwater stomped over with Anna, her hand clamped on Ted's daughter's shoulder.

Tears streamed down Anna's face, her eyes wide with fright, her breath coming in hitches. All conversation ceased.

Elizabeth grasped Anna's hand and caught

288

her gaze. "What's wrong, Anna?"

"She took a big hunk out of my cake, that's what's wrong."

Anna shook her head, her body shaking even harder.

Robby tapped Elizabeth on the arm. "Anna didn't do it." He swallowed hard. "I ate the cake."

"Robby, I saw you over with the men. You couldn't have done it." Her brother's bravado waned. But his attempt to save Anna warmed Elizabeth's heart. "Thanks for trying to help," she whispered into his ear.

Elizabeth knelt and pulled Anna into her embrace.

"I didn't do it," Anna said against Elizabeth's neck, her voice soft, pleading with Elizabeth to believe her. "Honest."

This wasn't the Anna with attitude; this child needed a defender, deserved one. Anna had her issues but she wasn't a liar.

"She was right there when suddenly a big hunk of my angel-food cake disappeared. My Betsy saw her take it. Do you have any idea how many eggs it takes to make that cake?"

Elizabeth rose and tucked Anna against her side. "I'm sorry about your cake, but Anna says she didn't do it. I believe her."

Mrs. Atwater's hands rested on her heart-shaped hips. "She's not above a prank like this, I'll tell you. Why, she's got a mouth on her, that girl. Everyone knows it."

Anna hung her head, tearing at Elizabeth's heart. "She's a girl with . . . opinions. Perhaps at times she needs to express them in a milder way, but she does not lie."

Mrs. Atwater harrumphed. "And what am I going to do with a cake that's half-gone?"

Rebecca marched down the table to Mrs. Atwater's cake and turned the missing part to the back. "It's only missing a chunk. There's plenty left."

"This isn't just any cake. This is a prize-winning recipe."

Elizabeth glanced at Mrs. Atwater's daughter, who ducked behind her mother's skirts, but not quickly enough. "Are those crumbs on Betsy's mouth?"

Betsy poked her head out and scrubbed a hand over her mouth. "I didn't eat the cake, Mama. I didn't!"

"Let me see that hand, daughter." Mrs. Atwater examined the small palm, dusted with evidence. "Betsy Marie Atwater! You've embarrassed me in front of my neighbors and accused Anna of something *you* did."

"Your cake is tempting," Elizabeth said softly. "Betsy probably couldn't help herself."

Betsy's head bobbed like a small sailboat on Lake Michigan during a storm. "I'm sorry, Mommy."

Apologies were given to all concerned. Betsy and her mother fell into each other's arms, crying. The ladies went back to unpacking their baskets.

Elizabeth felt a tug on her hand. She knelt in front of Anna and ran her palms over the little girl's damp cheeks. "You okay?"

Anna nodded, opened her mouth, shut it again.

"What?"

"You believed me." She leaned close and kissed Elizabeth's cheek, her eyes filled with regret for the trouble between them.

A lump swelled in Elizabeth's throat until she could barely speak. "You're a truthful girl. I had no reason to doubt you."

"I . . . I say . . . mean things to you."

"I know how hard it is to lose your mother, Anna. I understand. I understand it all."

As if they'd been given an order, Anna and Elizabeth flung their arms around each other, sharing the pain of their losses. When they pulled away, they shared something else — a new harmony.

Anna spun to Robby. "Want to play with us?"

Before he could answer, she led him to a

group of children kicking a ball across the way. Anna glanced back one last time and gave Elizabeth a smile, her gaze filled with warmth, something close to adoration.

Tears pricked the backs of Elizabeth's eyes. Her heart swelled with conflicting emotions that battled for control. What was she going to do now? She cared for Henry and Anna, cared more than she wanted to admit. She'd opened that door to Ted's children leading into her heart.

But she wouldn't open it for Ted. He didn't merely want a mother for his children. He wanted a wife. To kiss. To hold. To share his life. But loving a man could destroy her.

She pivoted, all but running into Ted, who blocked her way.

"I heard you stand up for Anna. I can't thank you enough." He tucked a loose strand of her hair behind her ear. "When I met you at the depot that day, I was afraid you wouldn't fit. But you're a terrific mother." He cupped her jaw with his large hand, his expression intense, full of longing. "A wonderful wife."

Elizabeth pulled away. Ted's words might have meant something if she shared his wish for intimacy. But she didn't.

She wasn't a wonderful wife at all.

■ ■ ■ ■

Around Ted, neighbors gobbled ice cream and cake, having a good time. Good people doing the best they could with very little other than love and hard work — two things that had been foreign to his family. New Harmony was such a welcoming place. Such a family place. But Ted didn't see the other families. He saw only his own. That Elizabeth had defended his daughter in front of the whole town rumbled through him.

His mother had been an ineffectual woman who'd never taken a stand. Not for her children. Not against her husband. Not for herself. He'd hustled over, ready to defend Anna. Certain with all the grief Anna had given her, Elizabeth wouldn't uphold his daughter. He felt like one penny short of two cents. His wife and daughter might clash at home, but when the chips were down, Elizabeth reminded him of a mother bear with a cornered cub.

"You're looking mighty sober, Ted Logan," Rebecca said. "An ice cream social is no place for that face."

He smiled. "Guess you're right."

"Now what you need to do is ask that pretty wife of yours to join you in the three-legged sack race. Lily can watch Henry and Anna." She took Henry out of his arms and gave Ted a little push toward Elizabeth.

"What about you and Dan?"

"He wouldn't miss the chance to be in the sack with me."

Ted laughed and headed toward his wife. Though he found her surrounded by women, he saw only her. The prettiest, most vibrant of them all.

The ladies stepped back when he arrived, opening a path to his wife. He took her hand and led her aside. "Want to enter the sack race?"

"What do we get if we win?"

He tugged on the brim of his hat, a smile curving his lips. "I heard the prize is a slightly dented angel-food cake."

Her eyes lit with mirth.

Couples donned the feed sacks, not an easy task with the volume of the women's skirts and petticoats. A chorus of giggles and chuckles peppered the starting line.

Ted grabbed a sack from the pile and laid it out on the ground. "Step into it."

Elizabeth did as he asked. "Wish I had on my pants."

Grinning, he joined his left foot to her right then pulled up the sack until it reached her waist and divided her skirts. "I'll hold it while you arrange your skirts. I don't want you to step on your dress."

Everyone lined up. The starter raised his hand.

He tucked her close in the crook of his arm. "Hold the sack with one hand and me with the other."

Her arm inched around his back slowly, as though she expected him to bite. Her gaze slid to his mouth then quickly returned to his eyes. "Which . . . foot do . . . we start with?" she stammered.

"Start on the foot in the sack. We'll try to swing them out together." He tucked his arm around her waist and gave it a squeeze. Their eyes met and collided, but only for a moment. "We'll go as fast as we can without falling. If we fall, we'll lose for sure."

The hand went down, a shout went up. In unison Ted and Elizabeth threw out their sacked legs. Gripping each other like their lives depended on it, they lurched ahead. Ted held Elizabeth tight, keeping her on her feet. The Wyatts went down beside them but they kept going, laughing from the exhilaration but never taking their eyes off the finish line. They sped along with only the Harpers in close competition.

At the rope stretched across the ground, Ted lunged, dragging Elizabeth with him.

They stumbled over the line, inches ahead of the Harpers, and landed in a heap on the grass, laughing while their neighbors clapped their approval.

Ted gave Elizabeth a quick kiss on her forehead. "We make quite a team, Mrs. Logan," he said, then extricated them from the sack and tugged her to her feet. "I've never had a better partner."

As he had earlier, he read the panic in her eyes. Why was Elizabeth afraid to get close?

Chapter Sixteen

The woman must have gotten up on the wrong side of the bed. Elizabeth had no other explanation for the harsh expression on the teacher's face as she stood outside the one-room schoolhouse swinging the brass bell. Children formed lines in front of her, girls on one side and boys on the other.

Not that Elizabeth didn't have some sympathy for her, grouchy face or not. She couldn't imagine facing all these children of different ages and intellects every day.

At least no one was telling her whom to marry or where to put the slop. Or pressing to get close. Like Ted.

Jason Harper leaped from the back of the wagon and trotted over to a group of boys while Robby lagged behind, head down, shuffling along like an old man.

Elizabeth tugged at Anna and Grace's hands. "Come along, girls. You don't want to be late."

Anna skidded to a stop. "I don't want to go."

"You have to go to school."

"Why?"

Because Rebecca is watching Henry for the day and I'm free as a bee on the first day of spring. "Because I said so."

Anna scowled. "That's a dumb reason."

Evidently, regret for past behavior didn't mean Anna wouldn't question Elizabeth's authority.

"Whenever I ask my mama anything she says 'because I said so, that's why.' " Grace rolled her eyes. "Every time."

Well, if Elizabeth sounded like Rebecca, then she must be doing something right. She retied the bow on Anna's pigtail. "Don't you want to grow up to be smart?"

"Why? To bake biscuits all day?" Anna thrust out her lip in a perfect pout.

She'd hit a nerve, that girl. Exactly the life Elizabeth had now. A biscuit maker, for pity's sake. Talk about lowering her aspirations. "No, so you can teach or be a nurse or a doctor. Education gives you freedom."

Anna arched a brow in disbelief.

"Education gives me freedom — when school lets out," Grace said, with a giggle.

Only six and already as smart-mouthed as Anna. "Well, go on, your classmates are marching inside."

The girls whirled toward the schoolhouse then took off at a run, barreling up the stairs, their boots clunking on each step.

Elizabeth pulled herself onto the wagon seat, vowing she wouldn't be a biscuit maker all her life and clicked to the horses. In front of the Sorenson Mercantile, she set the brake and tied up to the hitching rail. She'd sell the eggs, not much of a career but a start.

When she'd packed Anna and Robby's lunch bucket, she made a sandwich for herself. She couldn't waste money eating in town. Not that she knew exactly what she'd do with her day.

A sign caught her eye on a storefront next door to the mercantile: For Lease

This building was available for someone with gumption. Someone with ideas. Someone like . . .

Her.

Elizabeth peered through the grimy window into a room littered and dirty and in need of paint. But light streamed in the window, throwing patterns on the plank floor. Cleaned up, this would be a cheerful place. Elizabeth ran a finger down the pane. Here women could gather and exchange books and ideas, find ways to improve the community. For a brief time, free from children and homes and men.

She closed her eyes and pictured it all clearly. In front of the window a table, perhaps on the back wall a bookcase brimming with books and magazines.

Her eyes popped open. She'd collect books for a library, maybe start a book club. Ladies could gather once a week to improve their minds. To instigate improvements in the community.

On the back wall, a door led somewhere — outside or to another room? She hustled around the building and found a window. That meant a back room. Her pulse skipped a beat, then slowed as an idea planted itself in her mind, then bloomed.

This could be a place for her and Robby.

Maybe with just the two of them, she could give her brother the attention he needed. Perhaps get him to admit what bothered him, if he knew.

Even with Anna no longer giving him the cold shoulder, the forlorn expression in his eyes hadn't diminished. Ted treated her brother like a son, but Robby kept his distance, refusing his overtures, looking lost and miserable. Her brother's sadness tore at her. She'd given him everything she'd thought he wanted. And it wasn't enough.

In a way she understood. She felt hemmed in, suffocated by the demands of her routine. She'd gone from a life of ease to a life of endless responsibility, all thrust upon her overnight, giving her no chance to find her own way.

Ted was kind. Trying hard to get close. Too close. He wanted a real marriage when a business contract was what they'd agreed on. She had to keep him at arm's length. She knew with certainty that if she loved Ted Logan, she'd lose herself. She'd become dependent on his smile, on his affection, on the harmony of their marriage.

Then when he chose to withhold that smile, that affection, that harmony, she'd wind up like her mother . . . brokenhearted.

This shop was her and Robby's ticket to freedom, a chance for independence right here in New Harmony. Maybe here she'd find some air to breathe, some time to find her way.

Would Ted allow it?

Well, she hadn't promised to obey, only to try. And hadn't she tried and tried and tried? Lily and Richard would gladly help Ted with the children until Robby found his stride. She wouldn't be leaving Ted in the lurch.

She sighed. Ted would be upset, but surely

God understood her need to help her brother. Her shoulders slumped. But where would she get the money for the rent? *Lord, if this plan is all right with You, help me find a way.*

"It needs a lot of work."

Elizabeth jumped as if she'd been caught in a criminal act and reeled toward the speaker. Mr. Sorenson stood outside the back door of his store, a broom in his hand. He ambled over.

"Two years ago we rented the place to a lawyer but the folks of New Harmony didn't provoke enough lawsuits to keep him. It's been standing empty ever since. The missus and I've talked about expanding, but we got more work than we can handle now. My desk's buried under receipts and a pile of bills."

"I loved math in school. Bookkeeping sounds like fun."

"Fun? I'd sooner get a tooth pulled. And the missus can't add two and two."

Here was her chance. "I'm sure I could handle your books. How much is the rent?"

"What are you aiming to do with the place?"

"I'd like start a ladies' club, maybe a library, though I'd have to find some books."

He leaned on the broom handle and

scratched his head. "Sounds citified." He chuckled. "So it's sure to please the ladies. Normally, I'd charge —" He stopped. "Did you say you could handle my books?"

"I'm sure of it."

"In that case, it's yours for the price of handling our accounts."

"That's all?"

"You'll be doing us a favor."

Elizabeth reached out a hand and they shook. "You have a deal."

"Do you want to take a look around? See what you're in for? It's not locked."

Elizabeth opened the door. A three-inch shadow streaked across the toe of her shoes. She leaped back, pressing her hand to her bosom. "Looks like you already have a tenant."

Mr. Sorenson chuckled. "Mice included at no charge."

She pivoted and spotted dust and mice droppings everywhere. Nothing Tippy could help her with here. She'd wanted to escape the tedium of the farm, not add more work to her load. "Looks like I'll need to borrow that broom."

Mr. Sorenson handed it over with a grin, then thumped the window with a fist and lifted it with ease. "That'll improve the odor in here."

303

A small stove stood away from one wall. Cobwebs dangled between the chimney and the wall. She swung the broom, bringing down the webs.

"I'll fetch a bucket and some rags. There's a pump out back for water."

They walked to the front. Another small stove. More webs but no sign of mice.

"Will you need a table or two?"

"Yes, and chairs. I hadn't thought about those."

Mr. Sorenson waved a hand. "Got some grates out behind the store that'll make fine bases. Barrel lids will work as tops. I'll ask Cecil to nail them together. Covered with oilcloth, they'll look fine."

"You'd do that for me?"

"Not often New Harmony gets a new enterprise." He grinned. "Besides, the ladies might stop in for supplies once they're done chatting here. And Cecil needs something to do besides hanging out at the store, getting in the way." He rubbed a hand over his chin. "I expect the school will loan you a few folding chairs they keep on hand for programs and such."

"What a good idea. Thank you, Mr. Sorenson."

"Ted's a man I respect. I'm happy to help out his missus."

Would Mr. Sorenson be so generous if he knew her plan to move in here? "Could I trade the basket of eggs out in the wagon for oilcloth to cover the tables?"

"You've got a deal. I'll get them." He turned back. "It's a relief to get that empty store off the missus's nag list."

"Let me take down the sign." Elizabeth hurried to the window and then handed it to Mr. Sorenson.

"You know, Mrs. Logan, you're just what this town needed."

"I am?"

"A breath of fresh air. And a pretty one at that." He tipped an invisible hat, then ducked out the back, the sign under his arm.

Her chest filling with excitement, Elizabeth all but skipped to the front door and opened it, welcoming in the breeze and sunshine. She'd found something of her own, a place to exchange ideas and instigate change.

In her mind, she pictured the women coming in, sharing, laughing — making plans for the town and for themselves. And in the process, she and Robby would find a modicum of freedom, a place to find their way.

Mr. Sorenson cleared his throat, interrupting her daydreams. He put a bucket of water and the rags he'd promised on the floor beside her. "I don't see any more mouse nests, just droppings. The missus sent over a scrub brush and a jug of vinegar to cut the dust. Anything else you need, holler."

"Thank you."

"The missus is jabbering about your ladies' club. With you next door, I'll probably not get a lick of work out of her."

"We'll meet once a week, probably on Saturday. Women may not have much time or interest."

"Once the word spreads, you'll be swamped with members."

Elizabeth grinned. "When can you show me your books?"

"How about early Saturday? I can introduce you to my ledger, get you started. After you get that mess straightened out, I'd say once a week should handle it."

Elizabeth stepped outside with the broom and watched Mr. Sorenson head next door. She swung the broom and sent dirt flying. As Martha had always said: well begun is half done. For once the work didn't feel like a chore. Not when it meant she'd take a role in town.

"Excuse me." A familiar fellow she'd met at the café the night she married Ted appeared at her elbow, wearing a plaid shirt rolled at the sleeves, revealing a glimpse of long underwear. He removed his billed cap and squinted into the sun, deepening the grooves around his hazel eyes. "I hear tell you need tables, missus," he said, plopping the cap on his head.

"Please, call me Elizabeth. You're Cecil, the genius with hammer and nails who's going to make my tables."

A deep red blush moved up his neck and disappeared beneath his cap. "Yep. Cecil Moore's the name, but I ain't never been called a genius."

"A man that handy is a gift to womankind."

"Well, I ain't wearing no bow." He hitched up his pants. "How many?"

Stifling a grin, she took count. "Four should be plenty."

"If Sorenson's got that many barrel lids out back, I'll make 'em for ya. I'll be back."

"Please don't rush on my account."

"I only got one speed, missus. Rush ain't it."

Elizabeth watched Mr. Moore shuffle away. Clearly his one speed was tortoise.

Picking up the broom, she swept the store. Dust flew into her face and she coughed then sneezed, wishing for her red head scarf to cover her nose, especially if it would scare

307

mice as well as chickens.

Oscar, the other Moore brother, appeared at the door. Apparently word was spreading, all right, but not to the ladies.

"Cecil tells me you're going to form yourself a ladies' club, whatever that is."

The brothers didn't resemble each other. Oscar was portly, baby faced and short. Cecil was as thin as a reed, long faced and wrinkled.

"Yes, I am." She returned to her sweeping. If she kept getting visitors she'd never finish before school let out.

Oscar swung his head side to side. "Don't look like much."

"It needs cleaning," she said, ending on a sneeze.

He guffawed. "Yes, ma'am, it surely does." He grabbed the broom from her hands. "You'd better git some air. I'll finish this."

Elizabeth took a look at the man's thick waistline. A little work wouldn't hurt him. She grabbed rag and pail and walked outside to wash the window. When Oscar finished, she stepped inside to clean the other side.

"I hear tell you called my brother a genius," he said.

"Well, *you* are a knight in shining armor for protecting me from all that dust, Mr.

Moore."

"Shucks, weren't nothing."

"You kept me from a coughing fit or worse." She smiled. "I don't call that nothing."

The two men might not look alike but they both had blushes that would put a new bride to shame.

"Your brother is making tables out of crates and barrels. Isn't that the cleverest thing you've ever heard of?" she said, rinsing out her rag.

"He fancies hisself a carpenter, but hammering crates together don't make him a craftsman."

Apparently the Moore brothers had a competitive streak.

Oscar surveyed the room. "These floors could use mopping."

She gave the window one last scrub and then wiped a hand over her brow. "As soon as I get a bucket of clean water, I'll get started."

"I'll fetch it. It's too heavy for a dainty thing like you."

"Thank you. Your mother raised good men."

"We raised ourselves, ma'am. Didn't turn out to be Jesse James so I reckon we done okay." Oscar disappeared then returned with the bucket. "Where do you want it?"

"I'll start back here." She dropped to her knees and dipped her rag into the bucket.

"You'll mess up your dress," he said, getting a rag. "Can't hurt these here overalls."

Oscar started in the back and Elizabeth followed behind him, washing the woodwork. Her skirts kept getting tangled up around her. If only she had on pants, though the sight might shock the Moore brothers into apoplexy.

Mr. Sorenson appeared at the door carrying red-checked material. "Here are those oilcloths you wanted. Oh, let me do that. You'll ruin your dress. It's so pretty, too."

"I hemmed it myself — well, with a little help from Ted."

"It's hard to picture Ted with a needle in his hand —"

"He didn't sew —"

"Though I recall watching him stitch up a piglet's leg."

"Oh, my."

"Squealed its head off, but that didn't stop Ted. He clamped that squirming shoat between his knees and —"

Elizabeth gulped. "I've got the picture."

Mr. Sorenson grabbed the cloth and went to work. Elizabeth washed the back window, imagining curtains out front and trying to put out of her mind the image of Ted's pig doctoring.

Though there was one thing she'd learned. Farmers made do. Farmers were jacks-of-all-trades. Farmers weren't squeamish.

Nothing about Elizabeth fit farm life.

Around noon Mrs. Sorenson appeared carrying a tray with three thick slabs of ham between slices of fresh-baked bread and tin cups of hot tea. "Hubert, I left your dinner and the Moore brothers' on the table in the back. Mind the store. I'm eating with Elizabeth." Once they'd left, Lucille smiled at Elizabeth. "I can't tell you what a relief it is to have you handling our books. You've given Hubert a new lease on life."

"I'm getting the better deal." She nibbled on her sandwich. "Would you know where I could get two cots?"

"Well, sure, we've got some nice ones." Lucille frowned. "Why would you need cots?"

She couldn't tell the proprietor her plans. Not until she'd talked to Ted. She owed him that much.

But Lucille didn't leave the subject alone. "Are you planning on moving in here?"

"I might be." She swallowed a sip of water, flushing the food she'd eaten down her suddenly dry throat, and then explained her reasons for bringing Robby there.

"I doubt Ted will think much of the idea. No husband would —" Her gaze turned speculative, but she didn't ask questions.

Once Lucille took her tray and disappeared next door, Elizabeth heaved a sigh. Moving in here would cause people to talk, but helping Robby came first.

With an hour until she had to gather the children from school, Cecil showed up with the tables. "May not look like much but they're solid and won't tip, if'n the ladies put their elbows on 'em."

Elizabeth covered them with the oilcloth, not exactly linen but practical and cheerful. Though smaller than she'd like, the tables were sturdy, serviceable and cost nothing. Something she'd come to appreciate.

By the time she left, Elizabeth's club room shone. Cecil stayed behind, insisting he'd wait to help her with the chairs.

At the school, Elizabeth spoke to the teacher, who assured her the chairs wouldn't be missed until the eighth-grade commencement at the end of the month. Feeling optimistic, Elizabeth asked for twelve. Robby helped the older boys load them in the back while she herded Anna and Grace into the wagon.

Anna twisted on the seat to take a look.

"Where are we taking the chairs?"

Elizabeth couldn't very well explain about the ladies' club until she'd talked to Ted. "To a shop next to the mercantile."

Anna looked puzzled but forgot about the chairs when Grace mentioned the upcoming spelling bee.

True to his word, before she'd stopped the horses, Cecil lumbered off the Sorenson porch to retrieve the chairs. "Well, Anna girl, looks like your new mama is opening one of them fancy clubs for ladies."

Anna's eyes grew wide and she scampered down from the wagon and dashed inside the building.

Once she dropped off Jason, Elizabeth would talk to Anna. Ask Ted's daughter to give her a chance to talk to Ted.

About the ladies' club.

Soon to be her and Robby's quarters.

Was she making a mistake? Did God approve of her decision? He'd opened that door Ted talked about. Still, doubt nagged at her. She wasn't ending the marriage, but with every day packed with chores and children, she never had a minute to examine what she wanted. But if not for Robby's unhappiness, she wouldn't take this step. She had to find a way to restore his joy, even if it meant taking drastic action.

If she hadn't taken action in Chicago, she'd be married to Reginald Parks and Robby would be in boarding school.

A sense of peace surrounded her, as if God Himself had given her permission to flee. Would Ted see it that way?

CHAPTER SEVENTEEN

The minute Elizabeth drove in with the children, Ted took one look at her and knew something was up. He said nothing, not through supper, nor while they shared the task of putting the children to bed. But now as they sat at the table drinking coffee, separated by inches but miles apart, he had to know her plans. "Looks like you had a good day."

"Why would you say that?"

"You're different. There's a glow about you." She'd never looked more beautiful. "It's becoming." He took her hand. "What happened today?"

Her eyes lost their sparkle, becoming guarded, even wary. As a gambler, he'd mastered the nuances of expression. She locked her gaze with his. In that moment, Ted knew that he wouldn't like whatever she had to say. He squared his shoulders. "Tell me."

"I've found something of my own, something that will make me happy."

"You're unhappy here." It was a statement, not a question.

She removed her hand from his grip. "Not
unhappy exactly. Just not happy. It's not
your fault, Ted. Or the children's."

"Then what is it?"

Biting her lip, she looked away, a furrow
between her delicate brows. "It's hard to
explain." Her fingers trembled on the handle
of her cup. "I need freedom."

He could barely get the words out, but he
had to know. "You want a divorce?"

She shook her head. "I made my promise
to you before God."

Weak with relief, he slumped against the
back of his chair. But if not a divorce, then
where would this conversation lead?

"I've jumped into this marriage. I tried to
handle your and the children's expectations,
but the truth is I don't know what I want,
who I am. I need the freedom to find out."

"Doing what?"

"Mr. Sorenson will let me use the empty
building next to the mercantile in exchange
for taking care of the store's books. I plan
to form a ladies' club."

"So your head for figures will pay for this
adventure."

"I used to want adventure." Tears filled her sapphire eyes. "Now I just want . . . me." She sighed. "I'm confused."

Well, she wasn't alone in that. What did she want? How would a ladies' club give it to her? Where would her quest for freedom take her? His heart sank. No doubt farther away from him. Ted picked up his cup. "So what's your plan for this ladies' club?"

"Women need a tranquil place to enjoy one another's company and exchange ideas, find ways to improve their minds, the town."

"There's quilting bees and church functions —"

"No, not merely what they can do but to explore who they are." She laid a hand on his arm. "This isn't about other women. Not really. I'm doing this for me." She folded and refolded her napkin. "And for Robby."

"How will a ladies' club help Robby?"

"I have to figure out why Robby can't adjust and how to help him. Anna has accepted him. Tippy follows him around. You're good to him. Yet my brother's miserable. Maybe he needs time with me. Like me, time to find his way."

"I've tried everything I can think of —"

"I'm not blaming you. I'm not blaming anyone." Her mouth tightened. "Except maybe my father for forcing us into a new life."

Ted cringed. Elizabeth had been forced to marry him.

"Robby misses Papa and Martha, but he can't go back to Chicago." She sighed. "Maybe alone with me, Robby will speak freely. So . . . we're moving out."

A lump lodged in his throat. He set down his cup with a clink. "The children need you. I forbid it."

Her chin jutted, her eyes narrowed, her mouth thinned.

He might as well have waved a red flag in front of a bull but he couldn't stop himself. He didn't want her to leave. And it wasn't only the children who needed her. She'd brought life into the house. Into him. He cared about her. Yes, at times she rubbed him the wrong way, like rough sandpaper against his skin. But she also captivated him.

She rose. "You can't stop me."

He gave an imitation of a laugh, a scratchy sound. "Guess your escape from Chicago proves that." He stood and stepped toward her. "Have you forgotten we're married?"

"You're the one who called our marriage a business deal."

His fingers curved around her cheeks. "It's no longer a business arrangement to me." If he told her how much he'd grown to care for her, she'd get that haunted look in her eyes. Like a trapped animal facing execution. Why didn't she know he'd never hurt her? "But if it were, by leaving, you're breaking the contract."

"Robby and I need this. I won't give it up." She pushed his hands away. "I'm sorry."

"Have you prayed about this?"

She gave a gentle smile. "I have. I know it's not what you want, but in my heart, I believe I'm doing the right thing."

A part of him wanted to beg her to stay, but the other part understood the need to examine whether the path you'd chosen was the right one. Or if you had what it took to change course.

But why did he keep feeling God's Call to ministry when a pastor's wife didn't solve problems by leaving her family? He'd have to trust Elizabeth enough to let go, to let her find her way and help her brother find his. "I don't like it but I'm trying to understand."

She walked past him. "Tomorrow morning Rebecca will drop me off at the shop after she takes the children to school."

"Sounds like you've got it all worked out."

He heard the bitterness in his tone. Well, why not? Hadn't she wormed her way into

319

all their hearts and now would be leaving a hole as big as Gibraltar? He slowed his breathing. Tried to get a handle on his resentment. Keep that even keel he prided himself on.

Numbers 35:6 popped into his mind. "This ladies' club may be your city of refuge. For a time."

She gave him a beautiful, happy smile. "Thank you, Ted, for understanding how I feel."

Lord, how can I show her I care?

"Elizabeth?" She raised her gaze to his. "I'll ask Hubert to open an account for you and credit it with the egg money. For food or whatever you need. I wish I had more."

"You'd do that for me?" she said softly. "Help me when I'm leaving?"

I'd do a lot more if you'd let me. Instead he said, "I'm sorry for trying to make you stay. I was wrong." He took her hand. "You need to do this."

He understood how tired she must be of feeling forced into things. Of not getting to choose what she wanted. Not her path, not her husband. The only way she'd know if she'd made the right choice was to leave.

Tears flowed down her cheeks. "No one has willingly let me decide anything. Ever. Thank you." She rose on her toes and kissed his cheek.

Though Elizabeth pointed to Robby, he suspected the main reason for her departure came down to their marriage of convenience. He should've seen this coming. She'd married him to give her brother security, a happy home. That plan had failed.

Would their marriage also fail? Divorce wasn't the only way for a marriage to die.

Ted's pulse kicked up a notch. By giving her money, he'd made her flight easier. She might not miss him, but he counted on her missing his children. So much she'd come back. Soon.

Watching his wife retreat into the bedroom, he hoped their marriage would survive this test.

In his entire life, he'd never taken a bigger gamble.

Elizabeth slipped her and Robby's clothes and toiletries into the satchel while Robby slept curled up in the bed, unaware that tomorrow they'd move to town.

By leaving, she was adding to Ted's troubles. But she had to go. Or one morning she feared she'd wake up hating him.

He'd said she had a glow about her. The exact words Rebecca had said earlier when

Elizabeth had dropped off Jason from school.

Only, Rebecca had asked if she was pregnant — the biggest irony of all. She and Ted had no real marriage. Her leaving was merely an inconvenience for Ted, maybe an embarrassment. But with Lily and Richard still in town, he'd find a way to keep his life on that even keel he prized.

Elizabeth slipped out of her clothes and into her nightgown, and then crawled into the double bed beside her brother. Bunching up her pillow, she buried her face in it, her thoughts on Ted. She'd miss him. If only he'd court her, make her feel that he hadn't bought her with the price of a train ticket. She was so confused. If only —

No, what mattered was Robby's happiness. With God's help, she'd teach him to trust God, to build a foundation that would help him cope. Yet at the back of her mind a niggling suspicion plagued her. Her motives for leaving might not be as selfless as she pretended.

She and Ted were getting close.

A ragged breath heaved out of her. She had to leave before she got even more entangled with this man and his children.

Heaving a sigh of relief that Lydia hadn't

questioned him about Elizabeth's where-abouts, Ted thanked Jacob's wife. Though he suspected that she and half the town probably already knew his wife slept at the ladies' club. What kind of a picture did that paint of their marriage?

At the open study door, Jacob looked up, a broad smile on his face. "Just the man I want to see."

"Guess that means you've heard my wife and her brother moved to the ladies' club."

"I heard, but I don't think things are as dire as you look." He grinned, motioning to the chair across from his desk.

Ted took the seat, trying to gather his thoughts to explain, not that he understood his wife. "I'm trying to give her time. . . ."

"Have you told her about your past?"

"No."

"You know you have to."

Ted studied his hands. "If I do, she's gone for good."

"You're underestimating Elizabeth."

"I don't know why, but she hates gam-bling. I suspect gambling is behind the reason she married me."

"Ted, I don't believe in coincidence in the lives of believers. You prayed for a wife and God brought you two together. You are a perfect complement for each other."

He chuffed. "How do you figure that?"

"*If* she was hurt in some way by gambling, you've both taken action to start a new life. But, Ted, you've got to be honest with her." He rose and put a hand on Ted's shoulder. "I watch Elizabeth while I preach. She's softening to the Lord. I can see it."

"She's grown in her understanding of God, of His love, but something's holding her back. If I knew what to do —"

"Change yourself before you try to change Elizabeth."

Ted wobbled back in the chair. Jacob's words packed quite a wallop.

"She's got to sense you're hiding something. It's time to live what you believe. Trust God. He demands obedience. If you obey, He'll walk you through the consequences."

Ted met his pastor's gaze. "Now's not the time. Elizabeth has enough to handle."

"Don't wait too long," Jacob said, his words a warning.

Elizabeth opened the door of Agnes's Café, then hustled Robby outside. Their meal had been interrupted several times by friends coming over to say hello. Ducking his head, Robby appeared shy, uncertain, but his sweet smile won everyone's heart. Elizabeth hid her insecurity under flippant words and a spirited demeanor — far more like Anna than her brother.

Taking his hand, they walked to the nearby park not far from town, something they'd done every evening after dinner since they'd arrived four days ago. They sat on the swings and pumped toward the heavens, laughing as they sailed through the air.

Here Robby came alive, behaved like the boy she knew in Chicago, not the hesitant, downcast child he'd become at the farm. Why hadn't he adjusted when he'd practically begged her to live on a farm? Why hadn't the life met his expectations?

Later, sitting on a bench, the two of them leaned against the back. The sun, a bright orange ball, lowered in the sky. If she'd been on the farm, Elizabeth would've spent part of the day working under that glare. Hanging laundry. Picking lettuce or weeding the garden.

Ted, undoubtedly, tended the fields, the animals, all of them needing constant care, a wheel he could never stop turning.

She should be there.

Guilt panged in her chest. An impossible choice — her brother or her duties as Ted's wife. But to see Robby now, smiling, laughing, she'd made the right one.

"I like this park."

"Me, too." She sighed. They couldn't stay in New Harmony forever. She'd made a promise to Ted, to his children, to God, and she had to honor that promise. "Robby, we need to go back to the farm."

"I like it here." His face wrinkled up. "I don't want . . . Why can't we just stay here, Lizzie? Just you and me?"

"Ted needs me. I'm married to him, Robby. We're a family."

"I want our family to be just us." He swung his legs, scuffing the grass beneath the bench.

"You have Anna, and Henry will be fun to play with when he's older. And Ted will teach you lots, if you'll let him."

"Anna doesn't like it."

"Why do you say that?"

"Her eyes are sad when Ted's nice to me."

"Well, Anna's been through a hard time. Losing her mother hurts. You and I know how much. She doesn't like to share her father and her brother. But she'll get over it. And if you give the farm a chance, it will —"

"No. I want to stay here."

Elizabeth pivoted toward him. "Why? You've always loved being outdoors. The farm's a perfect place for a boy like you."

326

He bit his lip and shook his head. Mute.

"Tell me. What's bothering you?"

Robby said nothing. Elizabeth waited, sensing he needed time. Space. He kept scuffing lines in the grass, watching the blades flatten beneath his shoes. "What if . . . what if Ted loses all the money and the farm's all gone?"

In that instant, Elizabeth realized why Robby had refused to connect with Ted, Anna or Henry. Why he hadn't fallen in love with the land, the livestock, the dog. He'd learned in his short life how quickly those things could disappear. In the flick of a card, the flip of a coin.

"Oh, Robby." Elizabeth drew her brother near, until she could smell the soft-scented soap blended with the little-boy scent on his skin. "That won't happen. Ted isn't that kind of man. Everything will be there. Tomorrow and the next day, and the day after that."

He lifted his face to hers, tears filling his blue eyes. "Even . . . even the dog?"

She smiled, and her vision blurred. "Yes, even Tippy."

He burrowed closer to her, and she could almost feel the weight lifting off his shoulders. "Lizzie?"

"What?"

"Can we go home?" When he turned his face to hers again, the setting sun kissed his cheeks. "I wanna see the chickens go to sleep."

Elizabeth nodded for a moment, her heart too full to speak. "Tomorrow, Robby, after the first meeting of the ladies' club. We'll go home tomorrow."

CHAPTER EIGHTEEN

Ted had given Elizabeth five days to come to her senses, but she and Robby hadn't returned. He'd handled his household himself. To ask his in-laws' help would expose his wife's defection and give Lily another excuse to harp about raising his children, as if he couldn't handle the job.

He dropped Anna and Henry at Rebecca's on his way in to town, hoping she'd give them a decent meal while he dealt with his wife. Elizabeth shouldn't play socialite while he worked himself into an early grave. And, while she was at it, make him the laughingstock of the whole town.

His children had capsized his even-keel boat. Henry tested his patience. Anna opposed his authority. Only by the power of prayer had he met the challenge. Each day left him exhausted. His respect for mothers multiplied. Especially for Elizabeth, who'd managed his children and his household without the benefit of experience or the connection of blood.

When she'd married him, she'd taken on a momentous task. And now she'd run away, leaving him to handle it alone.

He'd planted the rest of the garden — taking on her chores as if he didn't have enough to do — and attended to his children, feeding them . . . something. Each day things had gotten worse around the house, more disorderly and chaotic.

Now standing outside the parsonage waiting for Jacob to join him, hands hung limp at his sides, he faced the truth.

He missed Elizabeth the way Adam must've missed his rib. Something essential had been ripped from him, draining him of vitality. Every word out of his mouth took supreme effort. If he'd thought he had trouble sleeping with Elizabeth at home, he'd found it impossible now that she'd gone. His decision to act, to enlist Jacob's help, wasn't just about his children.

Jacob opened the door, plopped his hat on his head and strolled toward him, his gaze somber. "Not sure Elizabeth is going to appreciate my interference."

"Probably not, but I'm hoping your presence will carry some weight."

"Have you forgotten she insisted I add *try*

to the obey vow?"

"Hardly." He sighed. "I must've misunderstood God's call. How can I pastor a church when I can't handle my wife?"

Jacob laid a hand on Ted's back. "All in God's timing."

"I hope God's timing includes my wife's return. Today."

Jacob chuckled. "You and Elizabeth are an exact match for the other."

"Match? Maybe as in struck and in flames. A man can get burned."

"I suspect this situation with Elizabeth is providing something you need to learn before you lead a congregation."

"Well, her absence is teaching me plenty." He stopped in his tracks. "You won't believe this. The gossip must've reached Agnes. She drove to the farm yesterday, bringing my favorite cherry pie and offering her condolences on my broken marriage."

Ted would've liked to refuse the pie but it meant something edible for supper. Besides, he couldn't blame this disaster with his wife on Agnes.

Jacob shook his head. "Shame on Agnes for trying to tempt a man when he's down."

"Worse, Henry toddles around the house, looking for Elizabeth, calling 'Mama.' Anna cries at the slightest provocation. Even

Rose's hanky no longer consoles her."

Well, he wouldn't let his children continue to suffer. He strode down the street, itching to settle things with his wife.

"Don't look so grim, Ted. You're attracting attention."

Sure enough, a flock of neighbors were converging on them. Why hadn't Ted remembered today was Saturday and the streets would be crowded? He lengthened his strides, eating up the ground on Main Street, trying to outrun them.

"If you expect me to help get your wife back home," Jacob said, panting, "you'll have to slow down."

"Sorry." Ted shortened his steps, moaning when the others caught up faster than a pack of starving wolves.

Jim Johnson skipped backward in front of them. "Where you going in such a hurry, Preacher? Did Mrs. Mitchell pass?"

"No."

"Where, then?" Jim persisted.

Jacob shot Ted a look of apology. "We're on our way to the ladies' club to try to convince Ted's wife to come home."

Ted gaped at Jacob. When a man shared a confidence, shouldn't he expect his pastor to keep it private? But no, Jacob had blabbed Ted's personal life to this mob. Not that any of these men had overlooked the fact his wife would rather sleep on a cot in one tiny room than stay home where she belonged.

Orville Radcliff whooped. "Yessir. The mare leaped the fence and moved on to greener pasture."

Will Wyatt guffawed, clutching at his belly. "Can't handle your woman, Ted, without bringing in the clergy?"

"Appears she's got a new man in her life."

Ted stopped in the middle of the street. He and Elizabeth might have their problems but she'd never get involved with another man. He shot a glare at Orville.

Jim scratched his head. "Who'd that be, Orville?"

"Not sure which, but one of the Moore brothers. Leastways they hang around her like flies on horse dung."

Ted wanted to slug someone, hardly God's way. But these men were having themselves a good old time, at his expense. And smearing Elizabeth's good name. Well, he wouldn't tolerate it. "Don't you have business to attend to? Supplies to buy? Milk to sell? Instead of making a nuisance of yourselves?"

Orville grinned. "Shore do, but this showdown's gonna be a whole lot more interesting."

"I'm going along because I want to know what my wife is doing at that club," Will said.

Great. Ignoring the occasional elbow jab in the ribs, Ted strode on, determined to keep his life from falling apart. In front of the shop, now whitewashed brighter than a baby's first tooth, he turned to the men. "I'd like to speak to my wife alone. Well, with Jacob here, but otherwise, alone."

Will folded his arms across his chest. "Reckon that's a decision for the ladies."

Ted opened the door. Women gathered at the tables while his wife stood at the podium, unaware of his presence. The ladies had come as Elizabeth had predicted. And from all appearances, they were enjoying the meeting. Elizabeth had captured their hearts just like she'd captured his.

His gaze swept the room. Shelves on the back wall displayed a few books. Red-checked cloths covered small tables with wooden folding chairs decked out in red-and-white-striped bows at the back, fancied up for a party of their own. A pot of violets sat in the middle of each table. White curtains fluttered in the breeze. The room was cozy and clean, with a smidgen of style that shouted Elizabeth.

His breath caught. Why hadn't he grasped how much she meant to him?

Wearing one of her new dresses, the blue gingham, hair coifed like the first time he'd laid eyes on her, Elizabeth made a fetching sight. His treacherous heart skipped a beat. Beautiful — and devious — that described his wife.

He walked in, the pastor on his heels. The room, abuzz with chatter, quieted. Doffing hats, the men crowded in behind him.

"Why, Ted. How nice of you to show an interest in the club," Elizabeth said, polite and sweet, as if she hadn't left him a week ago. "But this isn't a convenient time. We're in the middle of a meeting."

Heat scorched Ted's neck. "I'm sorry, Elizabeth, but this was when I could get away." He spun his hat in his hands. "I'm here to ask you to come back home. Jacob's along to remind you our vows said 'till death do us part.' There's no ladies' club escape clause in those vows, right, Jacob?"

Jacob nodded. Couldn't he at least thump the Good Book for emphasis? The man was worthless at spreading guilt. By now, his pa could've had Elizabeth on her knees. His lungs squeezed. Not that anyone should pattern himself after John Logan.

Ted surveyed the tight-lipped women. By the looks they shot him, he'd already ruffled their feathers. He was on his own with his rebel wife and a roomful of supporters eager to have his hide.

"Who are these men?" Elizabeth motioned to the crowd that had followed him. "The Break-the-vows posse?"

Cecil hooted and slapped his leg. "Ain't she something?"

The rest of the men chuckled. Ted clenched his jaw. It appeared Cecil and Oscar spent more time with his wife than he did. He gave the group a scowl. With a final snicker, they quieted.

Orville Radcliff cleared his throat. "Reckon you could call us a posse. It's got a nice ring to it." He hitched his pants up a notch. "Say the word, Ted, and we'll hog-tie her for you."

"That won't be necessary." Though the idea had crossed his mind. Ted took a step closer. "I can handle this on my own."

Elizabeth strode from behind the podium, eyes glaring. Had she read his thoughts?

Oscar snorted. "You're in for it, Ted." He plopped a foot on the rung of a chair. "Mercy, my bunion's killing me."

Elizabeth held up her hand. "Don't take another step." She parked her fists on her hips. "I won't have your dusty clodhoppers messing up our freshly mopped floor."

"It's time they gave a thought to the work they make," Gertrude Wyatt agreed.

Ted yanked off his boots, first one then the other, then stood there feeling like a fool in his stocking feet, his big toe poking through his sock. He covered it with the other foot, but not soon enough, from the smile on Elizabeth's face.

The other men complied and then fanned out against the wall in their stocking feet, all except for the pastor. His shoes gleamed, as if dirt didn't dare cling to his footgear.

"I worked hard on those floors," Cecil grumped. "But Elizabeth's biscuits are worth it. Why, I'd scrub the streets for a daily batch."

Ted's gaze darted to his wife. She was cooking for other men?

"I told you it was one of the Moore brothers," Orville said. "They may be getting up in years, but they ain't dead."

"Who said I was dead?"

Elizabeth patted Oscar's shoulder. "You're not dead. Not the way you eat biscuits."

"I see the womenfolk's point, gents," Cecil said. "You traipse in here without a thought to the mess you're making. As the man in charge of the town's streets, I have my hands full, I'll tell ya. I can sympathize with the ladies."

Elizabeth nodded. "A point well taken, Mr. Moore."

Cecil scratched his head. "What are you saying, missus?"

"I said you make a good point. As the street maintenance supervisor, you've seen the thoughtless behavior of your gender." Elizabeth gave Cecil a big smile. "The women of New Harmony are in your debt, sir."

Cecil puffed up like a rooster. "You can count on me." Then he scratched his head. "Now that gender part, I'm not sure —"

"She's referring to men, Cecil. Shouldn't you be on our side?" Jim said.

"I'm on the side my biscuits are buttered on." Cecil patted his stomach.

"What I want to know is why my wife's sitting instead of getting our supplies at Sorenson's?" Will Wyatt said.

Gertrude stood with her hands on her hips. Mercy, they all acted like Elizabeth. "I work hard all week, taking care of you and the children. I need time away. Like you — hanging out with the men, playing checkers and telling those tall tales of yours — only we're actually using our minds to solve the town's problems."

Will's eyes about popped out of his head. "I've never known you to speak to me that way."

Suddenly the men and their wives stood toe to stocking toe, ready for battle, except for Cecil and Oscar who had no wives, only bunions to keep them company. The whole thing had gotten out of hand.

If Jacob was right and God intended him to learn something from this standoff, He'd given Ted a whole series of sermons on marriage. But right now, Ted wanted life to return to normal, when the house had been peaceful — well, if not peaceful, interesting.

Ted edged closer to his wife. Her cheeks were pink, her eyes shining. His stomach knotted. Maybe keeping her on the farm was unfair. "Can I speak to you alone?"

Her eyes softened.

Around them couples argued. Ted could barely think above the din. A piercing whistle shrilled, shutting down every sound. All eyes swiveled toward his wife.

Elizabeth removed two fingers from her mouth. "Let's adjourn the meeting and serve refreshments," she said demurely. "Mrs. Johnson made the cake."

Soon the men joined their wives, sipping tea. Ted took a chair at an empty table. Elizabeth finally made it to his side carrying a slice of cake and cup of tea. She set them in front of him then took a seat.

He cleared his throat. "Where's Robby?"

"Over at the mercantile, helping unpack supplies."

"How's he doing?"

She smiled. "Oh, Ted, Robby's better. He's been afraid the farm, the dog, everything would disappear like our house in Chicago. I reassured him. He still misses Martha and Papa and grieves for Mama. But he's able to talk about his feelings now."

"I'm glad." He took her hand. "You were right about that. Right about a lot of things." He sighed, hoping he could make her understand how her leaving had turned his world upside down. "Anna and Henry miss you. A lot."

Moisture gathered in her eyes. "I miss them, too."

Hope for his marriage filled him, swelling in his chest until he wanted to shout with the joy of it.

"What about you, Ted? Do you miss me?"

He missed her, all right. More than parched ground missed rain and the grass missed the morning dew. He missed her like he'd lost a limb, a piece of his heart.

But he couldn't tell her that with Oscar and Cecil at the next table hanging on his every word like hungry dogs waiting for a scrap to fall.

"Of course I do. Last night's dinner was a disaster, worse than any meal you fixed."

She pursed her lips. "I can't tell you how much better that makes me feel."

"I'm sorry. That came out wrong." He lowered his voice. "I miss you. More than you could imagine."

Jacob appeared at their table. He clapped a hand on Ted's back. "Well, looks like you two are working it out. I'd better get back before Lydia sends out a search party."

In accordance with the pitiful help the pastor had been, Ted felt like subtracting a chunk from Sunday's offering.

He took Elizabeth's hand. It felt right in his — soft, feminine. Inside that delicate frame resided a strong, intelligent, vital woman. Already she belonged to the town more than him. He knew she could do anything she set her mind to.

He drew little circles on her palm with his thumb. "Hubert mentioned you're doing an excellent job managing his books."

"He did?"

"Yes." He chuckled. "He also said you bartered with him over the price of eggs."

"It wasn't all that hard. He's a softy really. And worn out handling the store."

341

Ted nodded. "He's talked about selling but can't find a buyer."

She flashed a smile. "He likes you."

"That's nice but I only care what you think of me."

"I think you're a good man, Ted Logan. A good father. A good citizen. But you don't know much about women."

"I know I'm proud of the job you're doing for Sorenson. I know I'm proud of your plans to improve this town. I know I want you to come home with me."

I know I want to hold you in my arms. But he wouldn't admit that when Elizabeth showed no sign of readiness to hear it.

She studied his face. She rose. "I'll go with you."

The weight on Ted's shoulders vanished. Leaning back in his chair, he watched his wife promenade around the room, speaking to her friends. He liked the way she moved. He liked the tendrils of hair teasing against her neck. He liked her smile, brighter than the summer sun.

The front two legs of his chair hit the floor with a thud.

His heart pounded inside his chest. He was in love. Deeply and totally in love with his wife. The knowledge scared him silly.

He watched Elizabeth chatting as if nothing of consequence had just transpired. Oh, how he loved her. Nothing and no one would keep him from his wife.

She went into the back room and came out carrying her satchel then stopped in front of him. "I'm coming home with you. Robby's doing better and we both miss Anna and Henry. And that cot's killing my back."

Not exactly the reasons he wanted to hear. Yet the softness in her eyes gave him hope she hadn't told the entire truth.

"But I'm not giving up this club." She raised her voice so all could hear. "We'll meet every Saturday. You ladies can count on that."

Cecil hung his head. Oscar toed the floor. "You, too, Oscar and Cecil."

The brothers' heads snapped up and smiles took over their faces.

"I'm ready, Ted, to pick up Robby and head to the farm. I hope you're up to having me around."

Ted opened the door. As she marched through, he glanced back at his neighbors. They grinned at him, as if he'd lost the battle. His wife was coming home with him.

He'd won, hadn't he?

CHAPTER NINETEEN

That night Ted sat beside Elizabeth on the swing, the soft squeak of the chain the only sound, pretending nothing stood between them. He knew otherwise. "There's something I need to say."

She turned toward him. Even in the dim light, he could see her eyes glistened. Were those tears? Neither of them would have any peace until they got things settled.

He cleared his throat. "That freedom you're looking for, Elizabeth. It isn't in a place. It's here." He laid a hand over his heart. "Inside you." He waited for her to speak. When she didn't, he pushed on. "I want you to be happy. What do you need from me?"

"I need to feel I'm worth more than how well I handle a list of chores."

"You think my opinion of you hinges on how well you run our household?"

She sighed. "I'm very different from Rose."

Was Rose at the root of Elizabeth's problem? Some false notion she didn't measure up to his deceased wife? He'd probably planted that seed. Not intentionally, but he was to blame.

"I won't pretend you haven't had struggles in areas where Rose excelled. But Rose never got involved with anything outside her family and church." He squeezed her hand. "I'm proud of the person you are. Proud of all you've set in motion to make New Harmony a better place to live."

She touched his cheek. "Thank you for listening and really hearing what matters to me."

"I like that you have thoughts on things." He grinned. "On most everything."

"I must drive you wild."

She did, but not in the way she meant. But if he admitted he loved her, she'd run. He didn't understand why his wife didn't trust love, but pushing her wouldn't work.

"You're vibrant. Fun loving. Smart. This town wants what you have. Needs it. Why, Cecil and Oscar are in love."

"With my biscuits." She chuckled. "Jealous?"

"Of the Moore brothers? No, they're old

345

enough to be your father. But I am jealous of what you've shared with them. How they've helped you while I've stood back —" he swallowed past the lump in his throat "— hoping you'd fall on your face."

The motion of the swing stopped. "You did?"

"I thought if you succeeded at the club, you'd stay away."

"I'm your wife. I couldn't stay away permanently."

"I wasn't sure what you'd do. You're not exactly predictable." Ted pulled her to him, giving her a squeeze in the crook of his arm, then kissed her gently on the forehead.

She stiffened and pulled away. "I'm tired." She got to her feet, taking her scent, the warmth of her skin, the essence he craved.

A second longer and he'd have kissed her the way he wanted to. He plowed a hand through his hair. Exactly the reason she'd gone inside. He'd thought he had his wife back, but she was as absent as if she'd stayed at the club. What could he do to ease the gulf between them?

As the Logan wagon pulled into church, Rebecca scurried over to meet it then took Elizabeth aside. Giving them privacy, Ted herded the children into the sanctuary.

346

"Valera Mitchell lost her mother yesterday," Rebecca said. "We knew she didn't have long. I thought we . . ."

As Rebecca talked about providing food for the wake, Elizabeth could barely concentrate, but nodded at whatever plan Rebecca suggested before hurrying off to join her family.

Elizabeth recalled once again the pain of losing Mama — her shallow, reedy breaths; the last gasp; the final goodbye. Closing her eyes, she tried to block the memories, but tears leaked beneath her lids. Now Valera was going through the same suffering.

Swiping at her tears, Elizabeth forced her feet toward the doors to the sanctuary. Mere feet from the door, she caught sight of Valera coming toward her, wearing black and a serene smile. Though she yearned to avoid Valera's grief, she waited to offer her condolences, her heart beating wildly in her chest.

When Valera reached her, through her clogged throat Elizabeth mumbled something about the sorrow of losing a mother.

"Thank you, Elizabeth. I'm at peace, knowing God was right there with my mother till the end. I'll always miss her, but it comforts me to know she's with God." She smiled. "Why, right at this moment, Ma's probably singing soprano with the choir of angels welcoming her into Heaven." She patted Elizabeth's arm, offering comfort instead of receiving it. "I'm grateful for my church family, especially at times like this."

Somehow Elizabeth made her way to the pew where Ted and the children waited. Henry reached for her and she tugged him onto her lap while Anna nestled close to her father and Robby leaned into her. As the song leader led the opening song, all Elizabeth could think about was Valera's peace with losing her mother.

If only she'd been close to God when she'd lost Mama. If only she could've leaned on Him, not just then, but during her troubles since. But her faith had been shaky, immature. She hadn't been convinced of the existence of Heaven. So much had changed. Now she accepted God's Word as truth. Now she believed God's promises. Now she recognized only God could fill this hole in her heart.

Since she'd come to New Harmony, Elizabeth had absorbed Pastor Sumner's words like parched ground soaked up rain. He'd spoken about God and His love. To think of God as a loving Father both startled and comforted her. Tears filled her eyes. God loved her even now. He knew what she needed. Knew she sat in this pew each week hungering for forgiveness, hungering for a clean slate, hungering for the peace only He could give. And He gave it freely. All she had to do was answer His Call.

Until now she'd hesitated to give Him her life. Perhaps pride stood in the way. Perhaps fear she'd embarrass Ted. Perhaps her struggle with obedience — something she'd fought her entire life.

When the congregation sang "Jesus is Calling," something inside Elizabeth softened. Her barren conscience bloomed in her chest, cultivating a desire to rid herself of that long list of her sins. She yearned to be forgiven. She yearned to be washed clean. She yearned to start anew.

Passing Henry to Ted, Elizabeth rose and walked toward the front, her legs moving of their own accord, tears streaming down her face. Before she reached Jacob, Ted had found a lap for Henry and joined her there. He took her hand and squeezed it, his eyes glowing with happiness while Pastor Sumner took her other hand. Standing between them, Elizabeth declared her faith in God's Son and accepted Him as her Savior.

After the final song, friends and neighbors gathered round, smiling and hugging her. They were her family now.

Her heart skipped a beat. One day she'd

see her mother in Heaven. No matter what had transpired between them, she knew Mama had loved her even when Elizabeth was most unlovable, just as Mama had loved Papa. Perhaps Mama's hope for Seymour would one day be realized. For after today, Elizabeth understood something she hadn't before. God never wasted love.

She no longer carried her burdens alone. She felt her heart would burst with the joy of that knowledge. Peace and a sense of security filled her. She no longer had to scramble to keep her footing.

To control the uncontrollable.

To fix the broken.

To fear tomorrow.

She had only to lean on God. To love Him. To love others.

Whatever happened between her and Ted and the children, God was in control.

With the children in bed, Ted and Elizabeth stood washing the supper dishes in the kitchen. He scrubbed the plates until they shone, until they reflected his wife's face as she dried them. She looked like the plates, washed clean. Shiny. Like new.

"You can't stop smiling," he said, and he couldn't stop looking at her.

"I'm happy."

He handed her the last plate. "You know we're united now. Not just by that marriage license, but by the love of God."

She met his gaze. "You've mentioned your Call to ministry. You know the Scriptures. You're an excellent speaker. You care about everyone in this town. All to say, you'd make a terrific pastor." She swallowed hard. "What's keeping you from answering? Am I standing in the way?"

How could she believe that? He opened his mouth to speak.

"Please let me finish." Her forget-me-not blue eyes brimmed with tears. "I'm assertive. Outspoken. Independent." She grimaced. "I don't even know all the Books of the Bible."

"You'd be your own kind of pastor's wife, Elizabeth, the best kind. You may not realize it but people are attracted to you." He smiled. "Your confidence in me makes you the perfect pastor's wife."

"So why do you hesitate?"

"The water's gotten cold." He grabbed the teakettle and added hot water. He could let her see a small part of his childhood. "My father was an evangelist. Our family traveled from town to town, holding revivals."

He paused, wanting to share why this

town, this church meant so much to him, yet uncertain of her response.

"Really? That must be where you get your love of ministry."

"Pa had the rhetoric." He almost couldn't speak the words. "Then we'd disappear in the middle of the night with the collection he'd promised to share with the host church, leaving behind a passel of confused Christians."

"Oh, my. That had to be hard."

"Most of those anonymous towns my father bilked mixed together in my mind, but one town stuck. New Harmony, Iowa."

Squeezing his arm, she met his gaze. "That's why you landed here."

"As improbable as it seems, Pa believed in God. He'd justified his stealing by saying he had no home church to support him. Conveniently overlooking many a preacher worked another job and rode circuit on Sundays."

As the memories crashed into him, he scrubbed the bottom of a scorched pot. Again and again, trying to remove the stain, but he couldn't. Any more than he could remove what his father had done to so many other towns.

Elizabeth laid a hand over his arm, stopping him, sending a shiver up his arm.

"Thank you for telling me about your father."

He had to tell her that his gambling also stood in the way of accepting that Call. That nothing would make him happier than serving this congregation. But they'd never allow him to step into the pulpit if they knew how he earned his livelihood before he met God. If they knew his pa had cheated them out of the offering all those years ago.

If only he could find the words to tell her, but she glowed with her new faith. She had no idea her husband wasn't the man she thought he was. He'd tell her, but not tonight. He couldn't bear to see that joy vanish from her face.

"But, Ted, your father's actions shouldn't keep you from answering God's Call. I'm sure a congregation would understand you had nothing to do with his actions."

Her attention flitted to a space beyond his right shoulder. Something bothered her, but what? She gave a weak laugh. "I'm a fine one to talk. You're not the only one with a parent you're ashamed of. When you asked how my family lost their money, I sugarcoated the truth, spoke of bad investments. But now that you're considering the ministry, I have to tell you." She cleared her throat. "Papa spent Mama's inheritance gambling. She watched him risk and lose everything she held dear — her money, her heritage, her position — and that slowly killed her."

Ted felt the blood drain from his face. *Why, God? Why did You answer my prayers with a woman whose life had been destroyed by gambling?*

"Why does a man do that, Ted? Why does he take such foolish risks again and again?"

His focus dropped to his sudsy hands. Hands that had made mistakes, now like these suds, covered by God's forgiveness, but would that appease Elizabeth? "It's hard to say. Probably different reasons."

"Maybe if Mama had stood up to him, had taken over the money . . ."

"Maybe, but dredging up the past can't undo it."

She nodded. "I'm trying to let go of things." She smiled. "I'm grateful I'm married to a godly man."

Her words slammed into his gut, twisting and carving him up with guilt. If only the past could be undone. If only he could bare his soul to Elizabeth. He would. But not now. Not tonight.

"If you think the church could handle my father being a gambler and your father being a hoax, then I'll try my best to be a good pastor's wife. God can use us, Ted. I'm sure of it."

He couldn't look at her.

She reached for his face and brought it to hers. "Put your faith in God, Ted. Rely on Him. It'll all work out."

Here he struggled with obedience, his faith in God's plan shaken. Elizabeth's faith was stronger than his. What an irony.

Fighting tears, he tugged her to him, dripping hands and all. This time she melted into him. Oh, how he loved her. But he couldn't say it, not yet. Not until he'd told her everything.

Not until he told her that John Logan had taught Ted everything he knew about poker — tells, how to recognize cheats. There in the saloons, his father was cool, levelheaded, in contrast with the raving, Bible-thumping, hell-and-brimstone preacher in the pulpit both scaring and fascinating Ted.

How could she bear that he'd followed his father's footsteps when gambling had destroyed her family?

Why had he lived such a life? He'd asked himself that question over and over. Why had he done the very thing he'd despised his father for doing? Was it easier than finding his purpose? Had he inherited it like his eye color? Perhaps he'd never know.

355

The prospect of telling Elizabeth clogged his throat, clamped his belly like a vise until the pain all but doubled him over. He'd told Jacob he'd tell her. But he couldn't find the words.

Tomorrow. He'd tell her tomorrow night after the party he'd planned. He couldn't risk ruining the celebration. He'd issued too many invitations to disappoint people now. But more important, he wanted to give Elizabeth a big party. He couldn't wait to see the surprise on her face.

But after that, he'd tell her about his past. Most likely, she'd honor their vows. But she might also resent him for the remainder of their lives, a prospect he couldn't abide.

If she could forgive him — and how he prayed she would — would his neighbors? Were all the offhand remarks that he sounded like a preacher, his strong sense of God's Call, the open door — was all of this from God? Or merely coincidences?

God, if this Call is truly from You, give me a sign.

CHAPTER TWENTY

With the library hours over, Elizabeth turned the key in the door of the ladies' club, anticipating the meal at the café Ted had suggested that morning. The prospect of a rare meal out put a bounce in her step as she headed toward the familiar team and wagon hitched to the rail in front of the mercantile.

Her breath caught. Could the harmony between her and Ted be too good to be true? Her parents' marriage had taught her not to rely on feelings that could change in the blink of an eye. But Ted was different from her father. She trusted him.

Yet deep inside, in a place she'd learned to heed, she waited for . . .

For what?

Trouble.

The thought shot through her, landing in her midsection, a cold lump of uncertainty. Her eyes misted. In less than two months, could she really know Ted? Hadn't she glimpsed a hint of guardedness in his eyes, in his manner, as if he held something back? Even last night she sensed he was under some strain.

Lord, please let this relationship be real.

Up ahead Ted emerged from the store with Henry perched on his shoulders, Robby and Anna walking alongside. When the children saw her, Henry's face lit up like a starry sky on a cold winter night. An odd little hitch took Elizabeth's breath away.

Oh, how badly she wanted the love and solidarity of a family. This family. No other would do. Yet, wanting so much terrified her, seized her throat and squeezed until she felt she'd choke.

No, she'd rely on God and ignore the uneasy feelings churning inside.

Anna ran to her. "Look what Mr. Sorenson gave us." She held out a candy stick, already pointed in the shape of her mouth.

"I'm saving mine." Robby looked pleased with his decision. Did he hang on to the good, thinking he might not get another?

Elizabeth forced a smile. "How nice. Did you thank him?"

Anna popped the candy stick out. "Yes. He said, 'You two are mighty sweet, but it can't hurt to add a little sugar.'"

As Elizabeth took in their beaming faces, her smile relaxed and grew. The transformation in the children bordered on amazing. Since Robby had tried to save her from Mrs. Atwater's wrath, he and Anna appeared joined at the hip. Robby now helped with chores, eager to please and do his part. They'd settled into the normal routine of family life.

Anna still had a stubborn streak, but most days she accepted Elizabeth in a mother's role. Most days Elizabeth loved her role. On other days, she wanted to scream. But Rebecca had assured her that was perfectly normal.

Ted stepped toward her, his gaze warm, intimate, only for her. At the tender longing in his eyes, her mouth went dry. What in the world had she been worrying about earlier? This man cared for her. He may not have told her he loved her yet, but maybe tonight . . .

Oscar and Cecil tromped out of the mercantile. "Howdy." They doffed their hats to Elizabeth. "We're off on our evening constitutional then heading to the café . . . for supper."

"What's a constitutional?" Anna asked.

"Means, little missy, that we're taking ourselves on our daily walk. Cecil here is checking the condition of the streets but I'm doing it for my health." Oscar patted his stomach. "I'm getting a paunch. Been eating too many of your mama's biscuits."

Elizabeth smiled at the Moore brothers, good friends and an enormous help around the club. "I'd hate to lose my best biscuit eater."

"I believe that's my position, Mrs. Logan," Ted said, running a teasing fingertip along her jaw.

At his slight touch, Elizabeth's heart thumped wildly in her chest. "I thought you were the one who turned that job over to Oscar."

A flash of frustration crossed Ted's face.

Chortling, Oscar slapped his hat on his thigh. "Elizabeth don't mince words." He plopped his hat back on his head. "See you soon . . . er, later."

The two men shuffled on as they did every evening. They might not have speed but they made up for it with endurance.

"I've got to agree with Cecil. I like a woman who speaks her mind," Ted murmured in her ear before tugging playfully at Anna's pigtails. "Ready for supper at the café, Anna?"

Too excited to stand still, Anna and Robby ran around Elizabeth's skirts. Henry squealed and clapped his hands at their antics. "Looks like we're more than ready," Elizabeth said, knowing full well that she withheld all the confusing feelings reeling in her head. But how could she harbor these doubts when all she had to base them on was the feeling Ted kept a secret?

"Then let's go." Ted shoved his purchases under the seat of the wagon then returned to the boardwalk.

In front of the café, Rebecca, Dan and their brood pulled up in their wagon. Their children scrambled down, two of the boys swatting at each other along the way. Rebecca clutched the baby to her bosom as her husband helped her down. "Sorry. We're late."

Elizabeth looked at Ted. "Late for what?"

"Why, ah, late for . . . spring. Here we've come to town to celebrate the first day of spring and we're a week late."

Elizabeth didn't believe a word of it. "What's going on?"

"Good job, wife," Dan mumbled, as he whisked Henry off Ted's shoulders, then herded his wife and all the youngsters into the café.

Alone on the street, Ted's large hand swallowed up hers and tugged her close. The gaze he turned on Elizabeth was tender, filled with hope and dancing with excitement. Lost in his silver-blue eyes, she held her breath, waiting for what he had to say. But instead he lowered his head and kissed her until her heart rat-a-tatted in her chest.

"Today is the two-month anniversary of our marriage. We didn't have a proper wedding so I invited our friends and neighbors to the café tonight to share in the celebration."

Tears gathered in Elizabeth's eyes. Ted had done this for her? How could she have doubted him? "I don't know what to say . . ." She rose on her tiptoes and kissed his cheek. "Except thank you."

"You deserve a party for all you've done for us, for all we've put you through." He grinned. "For the pain of flopping, pecking chickens, for a smart-mouthed daughter and damaged silk shoes — to name just a few."

He hauled her to the café door and opened it. A cheer went up. Half the town had gathered in the café, grinning and clapping. Robby and Anna darted toward them. The Moore brothers had cut their walk short, the Sorenson, Sumner, Wyatt, Radcliff, Johnson and Harper families — everyone who'd befriended her, gathered round, thumping Ted on the back and giving Elizabeth a hug. Lois Lessman and her husband stood on the fringes smiling. In the far corner, Lily and Richard even beamed their approval.

Elizabeth pressed a hand against her mouth. "I can't believe this!"

Ted touched her cheek. "I know how hard it's been, being away from the city, away from the polite society you've been accustomed to." He tucked a curl behind her ear. "I want to show you how much . . ." He paused. "How much —"

"You've become an important part of this town," Lydia Sumner broke in. "Not just by marrying Ted and giving that man some joy, but by starting our library and rallying us ladies to make changes in town. And you know what? That's made some lovely changes in us, as well."

"Oscar brought his fiddle and I got my harmonica," Cecil said, and both produced the instruments to prove it.

Like a mother hen with outstretched wings, Rebecca shooed the children in front of her to a table along the back wall. The group dispersed, moving toward their seats, laughing, no doubt, at the shock still lingering on Elizabeth's face.

"And I knew it wouldn't be a proper celebration without your family," Ted said, and then opened the door. There in the opening stood Papa and Martha. "Your father wired me while you were staying at the club and asked to come here."

Her heart leaped into her throat. She ran to them, throwing her arms around them, nestling into the warmth of Martha's girth, drinking in the love in their eyes, inhaling the familiar scent of Papa's aftershave on his handsome, smiling face.

"Princess, I've finally grown up." Her father's smile faltered. "I'd like to start over in this town if it's all right with you. To give you and Robby the love I was too . . . preoccupied to give."

"Only if you stop calling me princess!"

When she finally disentangled herself, Elizabeth noticed Martha had stepped back into the circle of Papa's arm and the two of them stared into each other's eyes, like love-struck youngsters.

That's why Papa finally understood love. He shared it with Martha. Elizabeth couldn't stop smiling. She hoped the temptation to gamble wouldn't take Papa over and ruin what he and Martha had.

Bubbling over with joy, Elizabeth introduced Papa and Martha to Ted.

Her father extended his hand. "Good to meet you at last, Ted."

Ted shook hands with Papa then took a step away. "We should get seated. Agnes has lots of food waiting on us."

But Papa hadn't released Ted's hand. "I know you from somewhere."

"Me? No." Ted pulled his hand out of Papa's. "Let's —"

"I remember now." The friendly look dropped from Papa's face. An ominous huff slid from his lips. "You're that gambler."

People pivoted their way, quieted. Watching. Listening.

"Sir, I'm —" Ted didn't finish.

Elizabeth grabbed hold of her father's arm. "You're mistaken. Ted's no gambler. He's a farmer."

Papa snorted and draped a protective arm over her shoulders. "Then he's bluffed you. You're not married to Ted Logan, farmer." He paused, his gaze connecting with Ted's — cold, hard, accusing. "You're married to Ted 'Hold 'Em' Logan, a no-account riverboat gambler!"

A collective gasp rose from their neighbors. Rebecca gathered the children and ushered them out of the door, shooting one last glance at Elizabeth.

The words tore through Elizabeth with the impact of a gunshot. The blood drained from her head and she staggered. Papa kept her on her feet.

Ted took a step back, his face pale beneath his farmer's tan. Their gazes locked. The repentant look in his eyes said it all. Bile rose in Elizabeth's throat, choking her as hope for their future drained out of her.

She'd been right. She couldn't trust this man.

Will Wyatt scratched his head. "Ted's a riverboat gambler? You must be mistaken. Why, he's a pillar of the community."

Jim Johnson slapped his hat against his leg. "Ted's lived in New Harmony for what, nine years? Never left except'n to pay a visit on Rose's folks and that ain't near no river."

A knot of pain settled in Elizabeth's chest, squeezing against her lungs until she fought for air. Her husband, the man she'd given her heart to, was just like Papa. Ted might not have gambled in the past two months while she'd lived in his house, but what did that mean? Two months was nothing.

Her father had stopped on occasion, each time promising a new start. But in the end, he chose the thrill of risking everything over his family. That craving had killed her mother. Ruined their lives. Driven her to marry Ted.

At the irony, a harsh laugh left her lips, the sound bitter, defeated. Ted reached for her. She slapped his hand away.

"Elizabeth, you have to believe me. That's in my past."

"Why should I believe you?"

"I thought you knew me," Ted said.

"I thought the same." Tears spilled down her cheeks. "After everything I told you, how could you hide this from me?"

His pale blue eyes filled with misery. A calculated bluff, no doubt, to win her sympathy. Well, she wasn't stupid.

"I was afraid of your reaction. Afraid of what it would mean for the children if the truth came out. Please believe me. I'm not the man your father remembers."

Seymour gave her shoulder a squeeze. "I wasn't the father I should've been, but I won't let you remain under this man's roof. You and Robby are coming home with me. I know better than anyone — a man like that can't be trusted."

"Just where would home be, Papa?"

Her father looked as if she'd slapped him, gnawing at her conscience. But Elizabeth was sick of all this posturing. Papa. Ted. They'd both caused her enough pain to last a lifetime.

"I'd thought it would be here in New Harmony. But home will be wherever we make it. Martha, Robby, you and me," he said.

Richard Stevens pointed a finger at Ted. "Did Rose have to live with that burden? It must have hastened her death. Lily and I aren't inclined to leave our grandchildren with a gambler."

Soon neighbors surrounded them, all taking sides. Pastor Sumner waved his hands, trying to calm the crowd while Lydia's lips moved in silent prayer.

"Stop it! This isn't your fight." Elizabeth turned on Ted. "I've been such a fool, worrying that a *godly* man like you, a man called to *preach* wouldn't understand my father's compulsion."

She snorted. "You told me once that the truth sets a man free. Every word out of your mouth was a lie!" She pounded her fists on his chest, watched him flinch, but he made no attempt to stop her. "Did you find deceiving me amusing?" Her hands fell away. "Well, I won't be fooled again." She wheeled on her father. "Not by any man."

She looked around the room, so quiet she could've heard a pin drop. "I'm sorry for flinging our dirty laundry in your faces. There will be no celebration, but please, stay, have dinner. It's all part of the show."

With that, Elizabeth strode out of the café

on wooden legs, holding herself together with her fury, and walked the short distance to the ladies' club. Her hands shook so badly, it took three attempts before she could get the key in the opening. Once inside, a moan escaped her lips. She clamped her jaw, then sank into a chair, numb, sick to her stomach.

Tears slipped past her cheeks. She swiped them away with a hand. Why cry? Why mourn the loss of a man she never knew? Even as she thought it, her heart shattered. She thought she'd found love, home, family.

Why had she fallen in love with her husband?

Look where love had gotten her. She knew better. She knew the risks. She knew she couldn't trust him. But no matter how much she'd kept expecting that shoe to drop, the reality hurt. Hurt more than she'd ever imagined.

Now she lived Mama's life.

Well, she wouldn't take to her bed. But what would she do? Where would she go? She was caught in the same trap as Mama.

"Elizabeth, can I have a few words with you?" Hat in hand, Pastor Sumner stood in the doorway. "I'll only take a minute."

"I don't want a lecture on forgiveness."

"I've learned hurting people need a good meal or a helping hand or maybe just someone to hold their hand. What they don't want is advice. But I can't seem to stop myself. I apologize for that in advance."

"You're right about all that, you know." She sucked in a breath. "So what's your advice? Besides to forgive. Besides submitting to my vows until the marriage destroys me?"

"Marriage is a holy bond. And yes, forgiveness is a command. We're forgiven as we forgive, but there's something else I need to say."

She raised her head, daring him to sermonize when her world had turned upside down. Yet she wanted an answer, a way to get through this mess. "What?"

"A couple weeks ago, Ted told me about this strong Call to ministry, certain he'd misread God's will. Then he told me why. I wasn't as shocked as he'd expected. You see, I've got a past I'm not proud of."

He let that statement hang in the air between them.

"I pointed out that many men God used in the Bible had done shameful things. Yet God used those imperfect men. In fact, He handpicked them for His service."

Elizabeth didn't speak. She didn't trust

370

her voice or the words shoving to get out of her mouth.

"There's a story in Luke's seventh chapter of the sinful woman who washed Jesus' feet with her tears and wiped them with her hair. The woman proves that those who are forgiven much love much. Ted's a grateful, changed man. I believe him, Elizabeth. Ted gambled in the past. He's not a gambler now."

He peered into her eyes. "Can you find it in your heart to forgive him?"

"He's lost my trust. He could return to that life. My father did time and again."

"Do you really believe Ted would return to a life that would put his family's security at risk? Do you believe he loves gambling more than he loves his family? More than he loves God?

"You're strong, Elizabeth. Lydia said she'd never have had the courage to leave her home, her family and travel alone without money to marry a stranger. But you have more than courage, Elizabeth. You have God. He'll get you through this. Talk to Him."

"Why didn't Ted tell me?" The words ripped from her throat. "Especially after I told him about my father's gambling."

"Ah, that would be fear. Fear of losing you."

"Ted doesn't care enough about me to hold such a fear. Our marriage is a business arrangement, a convenience for us both."

"Oh, Elizabeth, I wish you could've been there when Ted asked for my help to convince you to come back home." Pastor Sumner patted her hand. "Let me pray with you." He bowed his head and beseeched God to give her wisdom, strength, all she needed. "God will reveal the truth." He opened the door to leave. "Will you talk to Ted?"

What was the point? Papa's gambling had taught her how easily the dice could flip. "I'll talk to him, but I won't be taken in by his promises."

Pastor Sumner nodded. "Pray, Elizabeth. Talk to God. He loves you both," he said, then closed the door behind him.

Feeling drained, she rose and walked to the back room where she and Robby had stayed. She'd stay here tonight until she could think. She looked out the window at the creek running along the edge of the property, low from the lack of rain.

On past the mercantile she glimpsed a man sitting on a rock, hunched forward, his elbows resting on his knees and his hands dangling in front of him, staring down into the creek. Even from here those powerful shoulders and that windblown blond hair told her the man's identity. Ted. Probably praying.

Tears streamed down her face. Ted's arms had come to mean acceptance. Home. Joy.

How could she ever trust him again?

What did God think about all this? As Pastor Sumner said, she needed to talk to God. Then she'd talk to Ted.

Though talking to Ted would be a waste of time.

Ted rose from his position on the rock and Elizabeth stepped back from the window, not ready to talk to him. Yet.

Papa wanted her. Martha, too. But had Papa changed, really? "Lord, I don't know what to do. Show me the way."

A gloved hand clamped over her mouth, stifling the scream pushing up her throat. Rough hands hauled her back against a man's chest.

Fear gripped her and confusion muddled her thoughts. Who had her? What did he intend? Nothing good.

Heart pounding and tasting blood, she thrashed against him. Failing to get free, she bit the gloved hand covering her lips but didn't reach skin.

A mouth lowered to her ear. "If you're smart, Elizabeth, you'll forget about God and take orders from me."

Adrenaline shot through her. She twisted, turned, battled against the viselike grip, lurching until she heard the sound of ripping fabric. Pins fell from her hair, clinking against the wooden floor. *God, help me!*

She smashed her heel into a shin. Her captor cursed, then slammed her to the floor and pulled a bandanna between her lips. Dragging her into a sitting position by her arm, he shoved her hands behind her back and bound them with a length of rope he'd tugged from his jacket. Then, smirking at her, he tied her feet.

Her efforts to scream sucked the fabric into her mouth, gagging her. The man scrambled to his feet and pulled a gun, a snarl on his face. "Shut up that bellyaching! You're making my trigger finger jumpy."

She quieted.

"That's better, doll face," he said with an ugly smirk. "Now I can introduce myself proper like. I'm Vic Hammer, remember? We met in Seymour's library in Chicago. I'm here to collect the gambling debt your pa owes me."

Heaving for breath, Elizabeth eyed her captor warily, a little snake of a man, full of self-importance. Anger. Greed. By the shabby clothes he wore, he, and most likely his family, paid a high price for his habit.

Ted had rubbed shoulders with such a man. Rubbed shoulders with her father, a man blessed with every material advantage, yet for some reason had been determined to throw it all away. Rubbed shoulders with every sort of a human being who believed a life of ease could come from the turn of the cards.

Vic walked to the window. "Just what I need — a messenger," he said then slipped out the door.

Ted stared into the creek. Much-needed rain would fill it to overflowing but only a trickle of water ran through it now. He felt numb. Just when he and Elizabeth had gotten closer, everything good he'd tried to make of his life had blown up in his face. Not that he blamed Seymour. It was his fault for not telling Elizabeth before this. His throat clogged. The town would never accept him as a pastor now. And Elizabeth . . .

He'd lost his chance with her.

She fit him, her shape, her lively mind and her energy. Everything about her fit him perfectly, as if God had ordained their marriage.

Last night he'd come close to telling her he loved her. But knew he couldn't until he'd told her everything. He dropped his head into his hands. From the look in her eyes as she learned about his past, all her feelings for him had been shattered. He'd deceived her, given her half-truths, omitting things he'd feared she'd discover.

How had he fallen into this trap? The same trap of deception his father had lived? He'd told Elizabeth truth would set a man free. Yet he hadn't behaved as if he believed it. He'd kept silent to protect what he had, a dangerous motivation.

Why had he taken the same path as his father and turned to gambling to earn his way? He hadn't intended to. He'd hired on to the riverboat as a deckhand. But one night he'd sat in on a game and won. Then he competed every night, getting little sleep. Unlike his father, Ted had a knack for sensing when to hold and when to fold. He lost, sure, but the money piled up.

One windless night his life changed forever. He'd left the game, walking along the upper deck toward his quarters, listening to the raucous laughter from the gallery, the faint call of an owl on shore, the soft slap of the paddles as the boat moved through the murky waters of the Mississippi.

He heard footsteps behind him. Smelled whiskey. Then felt the end of a barrel in his back. "Hand it over, all of it. Or give me the great pleasure of putting a bullet in you."

Ted whipped around, caught the man with an elbow to the throat, tossing him against the hull. The gun clattered across the wood as Ted trapped him against the side of the boat. In the faint glow from the half-moon, he recognized Alex, the red-haired, mouthy kid who'd lost every dime — then accused Ted of cheating.

"Go on to bed, Alex. We'll forget this ever happened."

"You ruined me!" He sprang at Ted, hands reaching for Ted's throat, coming full tilt. The intoxicated young man stumbled and teetered to the right. Before Ted could get hold of him, Alex tumbled over the rail and sailed down the side, arms and legs flailing. Down, down, down into the water. In his nightmares, Ted still heard the boy's screams. Still felt the whisper of his shirt as he tore out of Ted's grasp.

Ted grabbed a life preserver, tossed it to the river, then dashed to the deck below and dove into the water. Time and time again, he dove, searching. But Ted never found him.

Weak with exhaustion and shaking from the cold, he'd been forced to give up, barely making shore with the last ounce of his strength. He was certain Alex had gotten entangled with the paddlewheel and died.

He collapsed on the bank of the river. As he sputtered water out of his lungs, half-frozen, Ted did what he'd never done before. He prayed. Under the stars, weary with guilt and grief at the terrible end of this young man's life, Ted pleaded for God's forgiveness. In a moment of total surrender, he felt the peace of God wash over him. He met God that night and knew he'd never be the same again.

The next morning, Ted made it to the nearest town and heard from a shopkeeper that a young man named Alex had arrived half-drowned after falling overboard. God had brought this second miracle into Ted's life. He hadn't caused the young man's death.

Sick at how close he'd come, Ted boarded the riverboat one last time. He packed his belongings and got his money from the safe. He'd found Alex huddled over the rail and returned every dime he'd won from him, reminding him that gambling had almost cost him his life.

From that moment with God the night before, he made a clean break from his existence as a riverboat gambler and gave his life to the Lord and never looked back.

In one of the many towns he'd traveled to, looking for a new beginning, he'd met Rose. She wanted the same thing he did. To work the land. To rear a family. To love God. He'd been drawn to her goodness and proposed. He'd found a farm he could afford in New Harmony and a niche in the community. A chance to give back what his father had stolen from the good people of this town.

He and Rose had been content, something he prized. He'd seen little evidence of it in his father's life and among the gamblers he'd known. He'd grieved when Rose's life had been cut short. He cared for her and she'd believed in him.

But then gambling hadn't destroyed Rose's family as it had Elizabeth's. Whatever feelings Elizabeth had for him, he'd destroyed them now.

He hurled a small stone into the water. It skipped across the creek then disappeared beneath the surface. Waves flowed out in ever-growing circles wherever the stone had touched. Ted's silence had produced ramifications that rippled outward, affecting the good folks in this town, all three children but most of all Elizabeth. If only he'd admitted his past.

Well, he couldn't change that now. Could he and Elizabeth get beyond all the lies? Start anew?

There was only one thing to do.

Chapter Twenty-One

The rope was embedded in the skin of Elizabeth's hands and feet, cutting off her circulation. She battled against the fear tingling in her limbs and despair clawing up her throat by reminding herself God would protect her. God would save her.

But as she looked into the dark, ominous eyes of her captor, doubt whispered in her ear. Victor Hammer — Vic — demanded money Papa didn't have.

As he checked her bindings, she caught the sweet scent of whiskey on his breath, the thick stench of sweat, and something more — an odor of desperation oozing off him in waves.

She'd felt that same desperation when she'd come here. Knew it now. The hope fluttering in her chest a moment ago ebbed.

Vic stepped back. He was short, stocky, with a scar that carved like a scythe along his cheek, ending at his downturned mouth.

She'd never forget the man or his appearance. That he didn't hide his face now could only mean one thing. Nausea climbed her throat. He didn't intend to let her live.

He paced the room, his steps calculated like a panther circling its prey. With each footfall, the gun in his hand beat against his thigh. Tap. Tap. Tap.

She wanted to scream. To run. To do something. But he had all the power, and she . . . she had nothing.

No, she had the power of prayer. Closing her eyes, she raised her head and sent an entreaty to God.

"What you doing? Praying?" He snorted. "Waste of time. I ain't letting you outta here. Not until I get paid. I don't care if Gabriel and his hoard of angels come for me. I need that money. All those riches you're enjoying are about to be mine." He snarled. "Your father thought he'd hold me off forever. That ain't smart. You're my bargaining chip, to bring in what I'm owed. All of it this time."

Elizabeth shook her head, fought at the gag, trying to explain they had no money, but her words caught behind the muslin.

Vic smirked. "I don't care 'bout your problems. Got enough of my own." He planted his hands on the wall alongside her head, the gun clattering against the plaster. "If I don't get this money, my family's tossed out on the streets. All because your brainless father wagers money he don't have."

Papa had done this to them. A heavy weight squeezed against Elizabeth's chest. No, she'd brought this trouble to Ted. To this town.

Lord, help us. Please. Before it's too late.

Ted gave his children a kiss then plopped Henry on Dan's lap and helped Anna scramble into the bed of the wagon between the Harper brood. None of the children appeared to grasp the significance of what had happened at the café. Thanks to Rebecca's quick action, they hadn't heard much. "Thanks for taking Anna and Henry home with you. If it's not too late, I'll pick them up later."

"Wait until morning. Give yourself a chance to . . ."

Had Dan been about to say, *to repair your marriage?* If so, Ted couldn't see how. But he knew God could change his wife's heart, as he'd changed Ted's one momentous night.

Rebecca patted Ted's arm. *Give her time,* she mouthed.

He nodded and tried to smile, but his lips wouldn't cooperate. He waited until Dan turned the wagon and drove north toward the Harper farm. Once they were out of sight, he strode to the mercantile where Seymour waited.

He'd asked Elizabeth's father for a chance to talk to him. The Sorensons had offered their store as a meeting place then gone home. Ted dreaded facing Seymour's wrath. Not that he blamed him. If Anna ever married a man with Ted's past, he'd feel the same.

If only he could talk to Elizabeth. But both Jacob and Rebecca had suggested he give her time. "Let her calm down," Jacob had said. Ted had seen that chilling anger in her eyes. She hated him. Was it already too late for them?

A man who loved God should know better than to deceive. He was a fallen man, a miserable creature who failed God at every turn. What made him think he should pastor a church?

God had.

Well, if God wanted him to pastor, Ted needed His power to resolve this mess.

One step in the mercantile door and Seymour started in on him. "You aren't worthy to lace my daughter's boots, Logan! I want you out of her life. Out of Robby's life." He jabbed a finger into Ted's breastbone. "You hear me? Before you destroy my children —"

"Like you did."

There, he'd called a spade a spade. Not to retaliate, but to push Seymour Manning to face the truth. To face how his conduct, the mistakes he'd made had wounded his family.

Ted's gaze swept the back wall hung with every imaginable tool, many used to dig, to break up, to cultivate the soil. The time had come to examine the choices he and Seymour had made, even if that excavation unearthed a shovelful of regret.

Seymour paled. "I've changed."

"Then why can't you believe I've done the same? Nine years ago, I made a clean break with gambling. I won't go back. Once Elizabeth's had a chance to calm down, I'm hoping she'll find it in her heart to trust me." He swallowed against the lump forming in his throat. "But, even if I lose her, lose everything — I won't go back to that life."

If only he could get Seymour to understand God could change a man overnight, as He had Ted. "I love God, Seymour. I want to obey His teachings. I want to do

His will. I want to fulfill His purpose for my life."

Seymour scowled. "Why should I believe a word out of your lying mouth?"

"Why would I want that life? I have my children, my —" his voice caught "— wife. I cherish them. I don't want them to be ashamed of me, as I was of my father, as I was ashamed of myself for following in his footsteps."

Ted leaned his hands on the table. Before him lay the bolts of material Elizabeth had selected that first day. He smoothed a hand over the blue gingham, seeing her in that dress, and then paused at an unraveled bolt of black stripe. "Except for God, nothing is more important to me than keeping my family together," he said quietly.

Seymour rubbed a shaky hand over his eyes. "You're right." He sighed. "All these years, I've hidden from the truth. It's far easier to bluff." His distant gaze filled with regret. "I blamed you and all those I lost money to," Seymour said. "It was easier than blaming myself. Now my children are paying for my mistakes."

"I believe God has a plan for us, a purpose."

Seymour snorted. "What purpose?" His hardened face dropped away, and a whisper of vulnerability wavered in his eyes, like a man searching for something.

Peace? Forgiveness? Grace? Exactly what Ted had craved before he'd found God.

"You think a man like me has a God-ordained purpose?" Seymour said. "After everything I've done?"

Ted laid a hand on Seymour's shoulder. "I think everyone —"

The door of the mercantile slammed open with the impact of a gunshot. Ted and Seymour jerked toward the sound.

Red faced with exertion, Cecil Moore leaned against the frame, panting. "Someone's got Elizabeth!"

"Who?" The question echoed from Ted's and Seymour's lips.

"A man." Cecil sucked in another breath, a third. "Says he wants money to free her."

Someone has Elizabeth. *Oh, God, no.* His heart twisted. His wife was in danger. His mind scrambled to make sense of the threat. "Money, what money?"

Cecil turned to Seymour. "Said you'd know how much."

The color drained from the older man's face. "It's Vic," he said, his words a horrified whisper.

"Who's Vic?" Ted grabbed Seymour's arm. "What's this about?"

387

"Vic's someone I . . ." The pallor of Seymour's face gave way to crimson, then resignation. He dropped into a chair and appeared to collapse into himself. "I did this. I . . ."

And then Ted knew. This was about a debt — a big one. How many times had he witnessed these disputes? How many men had he seen lose their shirts, their horses, their homes? But this involved his wife.

Ted wanted to shake Seymour, demand how he could be so foolish as to lead this Vic to New Harmony, to practically lay a breadcrumb trail to Elizabeth. But Seymour's eyes had filled with pain, regret and bone-deep worry.

Ted reined in his anger. For now, he and Seymour were on the same side —

The side that would save Elizabeth.

Lord, protect my wife. Show me what to do.

Ted met Seymour's gaze. "Vic's here to collect?"

Seymour nodded. "I have nothing to give him. There's nothing left." A sob tore from his throat. "He'll . . . hurt her."

Not if Ted got to him first.

The *tick, tick, tick* of the wall clock chipped away at the tenuous hold Ted had on his composure, an unnerving warning that, while he and Seymour talked, Elizabeth was in peril. He turned to go then stopped, as a memory hit him. "Seymour, what's this Vic look like?"

"Swarthy, short . . ." Seymour hesitated then turned toward Ted. "Oh, and he has a scar on his face."

"Right about here?" Ted traced a finger along his left cheek.

"That's him."

It had been years, but some men stuck in your mind. Ted could still picture Vic as clearly as if it were yesterday. "Victor Hammer. Gambler, small-time operator."

Ted had thought him more pathetic than frightening. But get him mad enough and Vic was capable of anything.

He'd once seen him knock over a table and pull a gun when the cards hadn't gone his way. But Ted wouldn't say that aloud. Not to Cecil. Not to Seymour. Not to himself.

Seymour slumped forward. "If only she'd married Parks."

Fire shot through Ted's veins. Didn't he care that Elizabeth despised the man? "What does that have to do with any of this?"

"Vic threatened my children if he didn't get his money. I had to do something to protect them. When Parks agreed to pay the debt in exchange for Elizabeth's hand —"

"What kind of a father would barter his daughter?"

Seymour jerked to his feet. "A frightened father! Do you think I'd force my daughter to marry that old codger unless I had no other choice?" He threw up his hands. "Wouldn't you do anything to protect your children?"

"I would do anything *but* put my children's lives at risk." Ted shook his head. "I'm sorry. We're both worried and my temper —"

"No, you're right. I gambled away everything that mattered."

"It's not too late for a second chance." Ted laid a hand on Seymour's shoulder.

Seymour's face crumpled. "I pray to God you're right." Tears flowed unchecked down his cheeks.

Ted gave Seymour's shoulder one last squeeze then turned to Cecil. "Where's he got her?"

"In the ladies' club." Cecil paled. "Ted, he's got a gun."

Ted's mind sped through possibilities. "If I bust in on Vic, he might panic. Hurt Elizabeth."

Seymour paced the room. He paused and veered toward Ted. "Where are your winnings? Surely you have some of that money left."

If only he did. "It's tied up in my farm."

"Once Vic realizes he's getting no money, he'll kill her. He'll kill my daughter!"

"Not as long as I'm breathing," Ted vowed. "You and Cecil round up as many men as you can. Have them arm themselves — handguns, rifles, shotguns, whatever they've got — then cover the exits to the ladies' club. Don't shoot unless I give the word."

Ted clamped on his hat and strode to the door.

Cecil trotted alongside him. "Where are you going?"

"First to the church to ask Jacob to gather everyone he can to pray. Then to the ladies' club."

"You ain't facing him without a gun, are ya?"

God keep her safe.

She needed — they all needed — a miracle. "I've got the power of prayer, Cecil," he said, opening the door. "And the weapons God gave me."

Ted's long strides ate up the distance from the church to the ladies' club. Around him, neighbors took up positions behind a wagon, from a rooftop, alongside a barrel. The town had turned out to help, either to offer up prayers or carry a loaded gun. As Ted knew it would.

Seymour crouched not far from the entrance, holding a pistol. Ready to do whatever he could to save Elizabeth. Even Cecil and Oscar carried shotguns, looking ready to blow Vic to smithereens. Ted's stomach twisted. He prayed it wouldn't come to that.

God, I love my wife. Help me get her out of there.

And he was sure that somewhere someone loved Vic. But if not, God did. *Let no harm come to anyone, Father. Not even Vic.*

Ted prayed his plan would work. A sense of calm eased the tension in his limbs. With God's help, he would not fail.

He thought of all he knew about Vic. The man was a wretched gambler. He couldn't sustain a poker face during a bluff. Or read tells — all the expressions, mannerisms and intonations that gave people away. But that hair-trigger temper of his posed a threat to his wife. He dared not underestimate the man.

Elizabeth's life depended on it.

Ted banged his fist on the door of the ladies' club. "Open up! It's 'Hold 'Em' Logan.' "

Ted caught a glimpse of Vic at the lone window in the front of the clapboard building. But he couldn't see Elizabeth. He covered his eyes with a hand to block the glare of the late-afternoon sun on the glass, searching for his wife. His stomach lurched. Where was Elizabeth?

"That's my wife in there, Vic. Let her go."

The man cursed. "Do you have the money?"

"I want my wife. I'm not showing my hand until I'm sure you're playing fair."

A pause. Ted's heart dropped ten times in that moment.

"Guns are aimed at the exits, Vic. The men behind them aren't in the mood to jaw. Now open up."

More cursing from inside. Vic sounded close to losing control. *Lord, calm Vic. Show him another way.*

Armed men and a sense of God's protection surrounded him. But where was Elizabeth? His heart stuttered in his chest. Had he hurt her? "I'm unarmed." He'd speak the language Vic understood. "Face it, Vic. I'm the only game in town."

Slowly the door inched open. Ted looked down the barrel of a revolver. "It is you," Vic said. "Raise 'em."

Holding up his hands, Ted stepped inside.

While Vic checked him for weapons, Ted's gaze swept the room. An overturned chair. The podium askew. Then he saw her.

In the corner next to the window, Elizabeth hunched on the floor, gagged, feet bound, hands tied behind her back. Her dress was torn and a section of her hair hung loose from its pins, covering part of her face, but praise God, she didn't look hurt.

Frightened eyes locked with his. He yearned to run to her, to hold her in his arms, to tell her he loved her. But that would turn Vic's attention onto Elizabeth instead of on him.

Vic found the deck of cards Ted had borrowed from the saloon. He cackled. "Looks like you're prepared."

"You all right, Elizabeth?" He'd tried to put all of his feelings for her in his tone, in his gaze, hoping she'd see and hear the depth of his love.

She nodded, made a sound he couldn't understand.

Ted wanted to slap Vic silly for abusing his wife that way, for reducing his outspoken wife to grunts or nods.

Why hadn't he told her he loved her before this? The truth rammed his gut. Hadn't it all come down to his expectation that she'd leave him? Wasn't that the real problem? One way or the other everyone, except God, had left him.

Vic finished his search. "I ain't hurt her. Yet."

Scowling, Ted leaned toward Vic, towering over him, every muscle geared to pounce. "If you've got a brain in that skull of yours, Hammer, you won't take that gamble."

Vic looked wild eyed, desperate, his fear palpable, though he tried to hide it with a smirk. "I'm not leaving till I get my money."

Ted had bluffed Vic successfully before. Meeting Vic's gaze with a steely one of his own, Ted crooked up the corner of his mouth. "Why not make this interesting?"

"Interesting? How?"

"You of all people should know what I'm talking about."

"A game."

Ted nodded again. "I haven't played in, what? Nine years? But I reckon it's like riding a horse. I'll put up the thousand that's owed you. And match it with another thousand. The bank's just down the street."

A crafty smile slid across Vic's face. "Winner takes all."

Elizabeth rocked her body, shooting daggers at him with those dazzling blue eyes of hers, now the color of stormy, wind-tossed seas. If he'd deceived his feisty wife into believing he'd returned to gambling, maybe he could do the same with Vic.

Struggling against her restraints, Elizabeth screeched, the sound muffled. Her eyes burned into him and her jaw worked against the gag, preventing her from giving him a piece of her mind.

If only she knew how much he loved her.

If only she knew she could trust him.

If only his plan worked.

Vic slammed his hand on the table and jerked Ted's attention from Elizabeth to him.

"I ain't got all day, 'Hold 'Em'!"

Lord, help me divert Vic's attention from the game to You.

"You're right, Vic. Your time's running out."

Cursing, Vic's gaze darted to the door of the ladies' club. "What do ya mean? 'Cause if you've got a trick up your sleeve —"

"You worry too much." Ted leaned back, crossing an ankle over his knee, trying to appear calm as every inch of him wanted to cross the room and help his wife.

If Ted hoped to succeed, he'd have to remember every ploy he'd used as 'Hold 'Em' Logan. Keep voice calm, demeanor nonchalant, gaze nonemotional. Vic must never suspect Ted had no money. That the only contest would be a battle for his soul. That was the only way to get through to Vic and to rescue Elizabeth without bloodshed.

Vic scrubbed a hand across his drawn face.

"You look tired, Vic."

His right hand danced near the gun's handle. "Not too tired to pull this trigger."

"Don't you get weary of courting Lady Luck?"

Vic snorted. "Luck ain't no lady."

God, give me the words. "So why do you do it? Why risk everything on the hand you're dealt?"

"Same reason as you," Vic said, glancing over his shoulder at Elizabeth.

Ted tensed, then relaxed when Vic swung his attention back to him. "I don't gamble anymore. Lost my taste for it. Why not give it up? Find a new path."

Vic hooted, the sound high-pitched, nervous. "Easy for you to say. You was a winner." He toyed with the deck but didn't deal. Could Ted dare to hope Vic was listening?

"I may've won pots, but I lost far more."

Vic chuffed. "Like what?"

"My self-respect."

"Crazy talk." Vic waved the cards in Ted's

face. "I'd swap my good name, if I had one, for one big pot."

"I did that," Ted said. "I wouldn't do it again."

"Yeah, you say that now with the winnings in the bank."

"You ever look a man in the eye after you've taken his last penny? Watched a young man fall apart right in front of you?" Ted shook his head, trying to dispel Alex's face as he'd come after him. "The gamble isn't worth the price you pay."

Ted could see the wheels turning in the other man's head. He leaned forward, rested his elbows on the table. "You're losing far more than you're winning, am I right?"

Vic's focus shifted to the floor. "Maybe. Still, this life's better than what I had growing up, which was nothing."

"You had a hard childhood?" Ted hoped the casual question would spur more from Vic.

Tapping the cards on the table, Vic stared into space. "Hard don't even describe it." He shook his head. "My parents came to this country full of dreams. Worked like dogs twelve-hour days, six days a week. For what? A single room in a dingy, drafty, decaying firetrap of a tenement with a single spigot on each floor and a bath down the hall?"

Vic's mouth turned down. "My parents died as poor as they lived."

Ted eyed that gun. Still too close for comfort. He glanced at Elizabeth. She leaned toward them, listening to every word, probably praying. He wanted this over for her sake. But he couldn't rush things. "Any good times growing up, Vic?" he said, hoping to soften Vic's mood and get that gun out of Vic's reach.

A smile played around his lips. "Yeah, we had some good times. Everyone was in the same boat. Neighbors would pitch in occasionally, pooling their food. And music." He grinned. "Pop had the voice of an angel."

Ted heard the nostalgia in Vic's tone. He'd try to build one more bridge. A bridge two men could find common ground to stand on. "You got a wife? Kids?"

"Don't everybody?" Vic's glistening eyes belied his tough-guy tone. "Four boys and two girls. They're the reason I'm here to get what's owed me."

"I'm guessing they'd prefer your presence over a hefty pot. I've lived the life, Vic. I know how much you're gone, how much of your kids' lives you're missing."

Vic looked away. "You sound like my old lady's nagging."

"She cares about you. If you want to be a

winner, place your bets on something that earns a wage, instead of paltry odds." He leaned closer, locking eyes with Vic. "Live a life. Not a bluff."

"I'm sick of your gibberish." Vic slammed a fist on the table, then picked up the gun and raised the barrel to Ted's chest. "I'm not here to talk. I want that money now!"

Worry gnawing in his gut, Ted's gaze flickered to Elizabeth. He prayed for words to restore the calm. To save his wife. "You don't want to use that," Ted said, motioning to the gun. "You shoot me and you'll get yourself hung."

"So what?" But the words shook as they left Vic's mouth.

"So what happens after that? After you die?" Ted raised the ante. "I'll wager your parents taught you where that leads."

Alarm slithered across Vic's face. Only for a moment, but long enough for Ted to know the man didn't relish hell. He cursed. "What did you do? Turn into some blasted preacher?"

"Not yet," Ted said. As the words slipped past his lips, a peace slid through him. "But if the town will have me, I will."

Not that anyone could stop a plan of God's.

Vic's jaw dropped. "Why? Why choose

that miserable life when you could go back to gambling?"

"I've found bigger riches in a life led by God. That life my children can respect. That life lets me hold my head up.

"Truth is, I didn't always win. But when I did, others lost. I saw the harm that caused. After a while, that eats at a man." Ted jerked his head toward Elizabeth, every muscle ready to pounce. "You've got a defenseless woman tied up, threatening her life." He leaned toward him. "Do you think God's going to smile on that?" He lowered his voice. "You're not a bad man."

The words hung between them, heavy in the air. Just when Ted thought Vic wouldn't respond, he saw a twitch in the other man's jaw. A slide of his Adam's apple. A few rapid blinks.

He reached across the table, connecting with Vic's forearm, a light touch for some strong words. "God loves you, Vic."

Vic shook his head, resisting the comfort, the grace. But then his face crumpled and the walls between him and God began to break. "God can't stand the sight of me."

"You're wrong there. God never stops loving us. He'll forgive us most anything. I know. He did for me. But He expects us to change."

"And do what?"

Lord, soften him. Help me get through to this man. "God gave you something, some talent you've overlooked. Farming isn't really mine. I'm going to put my hand to the plow, but this time it'll be to cultivate the hard ground of people's souls."

Vic's eyes widened. "You ain't kidding. You're a preacher."

A preacher. Ted smiled. He'd asked God for a sign. That sign was Vic's softening. He'd answer God's Call. Preaching was what he was meant to do. "I'm a man forgiven. God changed me. He'll do the same for you. Return to your family. Give your children another legacy. Show them another way. Before it's too late."

Vic picked up the gun by the barrel and handed it to Ted, then gave a weak smile. "I am tired. Those riches you're talking about sound a lot more reliable than these." He knocked the deck of cards to the floor. They scattered at their feet.

The door burst open. Dan Harper came in first followed by most of the men in town.

Someone handed Ted a rope. "No need for that. Mr. Hammer's had a change of heart," Ted said.

Ted ran to Elizabeth's side, weak-kneed and shaken now that the standoff was over, praising God no harm had come to his wife. The idea of losing her tore through him. It would be like losing his own heart.

He untied her gag, then her hands and feet and tugged her to him, holding her tight, never wanting to let her go. "Oh, Elizabeth, my brave wife. I'm sorry you've had to go through this."

She pressed into him. "I'm sorry that for a few minutes there, I thought you'd returned to your old life."

"I'd never go back to that life, Elizabeth. Not when I have everything — everyone — I want right here in New Harmony." He kissed her. "You."

CHAPTER TWENTY-TWO

Elizabeth's nightmare was over and Vic Hammer had a new beginning. Thanks to Ted and thanks to God.

"I'm sorry for treating you like that, Mrs. Logan. It weren't right," Vic said, then clapped Ted on the shoulder and headed out the door, a glow on his face. Looking as joy filled as Elizabeth felt when she'd found God.

She walked to Ted, smiling up at him. "You did it," she said softly. "You saved his soul."

"I had a lot of help . . ." Ted glanced heavenward. "From the Good Lord." When Ted had asked for a sign from God, he'd had no idea what he was asking for.

"You talked to Vic in a way he understood. By using your past, you got through to him. If I ever had a doubt, I don't now. You should become a preacher."

Ted took Elizabeth's hands in his. "Are

you all right with that? Being a preacher's wife isn't an easy life."

She grinned. "It can't be worse than skirmishing with the chickens."

The joy of a new future shining in his eyes, he brought her clasped hands to his lips and kissed her scraped knuckles. "It's so much better, Elizabeth, so much better."

Outside, half the town gathered, waiting for Ted and Elizabeth to emerge from the ladies' club. But they'd have to give them another minute. She had one more thing to say. "I think I always knew about the gambling."

"How?"

She searched for the words to explain her hunch that he hid something. Something big. As she'd grown to love him, she realized that if he did, he kept that secret from her for a reason. A reason she couldn't face. So all these weeks, she'd pushed those feelings aside, until her father had arrived and forced her to face the facts.

But that was in the past. They had a new beginning. It no longer mattered. She smiled. "You married me, didn't you? That was the biggest gamble of all."

He laughed, then sobered. "You have every right to be angry. I kept my past from you. I was wrong. I was . . . afraid. Afraid

I'd lose you."

Leaning into the strength of his arms, into the sanctuary of his broad shoulders, she smiled into his eyes. "You couldn't lose me, Ted Logan. Remember those vows we took? I'm here to stay."

He nuzzled her hair. "I love you, Elizabeth Logan."

Heart soaring, joy burst in her chest and she threw her arms around his neck. "I love you!"

The door opened. Papa and Martha crowded up beside her, followed by Rebecca and Dan with their children and Robby, Anna and Henry in tow. She caught a glimpse of all the good folks of New Harmony who'd been praying at the church heading to the ladies' club. These were her friends. Hers and Ted's.

As they entered, the men doffed their hats, looking proud of themselves while the women clung to their husbands and babies as if they feared a big gust of wind would blow them away. Vic Hammer's redemption had to surpass Ted's gambling, the town's biggest news until now.

Turning toward their neighbors, Ted's intense gray-blue eyes drifted from one friendly face to another. "It's time for all of it to come out. Past time. I remember someone commenting on my name when Rose and I moved to town." His gaze settled on Oscar Moore. "I believe it was you, Oscar." He let out a long breath. "Does the name 'John the Baptist' Logan ring a bell?"

Oscar's brow furrowed. "That no good swine —"

"Was my father."

The silence tore at Elizabeth. Her heart ached for the man who stood before them stripped bare, all the masks ripped away. Shocked, confused, people looked from one to the other, then at Ted.

Oscar scratched his jaw. "You're *Logan's* boy? That phony preacher who stole the church remodeling fund?" He shook his head. "I can't see it."

"Nope, you ain't his," Orville Radcliffe said. "You may carry his name, be his by blood, but you're nothing like your pa."

Will Wyatt moseyed over and laid a hand on Ted's shoulder. "You're one of us, Ted. Everyone in this town respects you. The way you took care of your younguns after Rose passed. The helping hand you give when it's needed. Why, you're someone folks come to for a dose of God's wisdom."

Pastor Sumner stood beside her husband. "Ted, it's time they knew." He turned to his parishioners. "Where do you think the money to rebuild the church came from nine years ago?"

Folks surged forward and pumped Ted's hand, slapping him on the back.

Ted held up a hand. "I've talked to Dan. He's willing and able to handle my eighty acres for a half share until I can get a buyer. You were right about that, Elizabeth. I'm no farmer." Ted tugged Elizabeth close and tucked a strand of hair behind her ear. "You were right about a lot of things," he said softly.

Elizabeth looked deep in his eyes. "And wrong about so many others."

"Never wrong. Different. Different is refreshing." He studied her face. "Once we sell the farm, I want to help Seymour repay Vic."

Unable to speak, Elizabeth hugged Ted, her eyes brimming with happy tears.

"Ted, as the chairman of the elders," Will said, "I'm here to ask you to fill the pulpit this next week while Jacob's off preaching at their home church."

Onlookers smiled and cheered their approval. Through the open doorway and windows, thunder rumbled off in the distance. Every eye and ear tuned in to the sound of the promise of rain, bringing smiles to their faces.

Papa stepped closer, tugging Martha alongside. "Ted, I can't let you repay Vic. It's time to take some responsibility for my debts. I saw the transformation in Vic. I know the only way I'm going to live the life I want with Martha, here, is if I stop living for myself. Stop trying to bring in easy money, hoping to be a big man."

He motioned to Hubert Sorenson. "I've talked to Sorenson. The store's too much for him and he's willing to sell it on contract. As soon as the paperwork's completed, Martha and I will own Manning Mercantile." He gave her a crooked grin. "Along with a series of payments for the rest."

"Papa, you and Martha are staying?"

Seymour tugged Martha close. "I think we can make a go of the place, especially with a smart bookkeeper of a daughter to keep us on track."

Elizabeth nodded and squeezed her hands together in a voiceless plea. Had Papa stopped gambling?

Seymour grinned. "We'll take ownership of the store as soon as we get back from our honeymoon."

Elizabeth enveloped them in a big hug. "I'm so happy."

"Speaking of weddings —" Ted ran a palm down her face. "Sometimes I marvel that it was you who came to New Harmony, the one woman in the universe who fits up against me perfectly. Who makes every plain day an adventure and treats my children like they belong to her. I'll admit you came to me in the strangest maze of circumstances." He chuckled. "Neither of us was exactly excited about the ceremony."

She laughed. "I marvel how God brought me into Sally's path when she lost her nerve."

"You were never the substitute bride. Elizabeth, you are the genuine article."

"I marvel that the man waiting at the end of the line, sight unseen, has given me more happiness — and grief —" she added with a laugh "— in the past two months than I've had in the lifetime before I met him. I love you, Theodore Francis Logan."

Ted raised her chin and looked deep into her eyes. "I love you, Elizabeth Manning Logan. I've got one more thing to say —"

"Get on with it, Ted. My bunions are killing me," Oscar grumbled. "I never heard a man go on so."

The room erupted with laughter.

"I will if our friends will hold their horses." He bent down on one knee and took her hand. "Elizabeth, will you do me the great honor of renewing our wedding vows?"

410

Tears stung her eyes. "Yes. I'll even agree to obey this time."

"And why is that?"

"Because I know you'd never ask anything of me that wasn't for my good and in obedience to God." She laughed. "Though I hope that vow won't go to your head, 'cause if you turn bossy —"

"She'll put you in your place," Oscar finished.

Ted grinned. "I'd never try to boss a woman who wears the pants as well as you do." He laid a tender hand on her cheek. "No more lies between us."

"None." She pursed her lips. "Well, almost none."

Ted rolled his eyes heavenward. "What now?"

"I'll speak the truth, except for the number of meals that go into the slop jar."

He chuckled and gathered her in his arms. "Jacob and Lydia are waiting at the church, ready for the ceremony as soon as we can get there. The café is decorated. After one false start, Agnes is expecting us to gather in for our reception. So if you haven't any objections, I'd like to renew our vows now."

"I'm not thrilled with my dress, Ted Logan," Elizabeth said. "Ripped cotton twill is hardly the stuff of weddings."

Rebecca grinned. "I finished that second dress I owed you, Elizabeth. It's yellow dimity, not a true bridal gown, but right pretty."

Elizabeth smiled. "In that case, Mr. Logan, I'll marry you again. Today."

"You've made me the happiest man in the world!" He lifted her off her feet and swung her in a circle until she was breathless and a bit dizzy.

Lightning streaked in the sky and the first real downpour in months soaked the ground. Rain meant the crops would grow.

With a smile on her face and her children crowding around her, Rebecca opened the door wide, letting in the sight and scent of rain. "A rainy day is the luckiest day for a wedding," she promised.

Elizabeth knew luck had nothing to do with it. "Thank You, God," she whispered, smiling through her tears at Ted. "Thank You for answering my prayers."

"And mine," Ted said, glancing to the sky.

Then for all the days they'd shared and all the days to come, he sealed their love with a kiss.

DEAR READER,

I find the history of mail-order brides fascinating. I've read numerous accounts of women traveling long distances to marry a virtual stranger, leaving behind everything and everyone they knew. Why did they take such an amazing step? For some, fear of spinsterhood, for others, a desperate need of life's necessities. Most couples corresponded, some sent pictures, but often they never met until their wedding day. To find their mate, men and women placed ads in newspapers, giving their physical description and who they sought. The outcome of these matches varied, but these courageous women made not only a home for their husbands and children but also improved their communities by establishing churches, schools and libraries.

Thank you for choosing *The Substitute Bride*. I hope you enjoyed Elizabeth and Ted's story and could empathize with their struggle to accept God's purpose in their lives, especially when that purpose took them out of their comfort zone. Many heroes of the Bible questioned their ability to answer God's call. You may struggle with that concern. We can step out in faith, knowing our great God will equip us to handle His assignment.

I love to hear from readers. Write me at Steeple Hill Books, 233 Broadway, Suite 1001, New York, NY 10279. Or e-mail me through my Web site, www.janetdean.net, at janet@janetdean.net. Visit my blog, www .janetdean.blogspot.com, and my group, www.seekerville.blogspot.com.

God bless you always,
Janet Dean

QUESTIONS FOR DISCUSSION

1. Marrying a stranger comes with a host of problems. What challenges did Elizabeth and Ted face because of their situation? Did isolation on the farm complicate or help?
2. Elizabeth is out of her element as a farmer's wife and must learn new skills. How do these experiences help her grow and change as a person?
3. Elizabeth had a love/hate relationship with her father. How did that impact her relationship with Ted?
4. Elizabeth and Ted were from very different worlds. What difficulties did that present for Elizabeth? For Ted? They both had gambling fathers in their pasts. How did that affect them?
5. Ted feels called to ministry, yet questions if he's worthy. Discuss his growth that eventually leads to the acceptance of God's purpose for his life.

6. What expectations did Ted have for a pastor? What colored his thinking about his worthiness? What helped him change that view? How was he the right man for ministry in the town?

7. Elizabeth ran from a marriage to Reginald Parks, a much-older man she couldn't abide, into marriage with a stranger. Why does she take this drastic action? Do you understand her decision? What factors influenced it?

8. Laid-back Ted and outspoken Elizabeth testify that opposites attract. How are they alike? What do they share at first? With the passing of time?

9. Marrying Ted threw Elizabeth into instant motherhood. What complicates an already unnerving responsibility for her? How do the children bring Ted and Elizabeth together and, at the same time, keep them apart?

10. Why is Elizabeth hungry for God? For what purpose? How did her view of God and prayer change?

11. Elizabeth married Ted to give her brother a good life on the farm. But when Robby comes to New Harmony, he's miserable. What does her brother's unhappiness drive Elizabeth to do? Do you approve of her decision?

12. What secrets does Elizabeth keep? What secrets does Ted keep? How do these secrets affect them?
13. When Seymour recognizes Ted, is Elizabeth truly surprised by Ted's past? What factors are at work in her? Do you understand her suspicion?
14. Do you feel that Seymour is a changed man? Why or why not? What influences him?

ABOUT THE AUTHOR

Janet Dean grew up in a family that cherished the past and had a strong creative streak. Her father recounted wonderful stories, like his father before him. The tales they told instilled in Janet a love of history and the desire to write. She married her college sweetheart and taught first grade before leaving to rear two daughters. As her daughters grew, they watched *Little House on the Prairie,* reawakening Janet's love of American history and the stories of strong men and women of faith who built this country. Janet eagerly turned to inspirational historical romance, and she loves spinning stories for Steeple Hill Love Inspired Historical. When she isn't writing, Janet stamps greeting cards, plays golf and bridge, and is never without a book to read. The Deans love to travel and to spend time with family.

The employees of Thorndike Press hope you have enjoyed this Large Print book. All our Thorndike, Wheeler, and Kennebec Large Print titles are designed for easy reading, and all our books are made to last. Other Thorndike Press Large Print books are available at your library, through selected bookstores, or directly from us.

For information about titles, please call:
  (800) 223-1244

or visit our Web site at:
  http://gale.cengage.com/thorndike

To share your comments, please write:
  Publisher
  Thorndike Press
  295 Kennedy Memorial Drive
  Waterville, ME 04901